Co-Pilot

A Trumpet & Gabe Adventure

KIM CRUMB

Co-Pilot
A Trumpet & Gabe Adventure
By Kim Crumb

© 2024 by Kim Crumb

Owl Creek Press
Ashland, Oregon 97520
owlcreekpress@gmail.com
owlcreekpress.com

Cover design: Chris Molé - booksavvystudio.com
Illustration: Kim Crumb

ISBN: 979-8-9907944-1-2

This book is dedicated to all of the dogs I have experienced. I have gained so much from their love and devotion.

I cannot thank my wife, Sherrie Owens, enough for her collaboration and many, many edits of this book.

Contents

Prologue

The long, straight Nevada desert highway defined perspective, its vanishing point disappearing into a sea of orange and red clouds at the crest of a distant hill. Though early in the morning, uneven waves of heat created the illusion of tiny blue-gray lakes forming on the shimmering blacktop.

About six hundred feet above the desert floor, three hungry scavengers rode an upwelling of heated air generated by the earth's parched surface. Their wings shifted slightly to conserve energy as they maintained a circular pattern over the object of their interest. From their vantage point, the vultures watched a fair-sized animal lying partially obscured by a large bush. The creature hadn't moved in quite some time; its proximity to the road boded well for the prospect of a hearty lunch.

In the vast stillness, a small dot appeared. At first, the dot grew in size without seeming to move, until resolving itself into a motorcycle sidecar rig, rising then falling over the road's undulating surface.

To anyone observing Aemea Rand astride the two-tone orange and cream Triumph with its matching sidecar, the rider presented quite a sight. Her coffee-shaded skin appeared to glow where it was exposed by the work shirt's open neck and rolled-up sleeves. Faded denim pant legs were carefully tucked into worn, but well-polished knee-high riding boots. Though in her early thirties, there were strands of gray in the jet-black hair banded into a long ponytail trailing back from the white open-face helmet. Behind the goggles, her otherwise smooth features revealed tiny lines at the corners of her eyes, affecting a combined look of world-weariness and kindness. At only five feet eight inches tall, and one hundred and thirty-some pounds, she didn't look strong enough to manage nearly seven hundred pounds of bike and sidecar.

Feeling the vibration and hearing the distant roar of the approaching bike stirred the animal lying near the road to life. A reddish golden retriever pulled himself to his feet and moved to the side of the road. He sat, watching as the rig approached. When the bike was within a hundred feet or so, he lifted his right paw in an unmistakable plea for a ride.

Ahead on the right shoulder of the road, the rider noted a red/gold form glowing softly in the sun's early rays. Drawing closer she recognized a large dog. Rolling off the throttle she allowed the rig to slow. When the rig rolled to a stop, he lowered his paw. The rider shut down the engine, lowering her goggles, she stood up on the bike's foot pegs. A long look around failed to reveal any hikers, cars, or campers in the area. Her eyes back on the red dog, she swung off the bike in an easy fluid motion. Removing her helmet, she tucked her brown leather gloves inside, then hung it by its strap over the throttle grip.

"Well, hello handsome. I suppose you're aware sticking out your paw is one devastatingly cute trick." The dog lifted his paw again until she knelt in front of him to take it in her hand. At her touch, his tail slowly swished a welcoming greeting.

"My pleasure, sir. I'm Aemea Rand," pronouncing her first name as "Amy." After solemnly shaking his paw, she gently turned it side to side while checking the pad. The dog sat patiently while she repeated the process on his other feet, continuing her inspection by running her fingers over his head and around his neck. "A couple of broken claws, a small cut on a pad, and what appears to be a singed spot on top of your head. Feels like you wore a collar recently. Hmm." She stared into his gentle brown eyes. "Let's see. Your ears are too short for an Irish setter, so I guess you're from the red end of the golden retriever line." Her hands moved along his back until her smile suddenly vanished as her fingers reached his left hip. "What's this?"

Whining slightly, the dog's muscles tightened when she carefully moved the hair away from an angry red mark an inch or so long. "This looks remarkably like a bullet recently grazed you. Someone probably thought a coyote was visiting their place last night." She gave him a reassuring touch on the shoulder. "You were very, very, lucky. Now, just sit tight for a minute."

Aemea returned with a small aluminum cooking pan from the survival kit she kept packed in the sidecar, along with an Army surplus two-quart canteen. The dog was instantly interested as she placed the pan on the sand, poured in an inch or so of water, and sat back. "We'll start with a little bit."

The vultures realizing their meal was not as promising as they hoped, moved onto another air current to seek out other possibilities.

While he eagerly lapped at the contents, Aemea folded her arms across her chest. "Well, my enigmatic friend, what on earth are you doing out here all by yourself?"

CO-PILOT

1

___

SECOND CHANCES

Three days earlier and hundreds of miles to the west, Trumpet the 'enigmatic' retriever, sniffed the air while gazing up at the clouds building to the north in the deep blue afternoon sky. Though partially obscured, the sun told him it was time for their evening walk. He rose from the old couch on the cabin's front porch, did a slow nose-to-tail stretch, and went looking for his friend. Upon reaching the front door he pushed down on the levered handle with his paw until it released, pushing the door with his nose he forced it further open with his shoulder and entered the cabin. After passing through the doorway a spring-tensioned mechanism quietly pulled the door closed behind him.

Gabe was quickly located sitting at the kitchen table, his fingers tapping softly at the keyboard in front of him. After waiting a few patient moments, Trumpet gently nudged the man's elbow.

"Easy there, I'm almost done." Eyes still intent on the small screen in front of him, Gabe's hand went to Trumpet's neck to give a brief, gentle rub. He resumed his typing.

"Walk," Trumpet thought. A mental picture formed of the two of them heading up the path to the woods. He nudged again.

This time Gabe turned in the chair to meet the steady brown-eyed gaze of his big red-gold dog. He spread the fingers of both hands in front of Trumpet's face. "Ten minutes. Okay?"

After nosing the fingers of one hand and snuffing softly, Trumpet's eyes searched Gabe's until the man relented with a resigned sigh. "Okay. Just wait five minutes. I promise." He dropped one hand, wiggling the fingers of the other for effect. "Great, I'm negotiating with a dog."

Temporarily satisfied, Trumpet reluctantly ambled out into the living room. "Wait" meant their walk would soon follow. When he reached the front door he took a short knotted length of rope dangling from the levered handle gently in his mouth, pulling down until the latch clicked. Still holding on, he took a step back. Once he tugged the door far enough for his nose to fit in the gap he released the rope. Using his head and shoulder he pried the door further open, allowing him to pass through before it closed behind him.

When Trumpet was a puppy, Sarah, Gabe's late wife, volunteered with an organization specializing in training dogs to assist people with disabilities. She and Gabe thought it would be fun to change out the doorknobs in the cabin for handles, and train Trumpet to open doors. The only downside was if they wanted any 'privacy' in the bedroom they needed to lock the door, or Trumpet would join them at inopportune times.

Walking down the porch steps, Trumpet headed toward the little garden in the front yard. After circling the garden for the second time he settled onto a small grassy rise. From there he could alternately observe the cabin's front door, the gravel drive leading out the gate, and the path leading up the hill to the woods. Letting out a breath, Trumpet lowered his head between his big paws. When a sizable cloud briefly cloaked the sun's rays, his sensitive nose took in the promise of rain.

❧

With Trumpet outside, Gabe returned his attention to the laptop. When he finished, he hit 'Save,' before printing a single copy to check over. Noting a few minor errors, he quickly typed the changes into the document. After printing out three copies he carefully signed and dated them, putting one into a folder in the bottom drawer of a large gray file cabinet. Another one was carefully folded, slipped into a hand-addressed and stamped envelope to be mailed to Bernard M. Pfeifer. The last copy was placed in a plain envelope he planned to take into town the next day to have notarized by his attorney and then put in a safe deposit box at the bank.

For a long moment, he stared at the envelopes, then arranged them side by side. Finished, he let out a quiet sigh. "Well Sarah, I just thought I'd have more time. After all we went through, I hoped somehow we would go together. Maybe I just didn't want to contemplate how things would turn out for us."

When he spoke, it was with what his late wife sometimes referred to as, his "Sam Elliot way of speaking." His voice was low, slow-paced as if he considered each word, and slightly hoarse. Her comment always made him laugh. He teased her about his physical resemblance to the actor being equally uncanny until the observer came within fifty or so feet.

Except for a slight limp from a bad knee, Gabe appeared to be in pretty good shape, for a man of sixty-eight years. Despite a downturn in his health over the last few months, his six-foot height was filled out with a solid hundred and eighty pounds. He still had most of his hair, though it was now thoroughly gray, matching his neatly trimmed mustache. Only his eyebrows still contained traces of the original dark brown. The area around his deep green eyes carried the well-earned wrinkles of a man who worked hard and smiled a lot throughout his lifetime. Above his left eye a scar ran down toward the left ear. The scar and a slight offset to his prominent nose were souvenirs of an Army helicopter crash some five decades past.

Gabe walked into the living room, staring thoughtfully out the picture window as a shadow crossed the yard from a cloud sweeping past high overhead. A few moments passed before a ray of sun caught the coat of the dog by the little garden, making his fur blaze against the grassy green background. Reaching for his wooden cane, Gabe sighed. "Thank God for you, Trumpet. You've held me together more than I could ever tell you." He didn't give much thought to not having children with Sarah until the cancer took her. He sometimes wished he possessed some part of her, something more tangible than a lot of good memories and photos.

Fortunately for both of them, there was Trumpet. During the early stage of her illness, Gabe was returning home from a shopping trip when a handmade sign declaring, "Golden Retriever Puppies" lured him down a quiet cul-de-sac. On the front lawn of an older but well-kept home, a dozen puppies cavorted inside a small fenced area. The owners came to the gate when the momma dog barked an alert. He was introduced to the rambunctious pups who were named for various musical instruments by the owners, who were jazz aficionados. Gabe almost picked a cute little female named 'Flute.' But when she left him to tussle with her siblings, Trumpet stayed, sat at his feet, and pawed at his ankle, capturing his heart with a series of enthusiastic puppy yaps. So, it was Trumpet who rode curled up next to him on the ride home. With the puppy's arrival, Sarah's cancer soon eased into remission. In his heart, Gabe knew the energetic red-golden ball of happiness had a lot to do with it.

Soon after the pup's arrival, they decided to sell their home in Santa Rosa, California, and move to their mountain getaway about twenty miles to the west, outside of the little town of Cazadero. Gabe purchased the cozy eight-hundred-square-foot cabin when he first left the Army in 1971. It was about two miles up (way up) a dirt and gravel road on a twenty-two-acre hilltop. There they enjoyed peaceful vacations and holiday retreats over the years. Though somewhat remote, they were still within an hour's drive of Sarah's doctors.

The top of the property held a majestic view to the south of the Russian River Valley, and to the west over the treetops, and through the canyons, the Pacific Ocean could be seen on a clear day. At the bottom of the property, there was a level patch of land with a natural spring feeding a small pond providing ample water for a garden. Water was pumped up to the cabin which was built on another level spot about 200 feet above the pond.

Once they moved into the cabin Gabe rebuilt the front porch while Sarah repainted the living room. There always seemed to be a project that needed tending, but they found time for hikes through the hills and took naps in matching hammocks hung nearby between the fir trees. In the evenings the three of them sat on the porch to watch the stars gather while the moon sent ribbons of light through the redwoods.

They regularly took trips to the ocean where Trumpet loved cavorting in the sand and playing tag with the waves rolling up the beach. He never tired of chasing the seagulls flying teasingly just out of his reach. They collected rocks, and he brought home carefully selected sticks of driftwood. After a day at the beach, they enjoyed feasting on fish and chips at a restaurant overlooking Bodega Bay, with Trumpet relishing his doggy bag.

Sarah was a tall woman at five feet nine inches and maintained a slender weight of one hundred and forty pounds. Her freckled complexion was highlighted by her red hair. As she grew older her hair faded to a golden blond, but Gabe still called her his "redhead." When she started to lose weight, and easily became fatigued, she knew the cancer had returned. New tests revealed their life together was ending. During this time Trumpet was a huge source of comfort. Sensing something different about her, as if some unseen foe was near and threatening, he took to staying protectively by her side. On days when Gabe drove the truck into town, Trumpet ignored his beckoning to, "jump in the cab and go for a ride." Instead, he would curl up against Sarah, or follow her inside until she began to call him, "my big red shadow."

Then came a windy moonless night when Gabe hurriedly carried a sleeping Sarah to the truck while ordering Trumpet to "stay." Trumpet remained alone at the cabin for many long days and lonely nights. A neighbor and his wife came by every day to feed him, trying a few times to coax him into the back of their truck. But each time, Trumpet refused to leave, parking himself resolutely on the cabin's porch until they left.

When Gabe finally returned, Trumpet joyously greeted the truck, dancing over to the passenger side, rearing up on his hind legs to bark a "hello" to his mistress. Gabe gave the dog a long sad look before peering out through the dusty windshield at something only seen by him. Finally, he shut off the engine, quietly sitting behind the wheel before getting out. "It's just you and me, Trumpet." Leaving the driver's door open, he absently scratched the retriever's ears before heading to the cabin. Trumpet climbed into the cab, settling onto the seat with his head on the passenger side where the scent of Sarah was faint but still present.

§

The months dragged by, during which Gabe attributed his lack of energy to his lingering depression. He thought the body aches were just a reminder he was getting older.

Finally, he decided to see a doctor when the dime-size mole on the back of his neck started to itch. It had been there for as long as he could remember, but it recently became larger and was tender to the touch. The doctor took a sliver out of the mole to send for a biopsy, and also blood tests. Gabe returned home to wait for the result.

Yesterday, after an urgent call from the doctor's office, he drove back to Santa Rosa to receive the news. Of all the doctor's words, "untreatable melanoma," and "beyond chemo," stood out in his mind like a flashing red neon sign. By the time, "could be weeks, possibly a month or so," came into the conversation, Gabe realized for some time he knew there was something seriously wrong. He just didn't want to hear the words out loud.

The well-meaning doctor gently suggested he put his things in order, which meant with Sarah gone his Will needed to be revised. In the old Will in case of their mutual demise, Gabe's brother, Dan, was named Executor. It called for the ranch to be sold after their death, with the proceeds going to the local Fire Department, school, and a few other charities. Sarah's sister in San Francisco reluctantly agreed to take Trumpet.

The new document continued to name Dan as Executor as Gabe knew he could trust him to honor his wishes. The big change was Bernard M. Pfeifer became the principal recipient of the cabin, under the provision Trumpet would always be loved and cared for, and Gabe's modest fortune was still to go to the Fire Department.

B.P., as the locals called him, was the third generation

from the town of Cazadero. When he was twenty, with a degree in law enforcement from the local community college, he joined the Army. He served five years, including two tours in Iraq with the 101st Airborne. The previous summer, B.P returned to Sonoma County and was subsequently hired as a County Deputy. He lived by himself in a rented cabin a couple of miles south of town.

Gabe was likewise a former member of the 101st, though his time was spent in Vietnam. Since the younger man's return and Sarah's demise, the two of them spoke often, sharing dinner in the town café on an irregular but consistent basis. When at times B.P. helped him with projects around the ranch Trumpet always enjoyed his visits. Gabe considered B.P. a good man who would make certain Trumpet comfortably lived out his life on the ranch. Since Gabe and Sarah had no children, it felt good to know someone would enjoy their home and think of them occasionally.

Also named in the document was Reggie, the resident raccoon. When Reggie first appeared, he regularly raided the trashcan on the back porch behind the kitchen. Trumpet wasn't too concerned and stayed out of his way when he encountered him in the yard. One evening, returning from a later-than-usual walk, Gabe and Trumpet entered the kitchen to find an enterprising Reggie who had worked the handle to the back door, let himself into the cabin, and was munching on Trumpet's bowl of food. Surprisingly, there were none of the barks and answering hisses expected by Gabe. Instead, Trumpet simply flopped down on the floor, watching a wary Reggie continue to eat. He became a regular guest, letting himself in at his convenience. According to the new Will, Reggie would also be fed and treated as an heir.

Trumpet was such a sweet, gentle guy. Each night the retriever slept on the foot of Gabe's bed, with his little teddy bear close by. While he chased the various critters living on and around the ranch, he never hurt one. Once, he cornered a young rabbit, which had somehow made its way into the fenced garden area. When Gabe arrived at the scene, Trumpet was on his stomach in front of the frightened animal, trying with soft woofs and yips, to entice it to play.

Trumpet could see Gabe staring out the window. With Sarah gone, Gabe sometimes stopped whatever he was doing to simply stare off into the distance. Rising to his feet Trumpet took a few steps forward and paused, when his friend was like this he would wait a bit before going to him. Watching him standing behind the window, Trumpet sensed the same unseen thing that took Sarah was now stalking Gabe.

2

A Walk in the Rain

Gabe descended the porch steps and met Trumpet in the front driveway. After hiking about a mile up the narrow dirt road Gabe and Trumpet made their way to an ancient stump at the far side of the road where the ground fell away to the valley below. Trumpet brought a stick hoping to initiate one of his favorite games. Using his wooden cane for support, Gabe bent to take the stick from Trumpet's mouth. Seeming to understand his master's difficulty, the retriever rose up a bit on his hind legs until the stick was easily taken.

"Thank you. You're a good one, Trumpet." Pausing until his wind returned, he gave the stick a toss down the hill. Tail flashing happily Trumpet bounded back up to Gabe dropping the stick at his feet. After a few more tosses and retrievals, Gabe straightened, waving him off. "Okay. You go sniff, go run."

Gabe found a comfortable place to sit on the stump to watch Trumpet trot and prance, envious of his effortless gait. "There was a time I could run with the best of them." Knowing no one was within a mile or two, Gabe felt free to muse out loud. "At least until a few years back when I wrenched my knee working on the tractor. Hell, I used to be six feet of muscle and blood." The saying brought a smile to his face. " 'Used to be,' being the operative phrase, of course."

Trumpet paused in his exploration, making sure Gabe was still in sight before bounding into the woods. Occasionally, Gabe could see flashes of his brilliant coat moving easily through the woods and undergrowth.

"I'm going to miss this." Memories curled around him like a pleasant warm smoke. "I married a fine woman, my life-long partner." His words softened as her image came to mind. "At first, there was love and passion. Gradually, over the years, the passion mellowed into a contented companionship, but there was always love."

When Trumpet reappeared at his side, Gabe was watching a dark series of clouds moving in from the coast, marching fast and heavy across the valley in his direction. At a light rumble from the approaching storm, the retriever nosed Gabe's hand anxiously before placing a big paw on his knee. "I think we're going to get wet, my friend." With his eyes on the darkening sky, Gabe rose from where he was seated and turned to follow Trumpet back the mile or so through the woods to their cabin.

The wind hit them when they were still ten minutes from the warmth of the fire left in the wood stove. Moments later the rain began in a disorganized splatter before slowly working into a heavy beating downpour. Sticking close to Gabe's side, Trumpet looked up, snapping off a sharp bark encouraging his friend to pick up the pace.

"Yeah, you're right. We should have headed back as soon as I saw the clouds."

The thunder came as a low grumbling wave across the

land. Trumpet had always been frightened by thunder. Tucking in closer, the fur on the ridge of his back bristled. Gabe could tell he was fighting the urge to bolt for the safety of their cabin. "It's okay boy, we're almost there."

The sky lit. The thunder boomed closer. This time Trumpet answered with a low growl and bared teeth, but kept moving. "That was close, less than a second away. Good boy, you're a brave dog." Gabe encouraged the retriever. "You keep it away from us."

Just a dozen yards away on their left, lightning struck a tree. From somewhere in the flash and thunderous boom, Gabe could hear the sharp crack of splintering wood. The smell of ozone permeated the air. Pressing close, Trumpet yelped, his head turning quickly side to side, his movements sharp and stiff.

Stopping, Gabe rested his fingertips on the wet fur of the dog's head. With the cane, he pointed toward an old burned-out snag. "After that one I'm guessing the lightning won't strike near us now. We'll head over there, hunker down to wait it…" His words were cut short by a growing sense of electricity in the air around him. Even his teeth seemed to tingle while the area turned a bright blue-white, the brightest white he'd ever seen.

❧

"Good God," Gabe thought the words as he opened his eyes. Something lay across his face, obscuring his view. A few moments passed before he recognized his hand. I must be lying on my back with my hand across my face. He tried to move it, but it didn't respond. His alarm increased when he realized where there had been dull aches and occasional shots of sharp angry pain, now there was nothing. He often wished to be free of pain, but not to lose all feeling. A panicked reckoning came to him, "I'm paralyzed!"

Gabe tried to take a deep breath to calm himself but felt an oddly disconnected sensation of 'floating.' *Okay, I've been struck by lightning and the paralysis is probably temporary. I don't hurt, I'm breathing, it could be worse.* The thunder was gone but he could see the rain; hear it splattering in a staccato into the pine needles inches away. The strike sharpened both his hearing and vision, but he couldn't feel anything.

Gabe heard a soft whining moan. Another thought came to him, *Trumpet!* The name shouted in his mind. "Trumpet!"

A moment later the hand slowly moved to one side, until vanishing completely, and he was watching the needles move away. *What the hell is going on?* He barely thought the question when his view moved and widened. *This is like watching through a camera lens with someone else holding it.* His view went sharply side to side before stopping again.

Gabe found himself looking at a body where little whiffs of white smoke arose from the singed clothes. It took him a moment to recognize the profile of the man's face. He wanted to turn and run, but instead tried for a non-existent deep breath. *Wait. Stay calm. This is some kind of an out-of-body experience, like something you've read about in* Reader's Digest.

There was another whimper he recognized as Trumpet's. Trumpet's panting calmed his mind as he moved in on the face. Yeah, it's me and this is incredible. Maybe, I'm dead and about to leave. He tried to visualize turning to see his dog. Instead, it came to him, he was looking down a long furry nose. Ahhhhh!

Gabe mentally shook off his shock and began to take stock of the situation. I'm in Trumpet's head; he may be able to hear me if I concentrate hard enough. "Trumpet, it's okay boy. I'm, um, right here." There was a brief glimpse of the woods, and then he was moving fast through the brush, dodging trees, his view Trumpet height above the ground. For what seemed an eternity, he merely experienced the passing scenery until they were approaching the split rail fence.

The forward motion came to an abrupt stop, but different parts of the forest flashed around him. Trumpet was circling around, confused and not understanding where Gabe's voice was coming from. Well, this isn't working, another thought came. "Home, boy. Let's go home!"

The fence rapidly approached until the upper and lower rails flashed by. The cabin with its small covered porch and welcoming drift of smoke from the chimney pipe appeared. Moments later they were on the porch, their eyes on the door handle. They stopped. His view of the deck swinging side to side. Good guy, shake off the water. Now, you know what to do. "Open the door, go on in."

Instead of hurrying inside, Trumpet reached back to retrieve his small stuffed bear from the porch rail. He turned his attention to the handle which drew closer, his paw pressed it down until the latch gave a click as it released, then his nose pushed the door open. Once inside he headed for the bedroom, carefully placing the bear at the foot of the bed on the light quilt.

Trumpet went to the far side of the bed and stopped abruptly. In one of the mirrored closet doors, Gabe found he was looking at the retriever. He was still wet, with a dark singed spot above his left ear. "Trumpet, that's us. I mean, we're together. This is us."

Oddly, the situation made Gabe feel like laughing. "I'm here."

Instead of continuing to stare, Trumpet moved to one side, quickly working the sliding door partway open with his nose. Peering into the dim forms of the clothes hanging there, he let out a pleading yelp.

"No. Back, boy. Back."

Once again in front of the mirrored door, Trumpet sat. Gabe watched the nose ease closer and closer to its reflection until they were almost touching. He looked deeply into the trusting brown eyes gazing back. "Good boy, Trumpet." Gabe thought the words in a soothing tone, imagining he was stroking the dog's head. "I'm right here with you. It's going to be all right."

At last, the events of the day left Trumpet wanting to retreat to a safe place to rest. Comforted by Gabe's words, he let out a gentle sigh. Jumping onto the bed he curled up with Yogi. As the retriever's eyes sagged shut, an equally exhausted Gabe wondered, if he fell asleep, would he wake up with Trumpet? The darkness beckoned.

The following morning, Gabe awoke in pitch-black darkness. He tried to turn over in bed, to open his eyes, but nothing was happening. In his struggle, he sensed a comforting presence, like finding a friend in the blackness of a deep cavern.

As he had since puppyhood, Trumpet's eyes quickly focused on the image in the mirrored doors of the bedroom closet and even before he stretched, his tail began to thump. But this morning, lying amid the tousled covers of the sun-streaked bed, his tail slowed.

Now fully awake, Gabe studied the reflection of the golden retriever while the events of the previous day suddenly flooded back to them. "Trumpet."

Trumpet sprang off the bed to stand again in front of the mirrored door, his nose pressed against the cool glass. His name came to him as clearly as if spoken.

"I'm here, Trumpet. Remember?"

Trumpet sighed, pressing his nose against the glass until his breath formed a foggy ring. He remembered.

The bedroom doorway flashed by, along with the living room couch and wooden magazine holder as the retriever made for the front door. This just-along-for-the-ride, Gabe mused, was going to take some getting used to. At the door, Trumpet stopped. Whirling, the retriever ran back to the bedroom looking above and below the bed, then poking his head inside the closet.

"Trumpet!" Gabe thought as hard as he could. "Good boy, good guy. I'm not hiding from you. I'm with you now."

"This is it." Gabe would have sighed if he could. "Come on; let's go out for a walk."

At the thought, 'walk,' Trumpet turned and trotted back to the front door. In his usual manner, he took the rope in his mouth pulling down until the latch clicked. Still holding on, he took a step back until the door was open enough for his nose to fit in the gap, and then he wedged the door the rest of the way open with his shoulder.

Making their way out onto the wooden porch, Gabe realized swapping from a knob to a handle may have been one of the smartest things he'd ever done. While opening the doors, and a dozen or so other 'tricks' were initially simply interesting behaviors to teach the obliging retriever, they could now be a matter of survival. While he was congratulating himself for his brilliant forethought, he noticed they were heading through the wet grass toward the apple tree at the edge of the yard.

Trumpet stopped, and Gabe was presented with a steady image of the cabin for a short length of time. He was beginning to worry when it suddenly came to him. Great, he thought, *now* who's going to shovel it up?

A sudden dizzying whirl accompanied by several sharp barks let Gabe know Trumpet wanted to play. Sure, I'll just pick up a stick and throw it for us. Another thought came to him. "Let's run!"

The dog lunged forward, treating Gabe to short sparkling tufts of grass flashing by, and then they were over the fence and on the narrow dirt road leading to the redwood water tank. Splashing through the puddles remaining from the preceding day's storm, they made a fast turn at the tank toward a spot on the ranch where each morning Gabe sat on an old tractor seat screwed to a six-foot section of railroad tie. With his dog and his coffee, he would watch the sun slowly rising over the range to the east.

Halfway there, Trumpet suddenly detoured back to the cabin. Making his way inside he took the stuffed bear from the bed. Carrying his friend, he headed back to the front door.

Realizing what Trumpet intended, Gabe chastised. "Come on Trumpet, you know the rules. Yogi stays at the cabin."

Trumpet lowered his head for a moment, the bear firmly in his mouth.

If it had been possible, Gabe would have laughed. "You have a point, you're in charge. I guess I need to accept that I am only your co-pilot."

Trumpet did however yield to Gabe's request and placed Yogi on the porch rail before heading back out to the tractor seat. The retriever settled in next to the empty seat providing Gabe a view of the eastern valley. "Well, Trumpet, we are still able to do this together." The peace of the moment was interrupted by Trumpet's enhanced sense of smell as he sniffed the air for the dead creature nearby. Though Gabe didn't want to think about it since technically he was still around, somehow they needed to deal with the matter of his body.

He'd been around bodies before, decades back during his tour of Vietnam. Gabe still felt a catch in his throat when he thought of the friends he lost. The idea of going back to his corpse; well, this would be beyond weird. The possibility of his mind jumping back into its old host kept nagging at him. From years of experience, Gabe knew the best thing to do was to confront the problem.

3

—

A Lovely Garden

"Hold it." From the cover of a small stand of pine near the cabin, Warren Theodore Bunting Esq. raised a hand cloaked in a camouflage pattern glove. Likewise clothed in camouflage fatigues, but with an open plunging neckline displaying a deeply tanned and generous cleavage, his wife, Tiffany-Jean, stopped in her tracks. From a few feet behind him, her eyes probed through the low branches of the trees ahead. "What is it?" She whispered back. "You *told me* Gabe was gone."

Bunting stiffened at the impatient tone of her voice. "I said, I *thought* he would be in town getting the paper. His truck is in the yard, but...Wait, the dog is there alone."

Trumpet trotted up onto the porch, and was inside for a minute before emerging and placing something on the porch rail, then heading out toward the road.

"What's the thingy in its mouth?"

"Quiet, the damned dog will hear you." Waving his wife to silence, Bunting kept his eyes on the cabin and his voice low. "It appears to be a stuffed toy of some kind."

"You said we would be downwind."

After silently clenching and unclenching his teeth, Bunting whispered fiercely to his wife. "Though the dog won't smell us, he may *hear* us if you don't remain quiet."

"You're using that tone with me. Again." She brushed at the sleeve of her shirt. "These branches are still wet."

Bunting screwed his eyes shut for a moment, taking a small breath before whispering. "I apologize. A little discomfort just adds to the thrill of the hunt."

"Oh, please. We're not hunting; we're just spying."

"Yes, yes." He again waved her to be silent.

Across the clearing, the dog was trotting past the deer fence protecting the small garden. He abruptly stopped, turning his head toward where the Buntings were concealed, his nose came up and his tail slowed its wagging.

To Bunting's relief, T.J. remained silent until the dog finally continued out the gate. At times like this, he almost missed his first wife, whom he divorced soon after he met the current Mrs. Bunting at a gentleman's club in Reno.

"The dog just took off. I'd guess he's catching up with Picket." Once certain there had been enough time for the dog and master to make the turn where the drive ran between a broad stand of redwoods, Bunting stepped cautiously into the open. "Wait here," he called over his shoulder, jogging over to the gate. Gabe and the dog were nowhere to be seen.

"Are they gone?"

Bunting cringed from T.J.'s shrill voice carrying over from the front of the cabin where she'd hurried to, ignoring his warning. "Sometimes, I wonder..." He muttered out loud.

She stood on the porch and waved gaily. Even from where he stood, a good sixty feet from the cabin, Warren could see the contents of her matching camouflage bra moving in such a way to remind him why he should cease his wandering. Clearing his throat, he headed over to her.

"Over here, this view will be our lovely Tucsony-style Italian garden." She gestured to the small pasture facing the west.

"I believe you mean, Tuscany," he offered. "Tucson is a town in Arizona…not, um, ah. Well, Italy." He smiled weakly as she fiddled with the only button on the shirt, her chin up, her eyes on his.

"You know how the outdoors turns me on?"

Actually, her definition of the outdoors was confined to the backyard pool at their home in town, and the large screened-in deck off the bedroom of their nearby cabin. "Um, yes."

"Just imagine, how turned on I'll be when you tear this dump down and build my dream house." Her eyes narrowed. "With, its…Tucsony, garden." Her fingers left the button fastened. "And a large redwood trellis in front, with lots of plants like the hanging gardens of… She nibbled at her lower lip briefly before brightening. "Bumble On."

"Oh yes. Just spectacular." Bunting winced and fought the urge to correct her with, "Babylon."

"Well." She turned and stretched her arms out. "How soon can you boot the old guy off of our perfect view?"

There, she had a point. The view was perfect. To the east and south, the land to the left of the drive dropped away revealing a broad valley with the occasional head of cattle dotting the low hillside a mile or so away. The forest bordered the land on the north and to the west, where a well-used dirt path eventually led to another long narrow valley.

By comparison, the small hunting lodge he purchased the prior fall on the adjacent property was located on a low finger of land surrounded by firs. Even if he went through the tedious and expensive process of having the trees removed, the surrounding terrain would limit their view to a few hundred yards in any direction.

"If I could only convince him to sell." Though he'd been over twice to see Gabe Picket, both times the stubborn old man turned him down flat. When he checked at the county offices, the taxes were current and there were no liens. Still, for a man in his profession, there were other options.

As if reading his mind, T.J. folded her arms across her chest and pouted. "Your law partner is his attorney. Can't you work out a deal, or just sue him for the ranch, or something?" She lowered her eyes demurely. "My big, hunky, attorney."

Making their way back to their property, Bunting considered not for the first time, his life was fast becoming the cliché his law partner warned him about. Well, screw him. With his eyes on T.J.'s shapely backside, Bunting shook off his momentary doubt. While my straight-arrow of a partner is taking his forty-something wife and three kids out on their bicycles, I'm running around in my Mercedes with a hot young... "Ahhh!" His thoughts were diverted when T.J. released hold of a low branch which whipped back into his ample stomach.

"What is it Trumpet?" The dog paused at the porch. After snuffing the steps, he lifted his nose toward the handrail. He moved Yogi carefully to the porch couch and continued to sniff around.

"Look, forget your toy and pay attention." He pictured his body and thought the words in a calm and soothing fashion, but Trumpet continued his investigation. "This is what we have to do."

By the dog's reaction, he was pretty sure Trumpet heard his words as if he were standing nearby.

When Trumpet opened the front door, it dawned on Gabe that with one glaring exception, they were going through their usual routine. The morning walk, sitting and musing before returning to the cabin, and food; this was what they both needed.

Back inside the cabin, Trumpet made for his food dispenser. With his nose, he nudged the handle to fill his dish to its normal level. At one point he paused, his eyes going to the aluminum pie pan assigned to Reggie. The empty pan was in its usual spot, as the raccoon normally appeared in the early afternoon for his feeding.

For some reason known only to the raccoon, Reggie traded for his meals. Everything from old soft drink pop-tops to partially intact glossy magazine covers were brought by the raccoon. With great dignity, he handed Gabe his 'payment' for the dog food placed there. Next to the pan lay a crumpled soft drink can. Reggie showed up yesterday for his meal, offering in hand, but no one was there to feed him. Trumpet picked up the pie tin in his mouth and placed it below the food dispenser, filling it for Reggie, then returned it to its regular location.

When Trumpet was finished with his meal, he scratched for several moments. Finally, letting out a resigned sigh, he headed into the living room for the front door and porch. With Gabe's encouragement, they trotted toward the woods.

"We're too late." Hidden by a thick stand of ferns a hundred feet or so from the body they watched Deputy Pfeifer return from his Sheriff's four-wheel drive with a small camera. Once the deputy had taken several shots from different angles, he slipped the small camera into a shirt pocket. "Ah, damn, Gabe." Tilting the black baseball cap back on his head, he squatted down and touched Gabe's body gently on the shoulder.

Yeah, damn. He could tell Trumpet was torn between running over to the deputy, and a fear of going near the body. B.P. would probably put the retriever in the truck, which wouldn't be all bad. Hopefully, he would go to the cabin and find the envelopes containing the Will.

From their remote vantage point, Trumpet let out a low throaty growl, and Gabe realized two things. Though his vision through the dog's eyes had been sharp from the beginning of this experience, sounds came to him in a muted, cotton-in-the-ear fashion. This morning, however, he was hearing more and more clearly. This helped quell the fear he might suddenly lose his attachment to the dog. The growl was not directed to B.P. as he rose to his feet, but to the black Mercedes SUV of Warren T. Bunting pulling up next to the deputy's vehicle. Of all the people I'd rather not see me dead, Gabe thought, Bunting is at least two of them.

"A problem, officer?" Bunting was about the only one around who didn't simply refer to the deputy as B.P.

"There's been an accident." Trumpet focused on B.P.'s voice as his attention returned to the body. "I'm afraid Gabe's dead."

The SUV's driver door burst open. Bunting nearly falling in his hurry to get out. "Not. Not, Gabe Picket?" In a moment, he was standing a few feet away, his head averted slightly. "Who would..."

"Not, a who. From the burn on his head, I'd say he was struck by lightning during yesterday's storm. A tree over there got nailed too. In fact, I stopped to check the tree out, when I spotted...well, if it hadn't been for the tree, I wouldn't have seen him from the road."

The deputy circled the body and then squatted down. "Interesting."

"Officer?"

Carefully, B.P. took hold of the right wrist and turned it slightly. "The fingers on his right hand are burned where the charge left him. There is a bit of burnt red fur fused to the skin." He lowered the arm and rose back up. "Gabe's dog, Trumpet was always with him. He may be around here too."

Bunting almost mentioned he'd seen the dog just that morning. Thinking better of it, he asked instead. "You're saying the dog could be dead too?"

"Don't know. I've only seen one lightning strike victim before. There was a guy out on a mountain bike a few years back. Fried both the rider and bike. Trumpet may be lying close by, or he could be alive and pretty shaken up. If he's alive I'm surprised he's not here looking after, well…"

"I see."

It came as no surprise to Gabe that Bunting didn't appear too broken up regarding his recent demise. Something in the attorney's tone warned him that while Trumpet may have survived the lightning, he was now facing a new danger. And there was something else, Trumpets' sensitive nose was picking up the same sickly perfume he smelled at the cabin when they returned from their morning run. Gabe would have groaned out loud if he'd been able. Bunting was out at our place a little while ago. The door wasn't locked. What if he found the envelopes?

As B.P. took a few more photos of the scene, Bunting asked if there was anything he could do before easing toward his SUV and mentioning 'pressing business.' Instead of continuing toward town, Bunting headed back to their cabin to pick up T.J..

Gabe urged Trumpet to quietly leave. Holding his ground, the red dog gave a few muffled 'whuufs.' "That's not me anymore, Trumpet. I'm still here with you." He wondered how to get the idea across to the dog, though he, himself, wasn't totally certain what was going on. "Look, we need to get back to the cabin."

Instead of following Gabe's commands, Trumpet lay watching the deputy take a small green tarp from his four-by and gently cover the body. For a time B.P. stood by the tarp, his arms folded, appearing deep in thought. At last, the deputy dipped his head slightly as if making a decision. He moved to a loose parade rest, then snapped to the position of attention. Eyes straight ahead, his body rigid, B.P. brought his hand up to the brim of his ball cap in a crisp military salute.

Gabe was completely taken aback. At once he felt proud and guilty. Proud, another veteran would render him a salute; guilty, because he wasn't actually, dead, but rather a witness in a dog's body.

B.P. dropped the salute with a quiet, "I'll miss you, Gabe."

A sense of loss washed over Gabe, as he watched the deputy heading back up to his truck. All the things he could no longer do played out in front of him like a long sad home movie. His wallowing in despair was gradually, peacefully, breached by a similar feeling he had earlier in the morning. There was someone very close by to comfort him. He could almost see an image of him and Trumpet sitting together, a gentle sun warming them.

B.P. made a radio call and returned from his truck with his insulated coffee cup. He made himself comfortable on a small stump at the base of an old redwood. Leaning back against the ancient tree, he closed his eyes, occasionally sipping from the cup.

Concealed by the ferns, Trumpet settled into a half-nap, his eyes mostly closed. All the urgency of getting things done left Gabe, replaced by a deep sense of peace surrounding him. He felt himself drifting pleasantly through many of the past's good times.

Trumpet, Gabe, and the deputy were roused from their

various thoughts when the Number One engine from the town's small fire department rumbled to a stop behind B.P.'s four-by-four. Apparently satisfied, Trumpet slowly rose to his feet and they moved back toward the cabin. The retriever felt content as Gabe pictured the two of them walking through the woods.

4

—

Careful What You Eat

"You're sure the sheriff won't catch us?"

Bunting turned to his wife as they pulled up in front of the cabin. "Deputy Pfeifer was going to call the fire department on his radio. He'll wait by the body until they arrive." The attorney looked at his watch. "That was fifteen minutes ago."

She looked anxiously over her shoulder. "This feels creepy."

"Think about your Tuscany villa."

They got out and slunk up to the front door. Finding it unlocked, Bunting led the way inside. "My partner is the late Mr. Picket's attorney, who mentioned he was going to write a new Will. As it hasn't appeared at the office yet, I want to see if he revised the document."

Bunting moved into the kitchen, where on the table was a laptop computer, and two envelopes. "Bingo." He picked up a plain, unsealed envelope from the table and held it up.

"There are two of them." T.J. picked up the second, which was addressed and stamped. Fanning herself with it, she smiled.

Wasting no time, Bunting opened and unfolded the paper. After reading the contents he noticed the computer was still on. Gabe left the document open, and Bunting

— 31 —

quickly deleted the file. He then noticed the file cabinet in the living room, with the key in place. He decided to examine it for any files pertaining to the Will. He easily located a folder labeled 'New Will' containing a third copy.

While he was reading the Will, his wife moved about the neat little kitchen. She ran her fingertips over the simple cherry cabinets, checking for dust before wiping them carefully on a fresh paper towel. On the white Formica countertops were jars with various labels, including one with Doggy Treats neatly penned on the lid.

"Ugh, dog food in the kitchen." She wrinkled her nose. "I just don't understand how people can live like this."

There was a small noise behind her.

When Bunting finished reading, he went to the porch to survey what he knew would soon be his. Suddenly a high-pitched blood-curdling scream filled the cabin. He turned in time to find T.J. clearing the front door opening at full tilt, hands high over her head, mouth wide open but now silent. Without slowing she threw her arms around her husband, pinning his to his side, launching them both off the porch and onto the gravel.

Lying on his back under her, the wind knocked from him, Bunting endured what seemed to be an eternity of his wife screaming in his face. When he finally caught a breath, he tried to force her arms apart to free himself.

"T.J.," he gasped, "get a hold of yourself. Do you want the sheriff to hear you?"

"Raaaacckee, raaaackee!" Was her frantic reply.

"Racket?" he asked, trying once again to free his arms.

"Rackeeeee." The word trailed to a whisper. Suddenly spent, she went limp.

"Wonderful." Bunting resumed his struggle. Finally working his way from beneath T.J., he staggered to his feet.

"Oh god, it was horrible." Suddenly aware of water dripping from her chin to her wet blouse, she sat up from where she leaned against the edge of the porch. "I'm wet."

"You passed out. I used a little water to bring you around."

"Not from here? Not plain tap water?" Her eyes registered a look of disgust.

Bunting averted his eyes from the old horse trough. "It's the only available water." He tried a different tact. "I was worried about you."

She let out a deep theatrical sigh, her eyes focusing on something in the distance. "It was horrible. It, it, walked toward me. It had beady, little, eyes."

"The, um, rackee?"

"Rackee?"

"You kept saying 'the rackee, the rackee.'" Under the narrowed-eyed gaze of his wife, Bunting cleared his throat. "I could be wrong."

"Raccoon. I was *saying*, raccoon."

"Raccoon. Of course."

"The filthy little animal came in the back door. It just walked toward me clutching a, a…" A puzzled look crossed her face, swiftly changed; then she fixed Bunting with a hard stare. "My God, the man keeps dog food in his kitchen."

"Well, you never know about people, do you?"

"We'll have to fumigate the place before we tear it down."

"Of course. You stay here and rest. I'll just go back in and take a look around."

On the way to the kitchen, he took a fireplace poker from its place next to the wood stove. The only thing he could see out of place in the kitchen was one leg from an old wooden nutcracker lying in the middle of the floor. "Odd." He picked it up and carried it out with him.

"Akk!" T.J. shrieked when she saw what he was holding. "It was holding it in its filthy little hands." She made a face. "And now *you're* touching it."

After making a show of throwing it out across the yard, he turned back to her. "You know, I didn't see the second envelope anywhere."

"Envelope?"

"There were two. I opened one, which contained a Will. I'm guessing the second also contained a copy which Gabe was about to mail."

"Oh. *That* envelope." She nibbled at her lower lip. "I remember. I threw it at the raccoon. The filthy little creature must have taken it."

"Hmm." Bunting quickly mulled over the chances of the copy of the Will turning up to haunt him at some later date. Warren, he mentally chided himself, you're a successful attorney and you're worried about a raccoon? He gave his wife a confident smile. "The little beast will probably use it for his nest. We will never see him, or it again."

"You left the front door open."

"We aren't done here yet. Do you have your anxiety pills with you?"

"It will only make him sleep?" T.J. peered at the contents of the dog dish. Bunting was emptying the contents of a second tiny capsule into a depression he pressed into a lump of hamburger taken from the refrigerator.

"Yes. The dog is about half the weight of an adult." He kneaded the meat for a few seconds until he was satisfied, then set the bowl back on the floor and went to the sink to wash his hands. "The sooner the dog shows up, the better. We'll just park the car down the road, and wait and see."

"What if the deputy shows up first?"

"Hopefully his help will be slow to arrive, and he'll do a very thorough investigation out in the woods."

"What did you do with your envelope?"

"Oh." He gave her a smug smile. "It accidentally caught fire, along with the one I found in the file cabinet, during my inspection of the wood stove. Just for good measure, I also deleted the original file from the laptop."

On the way back to the cabin Gabe tried to picture the actions needed to accomplish the tasks before them. They would take the letter addressed to B.P. from the table and go down to their mailbox on the road. Sarah had taught Trumpet to fetch the mail, so he knew how to open the mailbox, but instead of getting the mail he needed to insert the letter and nose up the little metal red flag. When B.P. received his copy of the Will, he would find the changes, and would surely honor his final wishes. Then, everything else would take care of itself, more or less.

Gabe figured he was not only in a highly unusual position but a tenuous one at best. With no idea what was holding him in the dog's mind, he continued to worry he might slip away into whatever awaited him. Just a day earlier he was preparing for his time to be up, but by getting caught in the storm he may have lost any possibility of helping Trumpet. He hoped for a second chance to help his friend.

"Damn. I can smell it too." Gabe was worried as Trumpet opened the cabin door. The strong perfume scent was everywhere.

Sure enough, as he feared, the envelopes were missing from the table. Without the new Will, the property would be sold, most likely to Bunting, and Trumpet would go to live with Sarah's sister in San Francisco. He really wanted Trumpet to live out his life with B.P. on this ranch, especially if he was going to co-exist with him. Now, things were leaning toward the mean side of desperation.

There was one more possibility, the third signed copy was in the cabinet. "Okay. We have to get into my filing cabinet and pull out a file." Gabe was keeping what he hoped was a positive attitude as they eyed the small key inserted into the cabinet's lock. As a matter of course, he almost always left the key there.

"Pay attention. We're going to turn the key like this." He pictured the dog turning his head sideways, gently taking the key between his front teeth, rotating his head back, and unlocking the cabinet.

Instead, he tentatively raised his paw, resting it against the key.

Gabe gave him a gentle, "wait, watch," and pictured the whole thing once again. "Come on smart guy, you can do it."

By the fifth failure to follow instructions, and his clawing at the key, Gabe understood Trumpet was simply trying to do what he watched Gabe easily accomplish in the past. Accompanied by a soft 'wuuf,' Trumpet dropped his paw and lowered his nose until his forehead rested against the drawer. His breath began to come in long ragged sighs.

Gabe pictured himself kneeling next to the dog, stroking his broad red-gold head. "I know Trumpet, I miss me too."

After a short time, Gabe became aware of a new, growing sensation, they were hungry. Trumpet backed away from the cabinet, stretched languidly, and entered the kitchen. The retriever went to his bowl and began wolfing down the hamburger before Gabe had time to think.

"Wait, boy! We didn't leave anything in the bowl."

It was too late. With the hamburger gone, Trumpet nudged the feeder, allowing a small amount of dry food to drop into the bowl. He ate at his usual pace while Gabe fretted over the meat.

5

JUST A DOG

"Oh man, this isn't good." Gabe stared through Trumpet's half-opened eyes at the kitchen wall, obscured by the chrome-plated grill of what he guessed to be a portable kennel. Fortunately for Bunting, the prior owners of his property raised border collies, and left behind a few kennels. One of which came in handy for confining the large, drugged dog.

"You're fortunate I have a decent soul. A less honorable man would have just simply poisoned you, buried your carcass out in the woods, and called it a day. I, however, am going to give you a chance to live out your little canine life in Nevada."

"You're not going to leave him at the God-forsaken property you have out in the desert? What about the pound?" Well, thank you, Tiffany Jean. Through Trumpet's bleary eyes, Gabe was treated to a view of her cleavage as she leaned close to the cage.

"If I leave the dog at the pound, questions could be asked which could very well eventually bring him back here." Bunting's voice became more earnest. "If the dog remains here, I might add, there will be no possible hope of your Tucsony Garden.

"Oh." Her eyes hardening she backed from the cage.

"Then you must go for the greater good. Of me."

Bunting was going to need T.J.'s help to get the crate into the back of the SUV. Together they dragged it through the house and bumped it down the front steps. The overweight, and out-of-shape attorney opened the rear hatch of the large vehicle, and with a considerable effort, they lifted the cage in.

Watching from the cage, Trumpet could see Tiffany-Jean back on the front porch. She gingerly lifted the teddy bear from the couch. "This is so disgusting." Holding the little bear at arm's length, she went over to the garbage can at the far edge of the covered porch. Lifting the lid, she turned her head away and dropped it in. The lid clanged, then slipped to one side; Trumpet let out a barely audible whimper.

"I'm sorry boy." Gabe's apology was interrupted by Bunting absent-mindedly speaking to the dog.

"If you possessed the mind to do so, you might be asking yourself, why Nevada?" He shook out a woolen Army blanket, eyeing Trumpet for a moment before draping it over the cage. "Because, as my lovely wife has pointed out, I own a modest amount of acreage out there. If the economy proved stronger, it would have been developable. I plan to let you lose where you might spend the rest of your days hanging out as the beloved adopted pet of some unfortunate owners of a desert-bound motor home. If the coyotes don't get you first." The rear gate of the SUV slammed shut.

Until they dropped T.J. at the Bunting's main home in Santa Rosa, a conversation between the couple centered around a timetable for tearing down the cabin, and getting an exterminator to deal with, in T.J.'s words, the "raccoon influxtation."

With his wife gone, Bunting became talkative. "You have to look at this as being a small sacrifice on your part for the greater good, as my wife so aptly put it. You're just a dog, a simple, stupid animal. You would never understand or appreciate the old guy's little ranch. On the other hand, for my friends and colleagues, the place will become a comfortable retreat from the pressures of our various professions."

At the beginning of the drive, Gabe alternated between seething anger and feelings of gloom. His plan was at some point to get free and encourage Trumpet to rip the attorney's throat out. The only reading he could get from Trumpet was a kind of melancholy acceptance of his fate, with occasional remembrances of better days. After a while, Gabe succumbed to the dog's point of view; they would deal with the situation as it came to be.

On the way, there were two stops for gas where Gabe could hear the sounds of slamming doors, kids laughing, or people talking. Trumpet let out several barks and a few howls, but no one came to the SUV. One stop took longer, and through the retriever's sense of smell, Gabe knew Bunting was at a restaurant having a meal. It irritated him to no end when the attorney returned to the SUV without scraps for Trumpet.

The retriever was content to doze, and at times, Gabe joined him. The little naps reminded him of the times when he would take an afternoon snooze at the cabin; Trumpet curled up with his back against him. The dog's warmth reminded him of snuggling with his wife; the memory comforted him.

At the gate by Gabe's cabin, B.P. stopped his truck and got out. Once the gate was unlatched, he drove through, stopping in the gravel drive by the porch.

"Trumpet!" The deputy stepped onto the deck holding a small box in his hand, shaking it slightly. "Come on, boy. I have your favorite cookies!" He peered about while calling the dog's name until finally he opened the box and placed several on the little wooden table next to the old couch.

He circled the outside of the cabin, even using a flashlight from his belt to peer into the dim area under the deck. Noticing the garbage can at the deck's end with its lid sitting to one side, he looked inside. "Strange." The deputy plucked the stuffed bear from the can, gazing at it briefly before placing the retriever's toy next to the cookies.

After looking around a bit more, he tried the cabin's front door. "Trumpet?" he called as it swung inward. Quietly, he stepped inside, his eyes sweeping the room for the retriever. After checking the kitchen, he entered the small bedroom. Like the rest of the neat and well-organized cabin, the room was empty, though the bed was a tangle of damp covers and pillows.

Back in the kitchen he took food from the feeder, filled Trumpet's bowl, and then topped off the dog's water. He even put some food in the pie tin he knew belonged to Reggie. When he decided nothing else could be done, B.P. locked the front door, paused, and then, his hand still on the door handle, gazed at it thoughtfully for a moment. Finally, he unlocked it before pulling it shut.

After a long time with the sounds of wheels running along a highway, the SUV slowed and turned onto what sounded and felt like a gravel road. More time passed and the gravel sound changed to what Gabe guessed to be dirt. Finally, the big vehicle slowed to a stop. The engine died, and leaving the headlights on, Bunting got out.

The rear hatch swung up, and the blanket flipped back from the end of the cage. It was after midnight, and in the darkness Bunting stepped back and smiled. "Last stop, Desert Rose Estates."

Gabe looked past the attorney where from the SUV's taillights he could see down a long dirt road, flanked by occasional clumps of sagebrush, and a vast desert expanse.

"You see, there's a good chance if the coyotes don't find you, you'll stray onto someone's property. If *they* don't shoot you, maybe they will adopt you. Try to think positive. You could have a good life, tied up to the broken-down deck of someone's old trailer." Bunting smiled as he dragged the cage to the edge of the SUV's tailgate, gave it a final tug, and allowed it to fall to the ground.

Trumpet quickly regained his feet after the rough landing. The blanket slid off completely, revealing in the moonlight a view of high desert brush and a nearby mountain range. Gabe had to agree with Trumpet's thoughts; things smelled fresh, and it took a few moments to understand, promising.

The retriever turned toward the front of the cage. The fall popped the door partway open and before Gabe could offer him any encouragement, Trumpet quickly nudged it the rest of the way and bolted through.

A few yards from them, at the edge of the dirt road, Bunting was facing away from the SUV, relieving himself.

"Trumpet, get the keys!" The dog paused, his eyes on Bunting and the mountains beyond him. "He'll have to come after us on foot." All it took was a mental picture of a tired and sweating attorney staggering through the desert to encourage Trumpet to dash for the open driver's door of the SUV.

"Hey!" Bunting was trying to zip his fly and hurry to the SUV when Trumpet found the keys lying in the center console.

"Gotcha, you dumb…" As Bunting slammed the driver's door closed, for a moment man and dog were facing each other through the tinted glass of the driver's window. Then, they both turned their heads toward the rear of the vehicle eyeing the still-open hatchback.

"Shit!"

Trumpet was over the seat, leaping through the vehicle, and out the back to the road, the keys jangling.

"Come back, you stupid mutt!"

Trumpet slowed and swung around to find Bunting stopped a dozen strides from the Mercedes. Red-faced and already sweating, he pointed to the ground. "Drop the keys and I'll let you go. Otherwise," The attorney made a throat-slitting gesture. "I'll get out my 30.30 and hunt you down like a dog."

At Gabe's urging, Trumpet lowered his head and dropped the keys.

"You know, you're smarter than you look." Bunting was walking toward them.

Gabe instructed Trumpet to paw the keys over so the buttons on the black plastic fob were facing up. Bunting turned his head as the horn of the Mercedes sounded, lights flashed, and the rear door slowly swung down.

Gabe heard the faint 'click' of the locks engaging. "Good boy. Now, get the keys, and let's go."

"No, No, No, No!" Running to the SUV, Bunting hurried around the black vehicle, trying to open all the doors.

Trumpet sat calmly, watching the attorney pause to bump his head slowly against a side window, one hand on the door handle. After a few moments, he turned his head toward them. Slipping his hands casually into his pockets, he smiled. "Good dog, good doggie. Bring the keys. You're a good boy."

"Trumpet? No!"

Picking up the keys, Trumpet took a tentative step toward the attorney. "Trumpet, what are you doing?"

"Good, boy. There's water in the SUV, boy." Bunting's smile widened, and one hand slipped from the pocket and thumped the door. "And doggie cookies. Lots of nice cookies for a good, good doggie."

Ignoring Gabe's pleading, the retriever continued toward Bunting until they were just a few feet apart.

"Okay, good boy." Bunting bent and reached for the keys. "I'll just take…"

Trumpet uttered a soft growling noise. With a shake of the ring, he backed up.

Bunting made a quick move toward him. He easily whirled away.

"Trumpet, this is no game." Gabe's repeated request to run was ignored and Trumpet easily dodged a second attempt to snatch the keys.

After nearly fifteen minutes of unsuccessful attempts for the keys, Bunting stood bent over, hands on his knees, red face dripping with sweat, his breath coming hard.

A few tantalizing steps away, Trumpet dropped the keys and yawned deeply.

After wiping at the curtain of sweat running down his face with the tail of his sports shirt, the attorney looked up into the night sky.

Trumpet flopped down on his belly.

"No Trumpet, this is not the time to let down your guard. He's going to..."

"Gaaaahaahh!" Bunting cursed. Flinging himself at the dog his fingertips grasped for the keys as Trumpet smoothly snatched them up and danced away.

They were back near the SUV, where Trumpet sat and snapped his head up several times. The keys jingled in the still desert air.

Sensing the dog was in complete control of the situation, Gabe began to enjoy the way the attorney pleaded as he chased him around the Mercedes. He fantasized about Trumpet somehow unlocking the vehicle's door, starting the engine, getting the transmission into drive, and leaving Bunting alone in the desert. He was trying to figure out how the cruise control might be used for applying the throttle, when he noticed Bunting sprawled full length in the dirt, having made another futile lunge at Trumpet. A mixture of dirt and sweat covered the attorney's face, and the man's comb-over was no longer remotely combed over.

"You're just a dog," the attorney wailed. "A miserable dog,"

Yup, Gabe thought smugly, but we're a dog with the keys.

Trumpet, having become bored with the game, began to trot away from the black SUV and the road, the keys still dangling from between his front teeth.

"I will not be beaten by a damn dog, you hear me?"

Trumpet kept moving, glancing back to see Bunting getting to his feet and lifting something from the edge of the road.

"Easy boy," Gabe cautioned, "he might just get lucky with the rock."

Trumpet picked up the pace.

"Warren T. Bunting Esquire will not be beaten by a dog, no matter what the price!" A short silence followed his scream, ending abruptly with the sound of the rock breaking glass. He rummaged through the vehicle until he found the loaded 30.30 rifle.

Running toward the top of a small rise, a bullet splattered rocks a few feet to their left. Bunting's voice carried over the growing distance between them. "You stupid dog, I'll pry my keys from your cold, dead, jaws." There was the crack of a second shot, but the round was wide to the right.

Gabe pictured the dog dodging side to side in an irregular manner, and Trumpet obliged. More bullets hit the dirt or sang past them, though none as close as the first.

Though there was some chance they could be hit, Gabe felt a familiar exhilaration.

Away from the vehicle's lights Trumpet's night vision provided adequate details of their surroundings. Just past a large scrub plant, they found cover in the form of a long shallow sandy wash. They angled one way as they dropped into it, then once out of sight, immediately switched directions. The wash curved off to the left, away from the mountains, and Trumpet slowed to an easy lope until they made the bend.

"Good boy, we showed him. The attorney may have a rifle. But, never in his wildest dreams could he know you were being coached by a one-time Army infantry sergeant." Gabe began to think ahead. Worst case, he chases after us, spots our tracks, and heads this way. The wash went straight for a way before heading back to the right. They continued to lope along, Gabe planning their strategy as Trumpet took in the new scents and sounds.

Just before the next turn in the wash, they slowed and made their way up the shallow slope. In the small depression behind a basketball-sized rock, they dropped the keys and covered them. With Gabe's encouragement, near the top of the slope Trumpet dropped to his belly and crawled up to the edge. To Gabe's surprise, the attorney was standing where they entered the wash, a point only a hundred or so yards away.

Nuts, I must be thinking in dog miles, Gabe chided himself. He considered the problem while Trumpet lowered his muzzle to the sandy soil.

Bunting continued to scan the area for several minutes before suddenly raising the rifle and firing two shots out into the wash. "He thinks the shots will flush us out, but we're smarter than that, aren't we?" The wash undulated down through the desert from where they were hidden. Gabe guessed it would eventually straighten out onto the broad lower plain and leave them exposed. The best thing to do would be to do the unexpected. Backing down from their position, they began circling back for the SUV.

The driver's door had been left open. After a quick look for Bunting, they jumped up into the driver's seat, mindful of the bits of broken glass spread out from the passenger side to the console. A nearly full half-liter clear plastic water bottle lay on its side on the passenger seat next to a white deli sandwich bag.

Knowing an animal could last a lot longer without food than water, he urged him to grab the water and then run for it. After Trumpet sniffed at the bag, he lifted his head to look outside.

"Okay, grab the water, and let's go. Let's..."

Trumpet slapped one big paw on the top of the bag quickly ripping it open. In seconds, the wrapper was mostly torn away, and he was wolfing down chunks of sandwich.

Gabe thought he could almost taste roast beef and Swiss cheese.

The still air was punctured by another shot, and Trumpet brought his head up. Bunting now stood less than fifty feet away, sighting down the barrel of the Winchester rifle. He took two steps toward the SUV, his eyes locking with Trumpet's. "You." The words were flat with loathing.

Trumpet ducked, grabbed the water bottle, and was out the door.

"Hold it, you sorry-looking animal."

Anticipating Trumpet's next move, Bunting stood with the gun trained on them. Once again, the three of them locked eyes.

Gabe tried to form a plan, while Trumpet whirled away.

The report of the rifle was punctuated with the retriever's yelp of pain, causing him to drop the bottle of water. The sudden burst of intense heat at his hip brought a raging thought to Gabe; "You son of a bitch, you shot my dog!"

Snatching the bottle, Trumpet broke into a hard run.

Instead of an expected and deadly second shot, Gabe could hear Bunting shouting, "You won't get far. I've got a glove box full of bullets." Bunting's voice cracked as he screamed, "Lots and lots more bullets!"

"Go Trumpet, go! Bunting has to reload. He wasted most of the bullets in the rifle trying to flush us." The ground dropped steeply as they plunged back into the wash. Disregarding the wound, Trumpet loped easily along. Gabe praised him for his bravery and cunning. The dog seemed to smile as Gabe pictured him teasing Bunting with the keys.

6

—

WATER RITES

Daybreak brought into view an alluvial fan with the mountain to their backs. Gabe hoped to see evidence of a road or traffic ahead. Instead, there was a second range of low mountains. Trumpet needed to rest from his injury, and soon the desert heat would be upon them. He thought their best plan was to find a shady spot and wait for the cool of the evening to continue. Moving by night would also help in their escape from the attorney, should he pursue them out into the open desert.

With Gabe's urging Trumpet carried the water bottle with him until he reached a small squat outcrop of crumbling red rock. On the sparsely shaded side, he dropped the water container and began to dig. When he created a sizeable depression, he retrieved the water and settled in. For a while he arched back, licking slowly at the wound until the throbbing began to subside. He was thirsty and now came the puzzle of how to get a drink from the screw-topped container. Gabe was at a loss for a solution. Trumpet nosed the bottle around, then settled for carefully chewing at the cap. When the liquid began to seep from the holes he made, he managed to lap up what water hadn't leaked into the sand.

Gabe thought they would now slip into yet another nap. But Trumpet simply lowered his chin to his paws, remaining alert and watchful. Surprisingly, there was a lot to watch. They lay contently observing a big set of clouds march across the clear desert sky. A jet passed high overhead, the contrails from its wings trailing back to the horizon. The sagebrush moved in a light breeze. A tiny mouse scurried from the cover of one unseen hole to another. There were ants, and the odd beetle trudged along on an unknown mission. Finally, they dozed off and on, waiting for darkness to fall.

They were making good time toward a mountain range he judged to be to their south. The stars glowed bright and glimmered in the night desert sky. Gabe wondered to himself if the retriever kept glancing up to the sky to please him, or if this was a natural dog thing he simply never noticed.

Trumpet was thirsty, and occasionally he paused, nose in the air, seeking a hint of water. The night desert scents were mostly unrecognizable to Gabe, yet strangely enough, some reminded him of a grassy field after a soft rain. Others simply puzzled him.

When the crisp night air was pierced by the howls of coyotes, which were becoming more frequent, Trumpet stood stock still, his ears up, eyes probing the terrain ahead of them before continuing on. Gabe long since ceased to advise him.

The stars marched halfway across the night sky when they reached the base of the low mountains Gabe viewed earlier. Trumpet's nose came up. After tasting the breeze flowing over the rocks, he increased his pace. They came to a spot where the rock retreated into a narrow canyon. The rain smell Gabe experienced through the retriever was strong here, along with something else. Cautiously, nose down, eyes flicking from side to side, Trumpet entered the canyon. There were other smells unfamiliar to Gabe, but the water scent provided the strongest effect on Trumpet. He halted abruptly when they came into what looked to be the bowl of an ancient waterfall, and found they weren't alone.

Several coyotes stood or milled around an area of the rock where a minute amount of water dribbled from a thin vertical crack into a small pool. Two of the closest animals spotted the dog. With warning growls, they began to circle toward them. Ignoring Gabe's advice to back off to find another source of water, Trumpet lowered his head as he padded toward the pool. Their warning growls increased as the other canines began to close in.

Trumpet's movement slowed, his legs and back stiffened. This unfamiliar change coming over his friend caused Gabe's worries to increase. Trumpet was never a fighter, but now he was staring down the six coyotes. "Okay, boy. You need to fight for the both of us. If they get us, we're finished." Though the dog probably had a good twenty pounds on the smaller animals, they were superior in numbers.

Trumpet raised his lips exposing his canines, at the same time letting out a deep rolling growl. The creatures stopped their advance. Looking about nervously, two or three whined. Near the water, a slightly larger coyote with a mottled dark gray coat stood observing the scene. Gabe noticed the one on their left resumed his approach, his fangs bared in a head-down advance. Suddenly whirling, Trumpet let out a blood-curdling yowl, charging the animal. Tail and haunches down, the animal scooted away.

"Good, now he's turning away, let's get out of here." Ignoring Gabe, Trumpet snarled a warning at a coyote moving in from the other side, then went for the leader.

"No, boy! Let's go!" Gabe's thoughts were unheeded. His jaws furiously snapping, Trumpet hit his target. The force rolled the larger coyote onto his side until Trumpet was straddling his victim, the animal's neck in his jaws. Growling deeply, glaring at the circling pack, he held his prey, his eyes flashing a warning to the others. Tails down, the pack began to back away. Moving nervously about, they gradually opened the circle.

Beneath Trumpet, the leader remained silent. Slowly, cautiously, the red dog eased up on his grip. Carefully, keeping his eyes averted, the coyote slunk from under him. Head down, he gingerly got to his feet. Instead of joining the others, who paced nervously, he began to lick Trumpet's muzzle.

Now what? Gabe could see the rest of the pack was watching the scene. The muzzle licking gradually stopped and the subservient animal backed away, joining the others. After letting out a few sharp barks, Trumpet headed for the pool where he drank his fill.

The coyotes were moving back out through the canyon and Trumpet chose to follow. The other animals occasionally glanced back or slowed until he was moving with them through the desert. Gradually, they fanned out, a couple moving ahead, the rest staying to the flanks.

The pack slowed and came to a halt. Like the others,

Trumpet's head and nose were up and Gabe could tell he found something interesting in the air. The pack shifted toward a rocky hill where something caught their attention. The closer the pack got, the slower they moved. Like a squad of soldiers maneuvering toward an enemy, one or two would ease forward, holding until one by one, the others would catch up or move ahead. Having given up offering advice or trying to influence the dog, Gabe resigned himself to the role of a bystander.

They were close to the hill when several indistinct objects developed into what Gabe guessed to be wild sheep of some kind. Two had large, curved horns of rams, while by their short horns, he took the other four to be ewes. They pawed at the ground, occasionally lowering their heads to nibble at whatever they exposed. Movement caught Gabe's attention and he could see a pair of coyotes circling in from both sides. He expected Trumpet to take up the hunt with the others especially since he was hungry and had been accepted into the pack. Instead, he could feel a vague kind of bewilderment emanating from the retriever.

Gabe chided. "Well, Trumpet, what did you expect? Did you think your new friends were stalking a wild bag of kibble?"

The coyotes stopped their ears up and alert. The scent on the night breeze was beckoning them to slink cautiously forward. One came up next to him, his eyes expectant. Trumpet ignored him until the other continued on. Gabe could read something else about Trumpet: disappointment. Well, of course, Gabe thought. The area surrounding their cabin had been home to rabbits, deer, raccoons, and other woodland creatures. When encountered they were a curiosity, rather than something to be killed and eaten, Trumpet had taken a cue from Gabe and Sarah in their respect for Reggie. The creatures were different than him, but somehow a part of his extended family. After watching for a few more moments, he broke from the pack, turning back into the open desert.

Quietly, he padded along, pausing here and there to sniff while occasionally breaking into a trot. Man and dog continued to move through the night at a steady rate, the direction selected by the dog. The ridge far ahead of them was backlit by what could only be the lights of a sizeable city. "Smart guy," Gabe pictured himself petting the dog's neck and added, "you've led us to Reno." Trumpet stopped and sniffed, standing with his nose up slightly, his ears slightly forward listening to the night whispering a veiled promise of the coming day. Come on, Gabe encouraged him, just head toward the city. Instead, Trumpet veered to their right, back toward some low hills, leaving Gabe to wonder what exactly he didn't know. Which lately, was about everything.

Just a few days back, he mused, I was just an old guy living out in the woods and missing his wife. Today, I'm trapped in my dog's mind, traveling across the middle of nowhere. The despicable Warren Bunting and his ditzy trophy wife will probably get the ranch, and that will be that. With nothing to do but watch the passing scenery, Gabe thought about Sarah and what she would have thought of his predicament. Probably, he thought, she would have laughed.

She was one of those women who laughed easily and often. He recalled how she lit up when he came through the front door of the cabin with a seven-week-old Trumpet wriggling in his arms. He barely got out his lame, "he followed me home, can I keep him?" when she was hugging the two of them. With a laugh and a kiss, she took Trumpet in her arms and proceeded to spend the next two years spoiling him, as Gabe had noted on several occasions, 'beyond belief.'

The first night, while Sarah played with their new puppy, Gabe set up a blanket bed in the kitchen. "He's so little. I'll take him out when he has to go," his wife had solemnly promised. After pets and reassurances, Trumpet happily curled up with a little stuffed bear on the foot of their bed. Three times during the first night, as well as on numerous successive nights, Gabe was woken by a tiny pink tongue licking his face, asking to be taken outside. Without any 'accidents,' the foot of their bed became his sleeping place. When Trumpet became a bit older he was able to hold it all night, and then later learned how to let himself out when he needed to. He was always a quick learner and eager to please.

Gabe thought about the comfort he received from Trumpet during the miserable days and nights after Sarah's passing, and then following her memorial service. At times Trumpet would sit by the front door, or run out to the truck, circling as if waiting for her to open the door and climb out. Through it all he was a bottomless source of encouragement and solace.

"Trumpet, what is it?" The sides of the retriever heaved while he let out a series of soft whines. With the desert before them, the whining continued. Instead of the warm reassuring feeling Gabe had come to expect, he was bathed in a kaleidoscope of pictures accompanied by a deep sense of longing. Sarah's face and hands came and went; there were bits of the cabin, the old porch couch, their truck, the seats on the stump, and she was in each. At last, there was just her face and eyes on him. Trumpet dropped down on his stomach. Laying his head between his paws, the whining grew more profound. Gabe at last understood. He too was grieving.

"I'm sorry Trumpet. I'm just feeling lost. I miss her so much." Gabe began to understand the canine depth of his sorrow. "I'm sorry," he repeated and brought up his own images of Sarah hugging and reassuring the two of them. In time, Trumpet regained his composure and pulled himself to his feet, and they resumed their quest for a road.

"Damn, Trumpet, you were right, I guess you must have smelled the pavement or maybe heard a passing car." With this thought came a sense of satisfaction from Trumpet, and Gabe wondered who exactly had the superior intellect here. At odd intervals along the road's wide dirt shoulder were thickets of sagebrush. After selecting the largest patch, Trumpet dug out a shallow wallow to settle into for the remainder of the night.

With the dog's eyes closed, Gabe was left alone with his thoughts. He was learning something interesting about his canine friend. Instead of mulling over his predicament, or worrying about the future, Trumpet appeared to take in the scents and sights, concentrating on the present.

7

AEMEA'S TRIUMPH

"Trumpet?"

A few moments passed in the pitch blackness.

"Trumpet," a familiar voice summoned. "You know I can't see without you."

Tired and sore from his long journey, Trumpet remained stretched out comfortably on the soft desert sand. Though awake, he kept his eyes tightly closed.

Gabe continued, "I'll bet it's going to be a beautiful day. This is going to be a good one, I can feel it."

Eyes still shut; Trumpet lifted his head from between his paws. Though he knew it to be a futile gesture, he growled a soft, "go away" growl before rolling onto his side. More dark moments passed. Then there was a brief mental image of a desert hare scampering away on a zig-zag course among the sage, closely followed by a kaleidoscope of desert scenery.

"Please? Come on you big red dog, it's still you and me. We need to get moving."

This time an image of the ranch appeared. Leaves on the old apple trees up the grassy hillside shivered in the morning breeze. The cabin's wooden door slowly swung open to reveal a trim sixtyish woman clad in well-worn denim work clothes. Smiling softly, she tossed a long golden-gray braid over her shoulder. Bending slightly, she tapped her hip in a beckoning motion with the flat of her hand.

"Yeah," Gabe sighed, "I miss her too. But she'll always be there, and if we don't get going we could lose everything. I have a good feeling about today." There was a smile in the voice. "We turned a bad day into a better one, didn't we?"

A flood of brilliant light melted away the image until, at an odd angle, there was a view of the dirt and rock-shouldered stretch of highway framed by a portion of a large desert tree. The view slowly normalized as the big red dog rolled upright. Trumpet yawned broadly, stretching his front legs forward. He looked around and snorted.

"I'm still here. We've got a road; we'll get a ride." The voice beckoned, "we need to get up and get going."

Trumpet sighed, his head dropping down between his paws.

To the east, the sun cresting the mountains sent long eager streaks of gold along the wide valley floor. The sound emanating from that direction increased until, as if racing for its share of the new day, a solitary speck of light appeared against the shadowed mountain backdrop. The dog rose to his feet and moved out to the side of the road.

"See? Someone is coming."

Trumpet sat watching the speck gradually materialize into a motorcycle with a sidecar attached. The rig slowed as it drew closer, prompting Trumpet to say 'hello' by holding up his right paw, a favorite motion that usually brought friendly words and pets from strangers.

Easing over to the shoulder of the road, the rig came to a stop, the rider lowered the goggles to hang from her neck, her eyes flicking to the bike's mirrors. After a moment she stood up on the bike's footpegs. Shading her eyes, she surveyed the surrounding desert. Finally, she smiled at them as she dismounted the motorcycle and removed gauntlet-style gloves. "Well, hello handsome. I suppose you're aware sticking out your paw is one devastatingly cute trick."

Taking Trumpet's offered paw, "My pleasure, sir. I'm Aemea Rand," pronouncing her first name as "Amy." She began examining his paws and ran her fingers gently over his coat, commenting on the spot of his head and the bullet wound on his hip.

After a trip back to the rig to bring them water, she sat back and asked, "Well, my enigmatic friend, what on earth are you doing out here all by yourself?"

Trumpet paused from his drinking, looked up at her, and let out a "Woof." If Trumpet was commenting on the appearance of their benefactor, Gabe had to agree. The tall, statuesque young African-American woman wearing blue jeans, high-top boots, and a faded work shirt was pretty enough to grace the cover of any number of magazines.

"I've got groceries in the nose of the 'car, but there's room enough for you." Aemea got to her feet. "What do you say?"

"Damn." Gabe smiled inwardly. The motorcycle was a recent model Triumph Bonneville, a late model ringer for one he owned prior to joining the Army. This could be a sign if one believed in signs. Well, why the hell not? He was a man's mind sharing his dog's body, why shouldn't he believe in signs? Just above the chrome tank badge, in the white area, "Aemea," had been neatly hand-lettered in black paint with an accenting orange drop shade which matched the bike's second color.

As she stood watching him, Trumpet got up and went over to the sidecar, sniffing at the open area. Apparently satisfied, he jumped in, arranging himself so he sat down facing forward. Through Trumpet's eyes, Gabe peered ahead through the windscreen. "Good guy. Now tell the lady, thanks."

Trumpet lifted his head and snapped off several rapid sharp barks.

"Well, okay then." After returning the pan and canteen to the back of the sidecar, Aemea got back on the bike, drew the gloves over her hands, and started the engine. "We'll take it slow at first to see how you do." She pulled the goggles into place. As the rig accelerated, Trumpet's pleasure was obvious by his nose held high and ears flapping in the wind.

When they were moving along at a good clip, Trumpet leaned out past the small windscreen allowing the wind to make his jowls fill and flutter. He turned his head toward Aemea so Gabe could see she was smiling slightly. When she noticed the dog watching her, she turned her head and winked.

They covered several miles when the bike slowed, Aemea turning the rig onto a gravel side road. The road meandered for a half-mile or so until they reached a broad stand of ponderosa pines. On the far side, they broke out onto a wide clearing at the base of a small cliff. Shaded from the afternoon sun by a few of the pines and one large palm tree, a shiny aluminum Airstream trailer sat surrounded on three sides by a wide redwood deck. Posts reached up to support a peaked metal roof over the top of the Airstream providing protection from the midday sun. The backside of the trailer was snug against the cliff's rocky base.

Aemea steered toward a large metal shed at the far side of the deck, expertly spinning a tight turn so the back of the rig lined up with the closed double doors. Apparently satisfied, she shut off the engine and turned to Trumpet. "This is it, handsome. My humble sanctuary."

Lowering the goggles to hang from her neck, she deftly unfastened the helmet strap. "Since I don't know your name, how about if I give you a temporary one? You acted like you enjoyed riding in my Triumph's sidecar. How about, Triumph?"

Close enough, thought Gabe while Trumpet gave a yip of approval. He leaped out and turned into the morning breeze. Nose up, he took in the smell of pine and other subtle scents.

"You check out the area while I see to the groceries." With her helmet and goggles left on the bike's seat, Aemea collected two bags from inside the nose of the sidecar and then headed for the trailer.

Circling back to the sidecar, Trumpet stopped to peer inside. Next to a six pack of root beer, a small paper bag with its top neatly folded over remained on the car's seat.

"What do you think, Trumpet, want to show her how smart you are?"

Trumpet tilted his head as he eyed the bag.

"Good boy, take the bag to Aemea."

Put off by an unpleasant odor Trumpet backed away.

"It's okay." Gabe studied the bag. "Looks like it's from a drug store. Come on, show her your stuff."

After a little more prompting, Trumpet took the bag by the folded top and trotted toward the deck.

"Well, aren't you a smart dog." After taking the bag, Aemea stroked the side of Trumpet's face thoughtfully. "I bet someone is missing you so much." Gabe noticed her voice didn't change when she talked to them. Instead, she spoke as if talking to another person.

When she went back to putting things away, Trumpet turned to check out the rest of the trailer. "Wow." The two of them stared as the retriever took a tentative step forward. An open set of polished wooden French doors in the far wall of the trailer led to a second small deck. Instead of an open backyard, the deck led into a large cavern.

"Pretty cool, isn't it? You wouldn't know to look from the outside. I rented a jackhammer to widen the opening, so it was big enough to walk through and provide light. A friend from the town helped me with the trailer's metal work, getting her set in place, and a few other things. When it gets unbearably hot in this neck of the woods the cavern keeps the trailer cool. I believe I have the only two thousand square foot trailer in all of Nevada." She flipped a switch to the right of the door causing a pair of lights hanging from the cavern's ceiling to come on and the fans above them to slowly spin. "All the comforts of home, huh?"Aemea gave him another friendly scratch behind his ears. "Let's see what kind of reward I can find for you for your help." She went to the refrigerator and opened the door. Before reaching in, she turned to him. "Unless you believe a good deed is a reward in itself?"

Trumpet sat, his long nose pointed at the plastic drawer.

Something came into Gabe's mind like a fuzzy picture. "Salami."

"I don't suppose you'd settle for salami, would you? I have to warn you, it's been there a while." She smiled when the dog thumped his tail.

I could smell the salami! Gabe's thoughts came tumbling excitedly as he considered the implications of what just happened. No words passed between them, but a sort of picture accompanied the faint aroma of salami. The whole time they had been 'together,' he was able to communicate his thoughts by imagining he was speaking the words out loud.

Each time he woke, Gabe considered it a blessing he still existed at all. He feared somehow the charge generated by the lightning would eventually dissipate to the point where he would simply fade into nothing. But he was getting signals, which were growing stronger and, if he were truly fortunate, might indicate a permanent imprint of some sort. If the human brain used only twenty-five percent of its capacity, maybe the same was true of the dog's brain, and he was present in the remaining part, or at least some part. The sensations he was experiencing seemed to be intensifying. The increases were coming in small increments, but they were steadily improving. Instead of simply observing the world through Trumpet's eyes and ears, it might be possible to eventually experience the world through all of his host's senses.

Aemea doled out several slices of the salami. As Trumpet gulped each down, Gabe tried to taste and smell the treats. At first, he could make something out, but, when he strained, the sense faded. Nuts. He gave up, retreating into himself. Suddenly, there it was. Not strong, but a taste and a smell he recognized as familiar, yet different. Could it be so easy, just relax and the sensations would come?

"Okay, now let's see how smart you are." She held a slice above his head. "Lie down."

Dropping to his belly, Trumpet gave her his best dog smile.

"Very good." She bent, handed over a slice, and tried, "Shake." When he looked puzzled she gave the command another attempt with her hand extended toward Trumpet. He translated the gesture to mean 'Say Hello' and raised his right paw.

After mastering 'roll over' for the second time, Aemea held out her empty hands. "That's it, boy." Trumpet got to his feet and diligently sniffed both hands, and she squatted down in front of him. With a wide smile, she ran a hand over the side of his face and down his neck. "Let's take care of your feet and the graze on your hip. You wait here."

Aemea returned from the bathroom with a large folded towel, and a small tray holding various items. At the French doors, she took a small remote from the top of a glass-faced cabinet and pointed it into the room. From hidden speakers, a female voice began to sing a soft country version of 'Me and Bobby McGee.'

Aemea gestured for him to follow her to a large oval rug near a pellet stove centered on the cave floor. Once the towel was spread over the rug she placed the tray to one side. She knelt next to it and patted the towel, "So, you lie here and relax while I clean you up and do your nails."

Trumpet sniffed the towel. She patted it again encouraging him to move in front of her, she asked him to 'sit.' With a little additional coaxing, he dropped down on his stomach, finally allowing her to roll him onto his side. He eyed her for a few moments before laying his head down. After a moment he let out a soft, "wuff."

"You know, I don't invite just anyone here." Her hands moved over him, pausing to further inspect his head and hip. The wounds on his head and hip were gently dabbed with something cool from a small bottle, and finally, a salve was applied.

Lying on his side, Trumpet sighed, closing his eyes while she began to carefully file and smooth his broken claws. This, Gabe mused, is the best I've felt in a very long time. He allowed himself to doze while she worked.

Finally satisfied, Aemea gathered up the bottle, tube of salve and the used cotton swabs. "Look, you just make yourself at home while I take a shower. Then we'll have some dinner. If you're not all done in, we can go for a walk afterward." She stroked the top of his head. "What do you think?"

Trumpet thumped his tail while Gabe studied her eyes. She was definitely a nice-looking woman, he thought; wide-set steady gaze, some tiny lines here and there.

Something about her reminded him a little of the photos he'd seen of Amelia Earhart. He wondered what she was doing out in the mountains living in a trailer. It was nice, with a huge rocky living room, but still a trailer in a pretty remote location.

She leaned close to him, tilting her head slightly as if studying a small detail in a painting. "Well." she got to her feet. "Give me ten minutes."

Trumpet trailed along until she reached the bedroom. With the door open, Gabe was tempted to coax him over for a quick peek. He barely completed the thought when the retriever abruptly turned away. After pausing to sniff at the boots by the door, and checking out the trailer with its tiny woodstove and tidy kitchen, he headed over to the cavern area.

The clean, swept floor area was covered in several well-broken-in area rugs, including the one they had laid on by the stove. A large barn-roof-shaped window framed in above the trailer filled the gap to the cavern rock above, lighting the area with a warm glow. Framed posters of various sizes dotted the mildly concave walls. They ranged in subject from a large photo of sunflowers to several antique aircraft and motorcycles. At the far end, a niche had been cut into the rock wall to allow a comfortable-looking hammock to hang a couple of feet off the floor. There were wooden bookshelves at random intervals, each filled with volumes of all sizes. A sizable couch and ornate iron glass-topped coffee table faced the one relatively flat vertical wall, against which sat an old wooden desk, angled so it faced toward the trailer.

Wooden bookends held several small volumes, including Gabe noted, 'The Pilot's Handbook' and at least two with 'Architecture' in the title. On the wall to the right of the desk, a large framed corkboard was covered with dozens of photos. Two cute little girls with coffee-colored skin held the hand of a tall, pretty African–American woman. In many of the photos a smiling young Caucasian soldier in his Army greens grinned for the camera. There were other photos of the same soldier; including one with him in the left seat of an Army Huey helicopter. In another, he was gesturing with a cigar to several holes in the Huey's tail boom. The expression on his face saying, "Oops."

"Hey, Trumpet," Gabe mused, "This guy could have been one of the pilots flying me and my buddies around. Man, those were tough days back then and…."

"They are my family."

Gabe did a mental jump, but Trumpet only turned his head and wagged his tail.

Aemea stood in the doorway, tucking the tail of a fresh work shirt into her jeans. She glanced from Trumpet to the board and back, a peculiar look on her face as she began to roll up the sleeves.

"My dad was a Huey pilot in Vietnam; he could fly anything. When he got home, he made the transition to a fixed wing. Former Warrant Officer Robert Rand now flies a corporate jet for some rich guy. When he has the time, he flies his own Baby Great Lakes biplane." Her words were spoken with obvious pride.

"This one." Aemea came over. Squatting down next to

him, she tapped a small photo of a red biplane with blue stripes along the sides. "My mother never learned to fly but loves to go out with my dad and do aerobatics, or just grind around." Gabe recognized the couple from the other photo, now older, still smiling, and leaning against the small biplane's lower wing.

"Teri, my sister, married a dentist. They live in Denver." She gestured to the board on the far side of the window. "That's me. Captain Aemea Amelia Rand and her very own ship."

Trumpet followed her gesture and Gabe was treated to a shot of Aemea in a flight suit and helmet, standing in front of a large and brutish-looking dark green aircraft. Beneath the canopy in official-looking black letters was 'CAPT. AEMEA RAND.' Below her name, flowing bright yellow letters spelled out 'WARTZILLA.' A cartoon lipstick print partially covered the front part of the 'W.'

She reached over, straightening the framed photo of her mother. "The spelling of my first name is a little odd because it's a palindrome. Mom is a high school English literature teacher and thought it would be cool to give me a first name spelled the same way forward and backward, instead of plain old 'Amy.' Sometimes it gets old having to spell my name for people, or correct their pronunciation when they read it."

Aemea tapped the aircraft in the photo with the tip of a neatly trimmed nail. "That, my friend, is the queen of the sky. She's an A-10 Thunderbolt, a 'Warthog' to the pilots and crews, and one tough aircraft. One time in Iraq, I was called in by a platoon from the One-Oh-First to…" Aemea suddenly stopped and sighed again. "Mom's right. I need to get out more and get a new boyfriend. I'm talking to strange dogs I've found along the road."

"Uuff?"

"I'm sorry, boy." She laughed softly. "*You're* not strange. I've been working some long hours, and I'm a little goofy from too little R and R." She rose to her feet. "Let's see what we can rustle up for a good listener, such as yourself." Dinner for Trumpet was Spam, chopped into bits and combined with a mixture of mashed potatoes, rice, eggs, and chunks of bread with a 'dash of milk.'

Later, Aemea led Trumpet out a path along the edge of the cliff to where it stepped back from a second rocky drop of fifty feet or so. She sat on the edge with her legs dangling while she gazed off across the broad plain below. Trumpet dropped down next to her. "I like to just sit and look sometimes, you know?"

Trumpet settled next to her and laid his head across her legs. He knew.

Sitting quietly for the first time since this adventure began, Gabe had a chance to appreciate his newfound senses. Trumpet raised his head, turning side to side, allowing Gabe to hear sounds of something nearby digging in a burrow. Another creature further in the distance was thrashing through the underbrush. Trumpet tilted his head skyward to watch a hawk circling, possibly looking for that creature in the underbrush. His nostrils flared to take in the profusion of scents drifting across the desert.

Breaking into Gabe's observations, Aemea quietly rested a hand on Trumpet's back. She smiled and then lifted his head toward her. "Do you know you have the most expressive eyes?"

Her gentle voice, coupled with an enthusiasm for her surroundings and the area, reminded Gabe of his late wife. Like Sarah had been from the first time she met the puppy, Aemea appeared to be completely taken with Trumpet. This wouldn't be so bad, he thought, living out in the desert with Aemea. He let his mind relax, relishing Trumpet's response to her touch, savoring the sensation of well-being and peace.

After their walk, Aemea built a small fire in the trailer's wood stove. It took little urging on her part to get him to settle onto the large, folded beach towel she placed in front of the stove. "You just wait here, fella. I'm going to draw your bath." She winked at them and headed outside.

At the word 'bath,' Gabe felt the dog tense. There was something he couldn't understand. He couldn't quite make it out, but there was an image of the cabin, a hose, and a sort of resigned feeling. He always thought Trumpet enjoyed his occasional bath, especially when he'd been rubbed down with an old towel.

"Triumph." Aemea stood at the side of the front door. She tapped the side of her leg and made a 'come here' motion with her hand.

With a quiet groan, Trumpet got to his feet and plodded to the door.

She led him to an old iron tub sitting in a bamboo enclosure at the shed end of the trailer. The front of the enclosure was a simple bamboo gate, which she swung wide open. "This will be a real treat." She gestured away from the trailer. "You'll get a nice bath while you watch the sunset. I bet you don't get this at home."

At the edge of the enclosure, Trumpet sat, his head turned away from her.

"Come on Trumpet," Gabe urged. "She's nice and you'll enjoy it."

Aemea dropped next to him. "I can lift you in if you want." She gently stroked the side of his head. The gesture melted the last of Trumpet's resistance. He got to his feet and hopped into the tub. The water was a few inches deep and comfortably warm. The retriever relaxed while Gabe felt a wave of guilt regarding his own method of bathing him. He simply used a hose and the spring-cold water fed from a spigot by the corner of the porch. Gabe tried to apologize, but Trumpet was too busy delighting in the sensation of Aemea pouring a warm bucket of water over his back.

After more water came baby shampoo with a firm but gentle rubbing of his neck and back. All the time she kept telling him what a good, patient, guy he was and how the girls where she worked were going to, "just love such a handsome, good-smelling fellow."

Gabe tried to recall when he felt such contentment, unsure if they were his sensations at all, or those emanating powerfully from Trumpet. At any rate, he was glad to share his feelings. While she rinsed him, Aemea pointed out the sunset over the mountains to the west.

The colors were familiar, yet strange. He thought he

could pick out the soft apricots and pinks of the cloud's undersides. This puzzled him because he always believed dogs saw only in black and white, and until this moment, he'd seen through the retriever's eyes. Possibly, Gabe theorized, just as Trumpet shared the ecstatic bliss of the bath, *he* was supplying the colors.

Once out of the tub came a thorough rubbing with the towels, punctuated by Trumpet's shakes, and Aemea's musical laugh. When the air began to cool, they moved inside. Aemea produced another towel, continuing to dry him as he lay by the fire.

"You know what?" She set the towel aside and got quickly to her feet. "Come on Red, we've still got some light left!" She hurried over to a cabinet and pulled open a drawer. "Come on now, out the front door." She held up a camera and a small tripod.

After telling him to stay on the deck by the trailer's front door, she made quick work of setting up the camera on the tripod, then hurried back to him. The shutter tripped as she sat cross-legged beside Trumpet, hugging him close. The next few were taken around the deck, some with him holding out a paw, but each containing the two of them.

"I haven't taken pictures for a long time." She gave him a hard hug after the last flash went off and darkness was complete, the stars bright in the sky. "There's something about you. Something which makes me feel relaxed, at peace with myself."

Aemea encouraged Trumpet to sit next to her chair while she skimmed the newspaper, looking for any mention of a lost dog roaming the desert. Instead, she found something else interesting. "Hey, fella, listen to this." Aemea shook the newspaper, folded it back and began to read. "The Golden Doubloon Hotel and Casino welcomes the Society of Golden Retriever Owners this weekend for the Retriever Rendez-vous. All Society owners will receive seventy-five dollars in chips plus drink and meal tickets...blah, blah." She leaned toward Trumpet, who lifted his head and was watching her. "I bet *the show* is where you were going!"

Trumpet got up and put his head in her lap so she could stroke his head. After several quiet minutes, she cleared her throat. "I suppose I could just run you into town, drop you off at the Humane Society. I'm sure they're nice people, and where your owners are bound to look. That would probably be best, wouldn't it?"

With a heavy sigh, he dropped down onto his stomach.

"Would you rather just stay here until the Convention?"

Trumpet's ears shot forward. Popping back up, he placed his paws on the chair's arm and began to lick the young woman's face.

"Okay, okay." The reluctant tone in her voice vanished. She scratched his chest, her smile broad and warm. "Look, tomorrow evening, I have to work in town. We'll go in early, stop at the pound, just to check things out. But you can stay with me until we find your folks."

8

ANOTHER BAD DREAM

"Lorazepam." Sitting on the edge of the bed, Aemea placed the water glass on the nightstand. After a few moments of consideration, she dropped a small white pill back into the plastic container she'd picked up from the VA Clinic the prior afternoon. Her lips formed into a contented smile. "This was a good day. Maybe I'll pass on this tonight." She spoke softly, admiring the big red dog stretched out on the rug by the stove. "A good day." She repeated.

The nightmare came on in its usual unhurried fashion. As always, Aemea was in the cockpit of Wartzilla. She responded to a radio call, and though not recalling the actual conversation, dropped the nose of the big aircraft toward a point on the horizon. Reaching out to a gauge that didn't look quite right, she gave it a tap. The move propelled her from the plane to her motorcycle and a familiar section of desert road. It's different, she thought within the dream, my plane is gone. She considered that something had changed, possibly for the better.

A bump in the pavement created a 'whoop' propelling her into the air. She easily brought the rig back down to the road. Two more whoops came and went before the darkness of the nightmare began to creep back. The third time the rig rose into the air she looked down to see the road a tiny gray strand far, far, below. She leaned back hard to bring the front wheel up. Instead, the rig fell off to her right, nearly throwing her from the saddle. On cue, an angry swirling mass of black sharp-beaked crows rose to meet her. The dream was disjointed moving back and forth between the cockpit and the motorcycle. This time, her plane with its armor and protective canopy, the weapons that always went inoperative, were gone. Her breath came in ragged gasps as the rig fell.

The fire had been reduced to a thin bed of coals when a sound woke Gabe. He was confused at first; thinking they were just lying on a comfortable rug in front of the fire with Aemea mentioning a hotel and a convention revolving around golden retrievers. From the bedroom came the soft whining sound of someone crying in their sleep.

Getting up, Trumpet trotted to the door. Peering into the dark room, he saw Aemea laying on her side among the rumpled covers, her body turned away from them. Every few heartbeats a tiny whimpering sound accompanied the jerk of her body. Before Gabe could make any kind of suggestion, Trumpet was on her bed and settled down so his back pressed into hers. Aemea's jerking stopped. After a bit, she rolled over in her sleep, draping an arm over him.

In her dream the rig was nearly on its side, hurtling downward toward the increasing hurricane of blackbirds rising to take her. Aemea wanted to close her eyes and scream. Instead, her breath was drawn out of her as if she'd been punched in the stomach.

"Arrk! Arrk, Arrk!" The barks became part of the dream

as her head turned to find a grinning red dog seated in the sidecar. "Triumph!" Her breath came back. Her eyes locking on his, any fear evaporating in the warmth and happiness of his steady gaze. Pointing his nose in the bird's direction, he let off another staccato of barks. They hesitated, their wings jerking uncertainly.

"Yeah!" She leaned toward him to rub his ears. The rig leveled. Instead of converging on her, their sharp beaks tearing at her, the black avian mass retreated under a barrage of happy, "arrks!"

"Easy, easy." The speed of the fall decreased until the rig hesitated a few inches above the pavement before gently settling to the surface with a soft 'chirp' of the tires. The dream faded until there was only the comforting image of Triumph's smile.

☙

The next morning after breakfast, he'd been trimmed and brushed until his coat gleamed like fire as he basked in the sunlight. Aemea tied a bright red bandana around his neck in place of a collar. "Hey boy, let's go for a morning ride."

Trumpet rode happily in the sidecar, his eyes protected by a modified set of goggles. As it rolled along the highway, pipes burbling a pleasant rhythm, the rig chased through the broad rays of the morning sun dancing across the valley. A turn of his head toward Aemea was rewarded by her smile and quick rub between his ears.

Life, Gabe smiled back in his own way, was not too shabby. True, he was caught in the retriever's body, but the pain in his other body had become a distant memory. Each day brought something new. Initially, he was only able to see and hear through his dog's eyes and ears. Now he could feel more and more. The hunger pangs had been real, the nip from the coyote he certainly felt. Each time Trumpet moaned softly at Aemea's careful attention to his neck and back muscles, Gabe was right there with him. Although Trumpet appeared to consider Gabe's advice, the dog still ran the show; a trait Gabe was beginning to think wasn't such a bad thing. It was like a guided tour of the world through a dog's eyes, and more.

He watched a rabbit spring from near a large rock a hundred yards ahead and sprint across the road. Trumpet let out a happy bark while Aemea tapped the bike's horn. Tasting the warmth of the air on his tongue and the sweet smell of the desert around them, Gabe decided life was pretty damn good.

"I'll just be a minute." From inside the building with its Reno Humane Society sign, came the sound of a myriad of barking dogs. Aemea disappeared through the front door. Gabe found the barks carried more than just animal sounds; he picked out feelings ranging from fear to despair. Except for an occasional uncomfortable whine, Trumpet sat quietly despondent in the sidecar.

When after a few minutes the door swung open and Aemea emerged, Trumpet wriggled with pleasure, until a second woman in the uniform of an Animal Control Officer stepped out after her.

"Uh, oh." Both Gabe and Trumpet seemed to have the same reaction.

Trumpet moved against the sidecar's opening as they walked up.

"It's okay, Triumph." Aemea's soothing tone failed to cover a trace of fear. "She's just going to look for a chip."

"Hi, buddy. I'm Sandra." From the woman's friendly brown eyes and equally friendly voice, Trumpet relaxed a bit, sensing a love of animals. Sandra squatted down, giving his neck a scratch, and holding out a plastic device for him to sniff. "This won't hurt. We're just going to see if you have a little thing that will help get you back home."

After running the device over him several times, Sandra got back to her feet. "Nope." Shaking her head, she addressed an obviously relieved Aemea. "If he were carrying a chip, this would have found it. Could be someone on the way to this weekend's show lost him. It's unusual no one's called, but you never know."

Gabe felt both guilty and relieved that he never had Trumpet chipped.

Aemea described Trumpet's condition when she found him while Sandra took a closer look at his head. "Funny. My cousin is an electrician. He got a similar burn one time when he stood up where he shouldn't have." She rubbed his neck again as she sized up Aemea. "I've got your number. If anything happens, I'll give you a call."

"Would you, um, mind?" Aemea held up her camera to Sandra.

Sandra nodded as she took the camera. After some brief instructions, she took a few shots of Aemea standing by the rig with Trumpet in the sidecar.

The two of them watched the officer return to the building, giving a quick wave before disappearing inside. Aemea gave Trumpet's chin and back a rub before remounting the bike. "Looks like you get to hang with me a while longer."

From the pound, Aemea took them to a small park where they played with a Frisbee, shared an early dinner of deli-made sandwiches, and napped contentedly in the shade of a row of trees.

9

—

THE T-TOP

"Here we are."

The rig slowed, allowing Gabe just enough time to spot a large, elevated sign with 'The T-Top' in yellow neon arching over a bright red neon Corvette. The sign's image suddenly changed, but Trumpet returned his attention to the street, and Gabe hadn't made out what the car changed into. They rolled down a narrow though brightly lit alley until an employee parking sign appeared on the right.

"Evening, Miss Bode." A deep and pleasant voice rumbled from a large young man standing just inside a small kiosk at the parking lot gate.

"Good evening, Barry." Aemea stopped the rig, pushed up her goggles, and smiled broadly at the young man. "The rest of the crew here?"

"Affirmative, Miss Bode." Barry nodded to the side car's passenger "New friend?"

Aemea reached over, affectionately rubbing the retriever's head. "For now. He's just visiting."

"You could use some company out there, you know."

Aemea gave a non-committal wave as she continued into the parking area, found a spot and nosed in. At the front was a small white sign with "Ms. Helen Bode" printed in neat black letters.

She removed the goggles, noticing how the dog studied the sign. "We all have, ah, stage names here."

Hmm. Gabe wondered what sort of job required a stage name. This being Reno, he had a sudden suspicion. She grabbed a black leather travel bag from the rear of the car and Trumpet eagerly followed her to the back door. After a short trip down a wide hallway, they came to a halt at a door labeled in the same style lettering as the parking space sign: Dressing Room.

"Oh, isn't he gorgeous!" A young woman in heavy eye makeup paused in fastening the strap on a high-heeled shoe. "Aemea, where did you find him?" The rest of her attire consisted mainly of a G-string and severely cropped tank top. Several other similarly clad young women stopped their primping to greet them with equal enthusiasm.

Gabe sighed to himself. So, Aemea's a stripper, she certainly has the body for it.

Trumpet failed to notice Gabe's assessment, his head and tail snapping happily from side to side while the women surrounded him with pets, scratches, and fawning words.

Though Gabe quickly lost track of Aemea in the endless sea of friendly hands, barely covered breasts, and butts, he could hear her explanation about their circumstances from further down the dressing room. The amicable banter continued until a heavyset thirtyish Afro-American man in a neatly tailored dark suit appeared at the dressing room door. The man's jet-black hair was cropped short. His sideburns led down into a tightly trimmed beard and mustache which added to his no-nonsense appearance. Below thick dark eyebrows, his deep brown eyes swept the room.

"Ladies, five minutes." He spotted Trumpet. "Who's this?" His voice was commanding, in a gravely, pleasant way.

"He's with me." Aemea pushed through the group.

"Woof," came to Gabe's mind. Aemea was stunning in very short black shorts from which rose a wide set of sequined black suspenders. Covering most of her breasts, they fastened at the back of her neck, though not leaving much to the imagination. Her eyes were made up like the rest of the girls, but oddly, Gabe thought, in sharp contrast to the spiked heels worn by the others; on her feet were plain black running shoes.

"I don't see a problem, do you?" Aemea locked eyes with the suit.

"Come on Aemea, you know the rules." His stare ended with a shake of his head. "Okay. Just make sure he doesn't do anything, ah, dog-like."

There were chuckles and a few snickers as the girls filed by.

"Nick, you're such a softy." One of the girls gave him a quick kiss on the cheek.

"Thanks, Nick." Aemea started to brush by.

"Wait a second." Nick checked down the hall to where the girls were hurrying up a short set of wooden steps. When the last was out of sight, he squatted down, taking Trumpet's head between his hands.

This can't be good. Gabe cringed. On the other hand, Trumpet was wagging his tail.

"Hey, hey, who's a handsome guy?" The stern lips parted into a wide friendly smile as Nick scratched behind the retriever's ears, his eyes and voice suddenly alive with the warmth of a dog lover. "Now, who's the silkiest big red dog I've ever seen?" From a pocket he produced a small doggie treat, giving it to Trumpet before going on about his 'beautiful flag of a tail.'

When the treat was finished, Trumpet was given a final rub on the nose. Nick rose to his feet. "Aemea," he nodded. His voice was back in its command mode.

"Nick." She smiled in return.

Followed closely by Trumpet, she headed down the hall. Trumpet paused at the steps, thinking Aemea would turn back. "Wrong door there." She touched his head. "I've got about ten years on most of those girls, but thanks for the compliment."

Instead of going up the steps, she continued around a corner, down another short length of hall. At another door she paused and looked down at them. "Okay, my big red friend, you have to be on your very best behavior." She spoke to him while making a last-minute check of her outfit.

"She's a bartender." Gabe wasn't sure why the thought of her being a stripper disappointed him. After all, the girls treated a strange dog with honest affection. Trumpet certainly hadn't made any distinctions.

He began to wonder what life would be like as Aemea's dog. Coming to mind were Bunting's comments regarding Trumpet spending the rest of his life chained to a rundown mobile home. So far, mobile home life felt like a pretty good deal. Their roommate was thoughtful, and considerate, gave great baths, and provided invigorating rides in the sidecar.

Considering his earlier options, life could have dealt him a much worse fate. If happiness to a human could be a warm puppy, as the saying goes, happiness to a dog could be a warm human.

The pulsing rock music came from somewhere out of Gabe's sight, which from the sound of it, was in pretty much every direction. The lighting was subdued, with colored strobes from overhead light cans shining toward where he assumed the stage to be. The constant catcalls and whistles let him know the audience was an appreciative one.

Two other women, dressed identically to Aemea, greeted her in a friendly fashion before returning to mixing drinks.

"Over here." Trumpet was led to the end of the long curved bar, where a wide wooden shelf was attached a couple of feet from the floor. He jumped up and quickly settled in, becoming a well-groomed red ball, his head facing down the length of the bar.

Aemea was serving customers at one end of the bar, as Nick appeared next to the shelf maintaining his all-business persona yet concealing something behind his back. He acknowledged several greetings by patrons, until, at an opportune moment, he turned quickly to Trumpet.

"Up, Red." He swiftly tucked a small dark blanket around Trumpet's space giving him a soft place to lie. "My pup's eyebrows are expressive like yours. It's loud in here, but you'll be fine." After a gentle rub of the dog's nose, Nick was again facing out across the bar, his arms folded across his broad chest.

Aemea finished placing drinks on a tray at the waitress

station. Noticing Nick standing further down the bar, next to Trumpet's spot, she joined him. "I never pegged you for a dog lover." She pretended to watch two girls dancing on the stage.

"I might say the same of you, Aemea."

Trumpet kept quietly curled on his blanketed spot, only his eyes moving to take in what little there was to see from his position. Most of the customers coming up to the bar never noticed him. Those who did made no comments, their eyes quickly leaving him for whatever was happening on the stage, or to Aemea's suspenders. She fielded the random lewd comment with a combination of grace and wit, tinged with a hint of bodily harm. Trumpet dozed off and on, and as the hours passed Gabe tried to keep awake behind Trumpet's closed eyes. A slurred voice carried over the music, bringing them both wide awake.

"Hey, baby, remember me?"

When Trumpet opened his eyes, Gabe felt a sudden distinct and dark impression coming from his friend. Ah, Gabe thought, so this is anger. They watched a drunk lean on the bar, a sloppy grin on his jowly face, his eyes on Aemea's chest.

"As I live and hold my breath, it's Harold Bassman." Aemea peered past him. "You come back for old times?"

He leered, pleased she remembered him. "While my lovely wife is minding the home front, I'm here on business, *and* looking for a fun time."

"How nice." She gave the top of the bar a quick swipe with a small white towel and tossed it into a hamper. "What will it be?"

"I was thinking I'd like..." His hand snaked out and caught one of her suspenders.

Before she could act, or Gabe think, Trumpet sprang from his spot to the countertop of the bar. In a flash, he was crouching with Bassman's wrist in his jaws, a growl coming from deep in his throat.

"There's a dog?" Confused, the drunk stared at Trumpet, his fingertips still clutching the suspender.

"Triumph." Nick appeared next to Bassman, his eyes and deep voice, icy. "Let him go."

Slowly, Trumpet opened his jaws. Next to him, Aemea's arm was cocked back with a heavy beer stein clutched in her hand, ready to deliver a blow.

"Aemea." The command voice was softer this time but still carried its authority. "I will handle this."

He delivered a chilly smile at Bassman. "You have your hand on my employee's attire. You may remove your hand, or my associate will remove it for you."

His associate, a large broad-shouldered red-headed man, appeared next to his boss. Standing well over six feet, his smirk conveyed there was nothing he'd rather do than remove Bassman's hand.

Bassman slowly opened his fingers and drew back. "That dog attacked me."

Nick eyed Aemea for a moment, then Trumpet. Their eyes locked, and Nick made a small nod of his head. Trumpet turned, dropped off the bar, and jumped back up to his blanket.

Nice, Gabe gave his buddy a hardy mental pat on the head. You didn't even break the skin.

"You assaulted my employee. The dog was simply protecting his mistress."

"I'll get an attorney, and I'll sue you."

"Mister Bassman, I'm sure my videotape of you accosting my bartender will keep things in their proper perspective." Nick took hold of the man's pale wrist, turning it side to side. "No bite marks. In fact, the skin hasn't been broken. Now, it's on tape, too."

He released the wrist. "Bernard, please see the gentleman to the door."

A few tables from the bar, a short, sunburned man dressed casually in charcoal slacks, a dark sport shirt and sporting a bad comb-over, lowered his sunglasses back in place. Because his attention had been bouncing back and forth from the stage to the tall comely bartender in sequined suspenders, he'd witnessed the entire episode from his table. "Too bad," Warren Bunting murmured to himself. "I would have loved to see what was under those suspenders." He turned his attention back to the stage, but disconcerting thoughts nagged at him.

Bunting felt comfortable in the T-Top. The place was clean, the girls young and pretty enough to lure him into the place numerous times in the past. This was his first time back since marrying T.J., and the first time since then to venture out to his investment property. Bunting nursed his drink, unhappy because he should have been celebrating. But instead, the damn dog left him in the desert, forcing him to endure a miserable hike until he was able to get cell phone service and reached a towing service. Yesterday, he spent most of the day by the hotel pool cooling his heels while the dealer repaired the window and provided him with new keys.

The damn dog cost him a five-hundred-dollar deductible, he reminded himself. Well, he was probably still wandering around in the desert, if the coyotes hadn't… He lowered his drink. No, not the dog that burst from behind the bar. It couldn't be. Naw, he just *looked* like a cleaned and brushed version of Gabe's stupid pet. Let it go, he thought. If it is *the* dog, he can just stay with the hot-looking bartender. The unpleasant events of the last couple of days closed in on him, and a little voice in his head at first whispered, then began to scream: 'Revenge!' He glowered into his drink before tossing the last of it down. He needed to get a better look at the dog. "Miss?" He held out the empty glass toward the young woman approaching him.

"Yes, sir?"

Bunting struggled to keep his eyes from ogling the young woman's minimally covered body. "Another of the same, please. I couldn't help but notice the bartender's dog. A golden retriever, isn't it?"

"I guess." She glanced quickly in the direction of the bar. "It's the first time I've seen him."

When the waitress offered nothing more, Bunting slipped a dollar bill on her tray "Thank you."

By the time his drink arrived, Bunting devised a plan. After all, he reasoned, the animal attacked someone. He placed a napkin over the glass and made his way to the pay phone by the restrooms.

Over an hour passed since Bassman was escorted from the club, when Aemea spotted Nick, accompanied by an Animal Control Officer, heading her way. "Shit."

Bunting watched the heated discussion between the three at the bar with interest.

"Damn." The officer muzzled the dog and led him out through the back door to the bar, not through the club as Bunting had hoped. After picking up his change from the table, he made his way unobtrusively out of the club.

Sure enough, the shelter truck was parked on the side street across from the sign. Bunting caught up with the officer and his captive as a door was being opened in the back of the truck.

"Nice dog." Bunting ventured. He peered down at the muzzled dog and caught his breath.

Bunting's voice had been as familiar to Gabe and Trumpet as cat poop on an old boot. "You!" Gabe screamed and Trumpet jerked back against the officer.

"Come on, in you go." The officer shoved them forcefully into the compartment and slammed the door.

Though the dog was bathed and well groomed, Bunting recognized the singed spot on the dog's head. He tried to keep his elation from his voice. "Officer, what time does the shelter open tomorrow?"

"Nine." The man gave him a friendly smile. "If you're looking to get a dog for the kids, we've got some good ones."

Through the louvers on the door to the compartment,

they could see Bunting staring back through them as the driver started the engine.

"You, are mine." Bunting made a little throat-slitting motion with his finger. He was smiling an evil smile as the truck pulled away.

The truck swung onto the main street, allowing Gabe a glimpse of the club's neon sign. The sign shifted from T-TOP to T-TOP-LESS, and the Corvette's top retracted. "Yeah, clever," Gabe sighed.

"There was nothing I could do." Nick spread his hands. "He filed a complaint. I can deal with the drunken customer, but not the County." At this hour, except for Animal Control dropping dogs off at the shelter, the place is closed. There is nothing we can do until they open."

Aemea ran a hand over her face, then gave her boss a tired smile. "I'll bail him out in the morning. Nine, you said?"

"Sharp."

"Nick?"

The manager turned back. "Yeah?"

"Thanks for saying, 'we.'"

"It will all work out."

For the next few minutes, Aemea concentrated on her work. Triumph, she assured herself, would be fine.

She placed a pair of cocktails on a tray at the waitress station, when Tammy, one of the other bartenders, placed two drinks of her own on the tray. Turning to her, Tammy smiled. "I didn't know you had a dog. He's beautiful. How long have you had him?"

"Not long." Aemea sighed. "He just sort of happened into my life."

Tammy nodded her understanding. "I have my handsome little Pug, Augie, waiting for me at home. It's nice having someone you can count on."

"I just found out Nick is a dog lover. Is there some secret society here I haven't been privy to?"

"Shana," she nodded to the curvy young woman twirling on the stage, "has Winthrop, a big black lab she rescued last spring."

"Taylor, tell Aemea about Stanley."

The waitress smiled as she swapped her tray of empty glasses for the full one. "My goofy gold lab? Just the best dog in the whole universe." With a wink and a smile, Taylor was heading back to her tables.

"Have we surprised you?"

"I, I guess." Suddenly Aemea was feeling some pangs of guilt about having kept her distance from the other employees at the T-Top. Basically, over the last five months, she showed up for work, changed into her work 'attire,' worked her shift, changed back, and left. Bringing Triumph into the club sparked the most conversation she'd shared.

"How's 'What's his name' taking to him? He doesn't strike me as a dog lover."

Aemea's look told her co-worker 'What's his name' was no longer in the picture.

"Ah."

"Yeah, 'ah.'" Aemea sighed. "He's pretty much last month's news."

Placing a hand over Aemea's, the woman smiled. "You're smart, exotic, and beautiful. If it's what you want, there's some guy out there who's right for you."

"Says another smart, beautiful, lady. Unless something's changed I haven't heard about?"

"I, have my Augie." This time, Tammy sighed but quickly followed up with a broad smile. "And when the right guy turns his head in my direction, Augie will let me know if he's the one."

Tammy spent several moments sizing her up. "Captain Rand, you aren't the only vet lugging around baggage from your time in 'The Sandbox'."

The sudden change of topic caught Aemea by surprise. "How did..?"

Tammy cut her off with a wave of her hand. "Me, Shana, Nick, Bernard, Tina, who does the books, we're all vets. We met through the local VA clinic. On Thursday afternoons we all get together at the dog park a few blocks from here. Bring your big red friend and join us."

"Right now, I'd just like to have my Triumph safely home with me."

"Your motorcycle?"

A group of customers arrived as Aemea finished an abbreviated version of her meeting her 'Triumph.'

"Fate." Tammy smiled over her shoulder as she hurried back to her own station. "Next Thursday!"

10
—

NICK'S BONNE

At the pound, Trumpet was led on a short leash to a cage. After his muzzle was removed, he entered the cage with no resistance. Ignoring the water in the metal bowl, he curled up in a forlorn ball on the cold concrete floor. Gabe could only recall a few times when he had been more depressed. Trumpet grunted in agreement.

"It's okay, Trumpet, you did the right thing. I wouldn't have tried to stop you. You're a good, brave, guy. I'm proud to have you for a friend."

With a heavy sigh, he closed his eyes. Soon he was asleep.

Gabe's mind was awake longer, listening to the occupants of the other cages, alternating from whimpering to an occasional howl. Great, he glowered, I don't even get a phone call.

Light was just spreading through the high windows when someone stopped in front of their cage. "Triumph?"

The familiar voice was Sandra's, the officer who checked Trumpet for a chip. She lifted a clipboard from its hook on the cage door. After studying it for a moment, she looked at the occupant. "Well, this can't be right."

Trumpet quickly rose to his feet, his tail wagging hopefully as Sandra hurried past the other cages and out the door at the end of the kennel. She returned with a blanket folded in quarters, opened the door, and put it to one side of the enclosure. After giving him a hug, she closed the door, disappearing down the corridor of cages. In the early morning light Gabe noticed the dogs in the cages he could see also had blankets. Trumpet looked after her and waited a few moments before curling up on the blanket and escaping back into sleep.

At eight oh-two in the morning, Warren Bunting parked his SUV a space away from a fire-engine-red fifties Ford pickup, the only other vehicle in the visitor parking area. "Now, that's tacky." He shook his head at the orange-to-yellow painted flames streaming back from the front of the old truck.

Walking toward the shelter, he paused to look back and admire his SUV. The Mercedes dealership replaced the side glass and detailed the vehicle until it gleamed in the early morning sun. They even cleaned up the dog crate sitting in the back. This time, their little trip out into the desert would end differently.

The door to the shelter was locked. Seeing activity inside, he thumped his fist on the frosted glass. A minute passed before there was a click of the lock. The door came open a few inches. "We don't open until nine."

"I'm an attorney, you have my dog. I want him now." He kept his voice low and commanding in the way he practiced for the last half hour.

"Okay, Okay." The man in the uniform relented and let him in. "There's a form to fill out at the counter."

The office wall across from the counter held several large corkboards topped with Adopt Me! Hand-printed in a whimsical fashion. The boards were covered with photos of dogs and cats. Ignoring the boards, Bunting went straight to the counter.

"My dog's here, and I'm in a hurry," Bunting told the female officer behind the counter.

"You don't fill out the papers, you don't get your dog. I'm sure you can spare a few minutes for your beloved pet." She tapped the blank form on the counter.

❧

Trumpet and Gabe woke to footsteps coming toward their cage. A heavyset man stopped and squatted down; Gabe couldn't bear to look.

"Hey, hey, who's a handsome guy? Who can wave his tail for his buddy?"

"Nick!" Both Trumpet and Gabe jumped for joy.

"Shush, Shush." Nick opened the gate, gave Trumpet's right ear a quick scratch then told him to "Heel."

Trumpet obediently moved to his side and sat.

Nick reached down. "My sister-in-law, Sandra, advised us to leave quietly by the back door. You be real chill, huh?"

When Nick opened the red truck's passenger door, a blond cocker spaniel with purple bows fastened to her ears gazed down at Trumpet. "Easy, Bonne girl." She responded with a low growl, then leaned out to sniff Trumpet's nose. After the red dog gave her a quick lick on the face, she looked up inquisitively at Nick.

"He's just a friend, beautiful. We're only giving him a ride." He held out his hands, palms up. "I swear."

Apparently satisfied by his explanation, she moved to the center of the seat and picked up a small stuffed pony. Trumpet looked longingly at the toy as he climbed in. Once Nick was in the truck, she settled in with her chin on his lap, ignoring their passenger.

They were leaving the parking lot when Bunting stopped in front of the empty cage. He rapidly checked all the others and then hurried back to the office.

"Somebody stole my dog!"

"I assure you, sir. No one has stolen a dog."

"Cage sixteen," Bunting blustered. "On the sheet you gave me it clearly states my golden retriever, um." The name he made up to avoid the possibility of a paper trail for Trumpet suddenly eluded him. "He is in cage number sixteen." The attorney jabbed his finger at the cage number printed on his copy of the form.

"In cage sixteen?" Sandra stood behind the counter, a look of concern on her face.

"Yes, yes. The damn dog is gone."

"Oh." She turned to the officer at the desk behind her. "You know what happened to the dog in cage sixteen?"

"Hmm, sixteen, sixteen. Oh, his owner picked him up a few minutes ago." The officer smiled before returning to her work.

"But, you don't open until nine."

"You're here."

Bunting fumed for a few moments. He had the distinct

impression they were somehow all in on this. "I want her name and address."

"Sorry, we can't give his or her information out."

"I am an attorney." Bunting thumped the countertop. "I, will obtain a court order."

"Ooh, a court order."

"Yes."

"I've never actually seen one." The way the woman smiled let Bunting know this wasn't going the way he hoped.

"Do I get my information?"

"So, when you bring your *court order* by, it'll be a first for me, won't it?"

❧

The rig hurtled down the wide road with Aemea keeping the speedometer at eighty-one, as fast as the bike would go with the sidecar attached. "Come on! Come on!" She returned home from the club at four-thirty in the morning, barely slept, then as the sun rose, drifted off for much longer than she intended or wanted. It was eight forty-eight, she'd be there in ten minutes, but she didn't want Triumph at the pound any longer than necessary.

All sorts of scenarios were playing through her head, mostly bad. She worried Triumph somehow escaped and was wandering lost in the city. Or they wouldn't give him to her. Or Bassman, in a fit of revenge, somehow... She blanked the thought from her mind.

Because she grew up in a military family, Aemea never had a dog of her own. She often thought about her friends, whose dogs were considered a part of the family, and wondered what it would be like having one. Triumph wasn't even hers; she only knew him for a couple of days, yet now she couldn't imagine not having him with her.

She coaxed the rig up to eighty-three when she noticed an old truck painted a bright red with a fade-away flame job parked up ahead in a turnout on the opposite side of the road. Leaning against the rear fender of the truck, a familiar-looking man in casual clothes was watching two dogs cavort a few yards out in the desert.

"Triumph!" In her excitement, Aemea stomped on the rear brake, causing the bike's rear wheel to lock up, the tire biting hard into the pavement. The rig swung hard to the left, snapped to the right as she corrected, and then slued side to side as she flew past them. As quickly as she could, she slowed enough to make a fast U-turn.

The man looked in her direction, smiled, and gave a casual wave of his hand.

"Triumph!" As the rig came to a stop Aemea shut it off and set the brake. She tossed her helmet and goggles into the sidecar and ran to where Nick waited by the road. A few yards away, Trumpet stopped playing with the cocker spaniel. For a moment he tilted his head to one side, then bounded over to her. She hugged and repeatedly kissed a jubilant Trumpet on the nose.

"She cares about us, Trumpet." Gabe reflected on his view, mostly filled with Aemea's expression of joy and relief. He was almost overcome by the feeling of warmth and love generated by Trumpet. His resolve about getting back to the ranch wavered. "I guess my friend, we could get to love trailer life."

When the little cocker spaniel let out several sharp yips, Aemea hugged her too.

"Looks like I brought the right dog." Nick's dark eyes sparkled, a broad grin replacing his usually stern look.

"I had all these…I was afraid somehow." Aemea wiped her eyes, "I'd be too late."

"Bonne insisted we go out for an early drive." He offered a what-could–I-do shrug of his broad shoulders. "We decided to pick up your buddy."

Aemea scratched the cocker's back. "Well, thank you, Bonne." She got up and hugged her boss, "Thanks, Nick."

While the dogs went back to their play, Nick and Aemea watched from where they sat side by side on the truck's dropped tailgate. Aemea told him about the gathering of retrievers at the Golden Doubloon.

"There's always the chance he's just a stray. Sadly, people dump their pets all the time."

"But he's such a good guy. He's not just a pet."

Her words brought a smile to Nick's lips. "*You*, are hooked."

"Yeah." Aemea suddenly changed the subject. "You know, I've never seen you in anything but a suit." She thumped the side of the truck's bed. "Where's your Beemer?"

"In the garage at home. It's my work car. Bonne wanted a truck to have for runs out into the desert."

"And what Bonne wants, Bonne gets?"

"Pretty much. Bonne's my little happiness on four paws." He watched her running after the bigger dog, occasionally nipping at his legs or his tail when he allowed her to catch up.

"She may look like a little priss, but she's a tough little dog."

Aemea chuckled. "And I used to think *you* were such a tough guy, a real hard ass."

His attention was still on the dogs, Nick allowed a slight smile. "We are what we have to be, when we have to be."

When Bonne induced Trumpet to chase her, he was more than willing to join in her contest. She dodged side to side, sometimes snapping a quick look over her shoulder to see if her new friend was still in pursuit. Twice she went down, rolled, then popped up to bolt off in another direction.

Aemea leaned forward, arms folded as if she were cold. "It'll break my heart if someone claims him."

"If you do the right thing, I have the feeling it will work out well for the two of you."

Trumpet began a new game where he flopped down on his stomach, slapping his long forelegs against the earth, before jerking his head up several times. Each time he let out a playful growl, clacking his teeth as he threw his head back. Bonne responded by charging over to him, nipping playfully at his flanks then dropping in front of him. Gabe had a close-up view of Bonne's open jaws and the sound of the two dogs letting out playful growls. The feeling Trumpet was generating was one of pure happiness and pleasure.

"Triumph is so much bigger, yet they play like they've done this all their lives." Aemea sighed, "They have such joy."

"I can have a rough night at the club." Nick grinned again. "When I get home, Bonne is waiting all happy and waggy just because I'm walking through the door. She does this kind of little dance where she circles me, her tail and whole hind end wagging. I call it her 'samba' move. I just can't stay in a bad mood when she's around me. She is really intuitive, she knows when I need her to be comforting. Some psychics claim they can read a dog's mind, but it is more likely that dogs can read human minds. Or maybe they are just more in tune with a human's smell, the sounds we make, or changes in body language or movements."

Both heavily panting dogs flopped down on the ground nearby, facing each other as if sharing a secret. They crawled closer to Nick and Aemea, quietly listening to the voices of their humans.

Gabe was following the conversation and understood what Nick meant by dogs having a sixth sense. Trumpet seemed to know when Sarah's cancer returned. He knew that she needed him by her side.

Nick continued, "Kind of makes you wonder about us being the superior of the planet's inhabitants, doesn't it?"

Nick rested a hand on her shoulder and gave her an affectionate squeeze. "Look, why don't you take some time off? One of the other bartenders can cover for you. You can see how things play out, maybe relax a little."

"I could be back tomorrow night."

Nick ignored her, "You'll want time to get to know your buddy. I'll expect you back in a week."

"You seem pretty positive about this."

Having regained their breath, the game was on again with Bonne whirling after Trumpet's tail. While observing their antics, Nick added, "I had a feeling about her, though at the time I wasn't looking for a dog, much less a friend.

Sort of like you and Triumph."

Finally, Nick scooped up Bonne and put her back in the truck. It was time for her appointment at the pet boutique for a bath and nail trim.

~

The rest of the day was spent back at the trailer, where Aemea fed, and then brushed Trumpet until his coat shone. In the afternoon they napped, snuggled together in the large hammock hanging in the cavern.

While Trumpet slept, Gabe mulled over how the situation with his ranch and Bunting seemed like something from another life. It bothered him to think the despicable attorney would probably end up with his property. Sarah's ashes were at the base of a big redwood on the property near the old tractor seat, and both versions of his Will specified his ashes be placed there as well. However, the chances of Bunting or his ditzy wife doing something to disturb the area were slim because of the tree's location a few hundred feet from the cabin. There was also a bronze plaque with the dates of their births and her death. By now he supposed his attorney would have begun the process to honor his wishes, the plaque would soon have both dates for him. In the matter of the cabin, the original Will planned to have it sold and the money given to various specified charities. The furnishing would most likely go to thrift stores. As for all the wall photos, well, the frames would be valuable to someone. With the pictures gone, the two of them would soon be forgotten until the only remaining memory would be the plaque at the tree, which read, "Sarah and Gabe, Forever in Love."

He pushed back against the impending feeling of depression with the thought of how pleased Sarah would be about him finding Trumpet a good and loving home. Ah well, Aemea would take them to the gathering at the Golden Doubloon; there would be no one looking for him, and they would live happily ever after. It was, after all, his ultimate plan for Trumpet: to have a long happy life. He'd like Aemea to know he too was behind the warm brown eyes, but it wasn't like there was a simple way of announcing his presence. He had no idea how she would take it, and that little bit of information would certainly complicate things. He began to fantasize about Trumpet pecking away at a computer keyboard with something like a pencil or chopstick held in his mouth when he too drifted off into a contented slumber.

11

GOLDENS GALORE

"Since you don't have a collar, and I'm hoping for the best, I've made a slight change to your bandana." Trumpet cocked his head, while Aemea smiled as she held it up so he could see. "I used a felt pen to put your name along the seam." In bold, easy-to-read letters, she printed AEMEA'S TRIUMPH. In the triangular area of the bandana, she drew a cartoon sidecar with a woman on the bike and a reasonable likeness of Trumpet in the car. "I draw sometimes, and I wanted this to let people know you're special to me. You know, in case..." She swiped at one eye with the back of her hand as she struggled to bring the smile back.

Trumpet needed no urging from Gabe to nuzzle the young woman's hand and then lick her face. Aemea's response was a fierce hug followed by a series of kisses placed on the top of his head.

The walk from the trailer was in silence, but Trumpet kept rubbing against Aemea as if to reassure her all would turn out well. Once they were aboard the sidecar, she let the bike warm up a little longer than usual. During the ride, she kept reaching over to give him a quick pet or straighten the bandana.

Just outside of town, at the same turnout where Nick and Bonne were waiting the day before, Aemea pulled over. After shutting off the bike's engine she slowly raised the goggles before turning to Trumpet. "I didn't think this would be so hard, you know? I mean, who could let someone like you get away? If you were mine, I'd move heaven and earth to find you, to bring you home." She ran a hand along the side of his face. "I've always considered myself a realist. I've seen how things don't turn out the way we want. It's selfish of me, but I'm hoping with all my heart, in a little while the two of us will be heading back this way to our home."

When Trumpet nuzzled her hand, she managed to smile tightly. "Okay then. Let's go see how things stand. And the best of luck to the both of us." She sucked in a breath, let it out, and lowered her goggles back in place.

Gabe was surprised and deeply touched by her words. He had no doubt they would have a great life together. His only concern was somehow Bunting, who kept turning up like the proverbial bad penny, would show his tarnished self and try to screw things up.

As they pulled out onto the highway, Gabe was reminded of the times in the past when he had been in a tense situation. Aemea certainly had a grim resolve about her, and even Trumpet seemed subdued. He recalled a time when an unexpected storm swooped down from the mountains and across the lake on which he and Sarah were learning to sail their small wooden boat. With the tape player in the tiny cabin cranking out Jimmy Buffet, they quickly dropped the jib and rode out the brief storm to the loudly played tunes of 'Changes in Latitude,' and 'Why Don't we get Drunk.' Though the little boat had been nearly knocked down twice, they laughed and sang along all through the whole thing. The singing had taken away their fears and lightened up their situation. "Trumpet," he called out to his friend, "give us a few barks."

When he obliged with a series of the sea lion-like, "aarks!" he used when he wanted something, Gabe could see a smile form on Aemea's face as she rolled on the throttle. A half block from the Golden Doubloon, Aemea spotted a car pulling out of a parking space and swung the rig neatly between the other parked cars.

"Okay now. You stay here and no trouble this time, okay?" She removed his goggles, flashed him a dazzling smile and rubbed his head affectionately.

They watched her walk off toward the hotel, her step determined. Twice she turned back to wave.

❦

"No, I'm afraid not. Everyone checked in yesterday. No one is missing their dog." The woman in charge of the booth, a striking redhead with 'Sherrie' engraved on her retriever-shaped nametag, smiled up at Aemea.

Aemea noticed what she had at first taken for flowers on the material of the woman's pale green sundress, were, in fact, small cartoon golden retrievers. She peered down at the booth's open registration book. "You're sure? He's got a redder coat than most of the dogs I've seen here." She found herself staring at Sherrie's long red hair.

"Like mine?" The woman noticed the look. Her smile

was warm and genuine; her green eyes danced. "My first 'golden' was from the red and slow-to-mature end of the spectrum. Sam was a wonderful dog." Her wistful look faded. "If he's being a bother, I'm a member of Retriever Rescue. I'd be happy to take him."

"No!" Aemea's hand went to her mouth. "I mean, if you're sure, I want to keep him."

Sherrie's smile indicated her understanding. "You might try an ad in the paper. But, sad to say, when the puppy wears off, some people lose interest in the dog. Or, perhaps the owner died, and no one wanted the responsibility. Unfortunately, this isn't an unusual situation."

After thanking the woman, Aemea hurried back to Triumph. The mood of the people and their friendly companions at the hotel was exciting and fun. Everywhere, there were people with "goldens" as she now thought of the breed. They ranged from pale gold to dark blond, with one or two who looked a lot like her Triumph. *My Triumph,* she thought happily.

∾

Bunting was edging forward in the downtown traffic. Everywhere he looked there were people with their damn golden retrievers. He scowled to himself; it was as if the entire world had gone mad; suddenly filled with the happy-looking animals slapping the events of the past few days in his face with a sea of wagging tails.

Well, in a few hours, he'll be home. Eventually, the Picket Ranch would become Bunting's Tucsony Paradise, or whatever they'd finally call it. "And *I'll* have the last laugh." As he uttered the words, he tried to recall the movie in which he'd heard them, knowing they had been spoken by yet another villain. Well, screw it, he thought, and let out a loud, "Bwahaaahahaha." With the vehicle's CD playing a boisterous jazz tune, the windows up, and A/C going, no one heard him. When he finished, he grinned to himself, "now, *that* felt good!"

The light turned red. Stopped a couple of cars back from the intersection, he idly gazed out the SUV's tinted side glass. A few feet away, from the sidecar attached to the motorcycle at the curb, a retriever with a red bandana around his neck was watching the people on the sidewalk.

"No, no." Bunting ran the window down for a better look. The dog turned its head his way. "Not you! Again!"

Trumpet needed no urging from Gabe. At Bunting's angry bellow, he was out of the sidecar and running for the hotel.

As the light changed, a parking space opened up ahead. Bunting honked and yelled his way in front of another car to park there.

Tucking in behind a couple with a pair of gold dogs on rhinestone leashes, Trumpet slipped inside the hotel and began to search for Aemea.

"Hey, whoa, big fella." Trumpet was pulled to a stop as someone grabbed hold of the bandana. "Not only are you supposed to be with someone, but you're also supposed to be on a leash."

Trumpet turned his head up to find a tall thin man with a kindly face smiling down at him. On the left pocket of his sports coat was a small discrete badge with SECURITY in gold leaf letters. Beneath SECURITY, also in gold, was BOB.

"'AEMEA'S TRIUMPH,' huh?" Bob angled his head to read the name on the bandana then rubbed the dog's head affectionately. "Good name. Cute cartoon. Now, suppose we locate your owner." With a finger hooked in the bandana, he straightened and began to peer around.

"I see you've found my dog." Warren Bunting stood panting a couple of feet away, his hands placed on his hips.

While Gabe wasn't pleased to see him, he was happy to note the sunburned face and peeling nose. Trumpet whined as he tried to back away.

"I'll take him now." Bunting reached toward the dog.

Trumpet growled, while Bob, keeping a firm grip on the bandana, stepped between them. "He doesn't act like your dog."

"Well, ah, because he's...he's my wife's dog." The attorney glanced quickly around. Smiling crookedly, he pulled out his wallet. "Look, she adores the big guy. But, hey, I'm just not much of a dog person."

The way Bob's eyes narrowed told the attorney he'd better try a different tact.

"What I mean is, I expect him to be a dog, she lets him sleep on the bed and other...Look, she's going to be pissed if she finds out he got away from me." He opened his wallet. Removing first a one, then after a moment's thought, a five, he held it out toward the security guard.

"Sir, I'm afraid we can't accept gratuities for simply doing our jobs." He fixed the attorney with a tight professional smile. "What is your dog's name?"

"Ah." Bunting glanced around at the number of people stopping to watch the three of them. "Trumpet. It's Trumpet."

Trumpet's growl deepened.

"Hmm." Bob's voice turned chilly. "Does he have a nickname, something your wife likes to call him?"

"Nickname?"

"Nick…name."

"Why, yes. It's, um, his is…" Not for the first time, Bunting regretted being a tax attorney because he never actually argued anything before a judge. He wondered frantically what Perry Mason would do at a time like this? Suddenly, it came to him. He straightened, and in a voice full of a confidence he didn't feel, Warren Bunting, Attorney, spoke. "Hunky. My wife often speaks to him with affection, as, Hunky."

The small crowd's eyes turned to Bob, who wore a thoughtful look on his face. "Your wife's name is?"

"My wife?" Bunting swallowed. "Tiffany-Jean?"

Finally, he gave Bunting a thin smile. "Sir, just give me your hotel and room number while we sort this out."

A few feet away, a little girl moved to the front of the small crowd. In one hand she held a small stuffed bear with its own little red bandana. Bright yellow letters spelled "Sonoma" on the red cloth, and the identical letters on a small plastic heart dangling from the bear's neck caught Gabe's eye. Bingo. It could be something helpful in getting them home. He gave Trumpet a hard mental nudge. "Trumpet, see the toy! Go see the girl, Trumpet." He pictured Trumpet running to the girl and the stuffed toy. "Go say hello."

As Gabe drew the dog's attention to the stuffed animal, the little girl's lips moved as she read the letters on Trumpet's bandana.

"Triumph! Like daddy's new motorcycle."

Bob turned toward the little girl. "Hi, honey, is this your dog?"

"Tawny?" A dark-haired young woman stepped next to the girl and took her hand. "You're supposed to stay close to me."

"It's Triumph!" She pointed to Trumpet and held out her arms.

"Good enough." Bob released his hold as Bunting began to protest.

His eyes fixed on the stuffed bear, Trumpet needed no further prodding and trotted to the girl. Sitting in front of her, he held out his paw to 'Say Hello.'

She gave his paw a quick shake, and, when Trumpet nudged the toy, the girl giggled. "Here, nice doggie." With both hands, she offered him the bear. Accompanied by "ohs'" and "isn't that cute" from the audience, Trumpet carefully took the stuffed animal in his mouth.

"Triumph wants to hold my bear." Releasing her hold, she gently touched his head. "He's a nice dog."

The crowd murmured their approval as the girl's mom knelt next to her. "Tawny, you know what I've told you about touching strange dogs."

"He's not yours?"

The security guard's question prompted Gabe. "Time to go, boy!"

"For cripes sake, I told you, he's my dog, not hers." The attorney snapped. "Just ask her."

"Ma'am is…"

"Run for it!" Gabe roared in Trumpet's head. With the toy still in his mouth he dodged around the girl and her mother, bolted through the crowd, then down between the rows of slot machines.

"Bye, Triumph!" The little girl, unconcerned by the loss of her bear, waved after them.

"Get the dog…get…." But the attorney was drowned out by the laughter of the people surrounding him. He pushed through them, storming down the aisle in search of his prey.

With all the noise of the machines combined with the people and their dogs, Trumpet became confused. Instead of making their way toward the door, they turned down a wide, less traveled hallway.

"Hey!" Bunting's voice echoed off the walls. Gabe caught a quick glimpse of the attorney running toward them. Trumpet nosed open a wide door and dashed inside.

Seconds later, Bunting reached the door. Flinging it open he yelled, "Gotcha!"

The large room before him was filled with tables occupied by golden retrievers, their people standing next to them with grooming shears, or scissors, in their hands. A number of off-leash gold dogs milled about or played.

The happy energy was completely lost on Bunting as he staggered into the room. "Nooo."

"Sir?" A tall woman called from the stage. "Do you have a question?" Clippers in hand, she was standing next to a table with an obliging golden looking on.

"A question?" His eyes frantically searched the room. Dogs and people looked back.

"Regarding our dog grooming seminar." With her clippers, she indicated a sandwich board sign on the stage.

A door off to one side of the room opened. Bunting watched helplessly as a woman entered the room. Before the door could close behind her, Trumpet exited past in a red blur.

"No, no don't let him…" Bunting dodged around the tables to the door, getting it open just in time to see Trumpet stop at an exit at the end of the hall. His quarry glanced his way. Rising up, he slapped a square red handicapped button with a paw. The door swung open, and he was gone.

"Argg!" Bunting charged for the door.

 ❧

"Hey, careful there, big red." A large woman snagged Trumpet by the bandana as he started into the street. Over her shoulder was a heavy-looking brown leather purse. In her free hand she clutched a life-sized toy raccoon.

"We can't have you getting hit." She smiled down kindly, noting Trumpet's little stuffed bear. "Nice toy you have there. I'm bringing this back to my Toby." She held out the raccoon. "He's with my husband while I shop."

Trumpet wagged his tail, bobbing his head several times to show off his toy bear to the friendly woman.

"You, you've got my dog." Breathing hard, the attorney

stopped next to them and snatched at the bandana.

"Your dog?" The woman pulled back on the bandana guiding Trumpet behind her. "Your dog? You let your dog run loose. He could have been killed just now."

Trumpet let out a muffled growl.

"Yes, well, just give me my damned dog." He snapped at her. "Is everyone here stupid?" Grabbing at her arm, he tried to reach around her. "Just give me the damn dog. Just…"

His words were cut off as the woman hauled back her arm. Using the raccoon as a boxing glove, she punched him full in the face. "Thief!" she screamed, hitting him again. "He's after my purse!"

12

SONOMA BEAR

Free of her grip, Trumpet bolted into the traffic. Gabe tried to calm him, to get them off the street, but the blaring horns and shouts from drivers urged him on. Trumpet dodged between cars and spotted the motorcycle and sidecar where they were parked. Aemea had just returned to the bike, and realized that Trumpet was missing, as he made a flying leap into the sidecar. Landing hard, the big red dog scrambled to get settled. The grateful look Trumpet gave her was returned with an expression of relief.

With the dog safely in the sidecar, Aemea skillfully pulled into the traffic. She drove until she found a quiet side street where she stopped next to the curb. Turning to him. "You were supposed to stay in the rig until I got back! When I came back out, and you were gone…" She took a breath. "You could have been killed back there." She ran a hand over the head of the panting dog who was still holding the toy in his mouth.

What's this?" She tugged gently at the teddy bear until Trumpet released it. "You got out for this? A stuffed bear?" After looking the toy over, she held it out to him.

Encouraged by Gabe, Trumpet nudged the heart-shaped plastic tag hanging from the bear's neck. "Woof."

"You are a very odd animal." Aemea read the tag before holding it out a second time. When Trumpet again nudged the heart, she read the two words on the tag out loud. "Sonoma Bear."

"Woof." Gabe managed to communicate through Trumpet.

After studying him for a few moments, she repeated the words. Each time receiving the same response.

"Hmm. Reno Bear."

Silence.

"Sonoma."

"Woof." Trumpet seemed to understand what Gabe was asking from him.

She thought for a moment. Other counties and names brought the same silence. But 'Sonoma' was followed by a soft "woof."

"Well, it's the sound of the word, isn't it? You just understand Sonoma, like if I said, 'walk,' right?"

When Trumpet remained silent, Aemea sat back on the motorcycle seat. After regarding him for several moments she shook her head. "This, is silly." Finally, after she glanced around, she spoke in a faint voice. "Can, um. Are you able to understand what I say?"

"Woof." Gabe was sharing his thoughts with Trumpet, and they were vocalizing together.

Aemea placed the bear on the seat next to the dog. Folding her arms across her chest, her eyes fixed on Trumpet's. After taking a deep breath, followed by some nibbling at her lower lip, she came to a decision. "Alright.

We'll make this simple, and then I'll be able to forget the whole thing. We'll do a 'woof' for yes, a 'growl' for no. Got it?"

"Woof."

"Oh, God." Aemea momentarily closed her eyes. "Are you part of a government experiment?"

At Gabe's urging, Trumpet let out a low growl.

"Hmm." She studied him for a moment. "In that case, are you from outer space? Kind of a cute Roswell alien with floppy ears?"

Gabe wished he could laugh out loud, but again carefully prompted Trumpet. "Arrourr."

"Let's try something more personal. Did you spend a night at the pound?"

This time she received a positive answer accompanied by a fast dip of his head.

"Okay. I live in a big house with a swimming pool."

Trumpet swung his head side to side. "Arrourr."

"Alright, how about a trailer with a cave?"

"Woof."

"Um." She glanced down to her open neck shirt to her cleavage, then back. You, um, don't...I mean back at the club..." She cleared her throat. "You actually understand?"

"Woof."

"Sweet Jesus." She brought her hand to her open mouth. "Is there something... do you want me to help you?"

"Woof." He reached out to touch her knee with a big paw. "What can I do?"

Trumpet nudged the bear's tag with several short jerks of his long nose.

The sound of car horns and tires skidding on the pavement back on the main road made them turn their heads. A black Mercedes SUV backed up against traffic, stopped hard, and then accompanied by the squeal of tires, swung its nose down the street toward them.

After a quick glance into one of the bike's mirrors, she turned to look over her shoulder. "Is he a bad guy?"

Trumpet loudly let her know yes indeed, the bad guy was coming after them. Quickly settling back into the 'car, he faced forward and let out several encouraging "arks" to get her moving.

"Good enough." She kicked the idling bike into gear, accelerating away from the curb. "Hold on!"

Hunkering down, Trumpet howled his encouragement.

The first right turn brought the sidecar into the air, with both Aemea and Trumpet leaning into the turn. A fast look back told him the SUV was just a few car lengths behind. The 'car slammed down, they dodged around a van backing out of a driveway on their left, putting the sidecar back in the air, then down again. Behind, tires squealed, car horns sounded.

"Hang on. We're about to make a real hard left." As they slid up to a stop sign, Aemea blipped the throttle as she downshifted, the sidecar's tire dug in and she executed a sudden tight U-turn, reminding Gabe of the old game of 'Crack the whip.'

Gabe caught a quick glimpse of Bunting's angry face as they shot by in the opposite direction.

She checked the mirror. "We can't outrun him in this.

We can only manage about eighty or so." She grinned. "Don't worry, I have a plan."

As they raced along the side streets, a few quick looks back told Gabe the SUV was staying within a half block. At a two-way stop, Aemea slowed slightly before running the 'Stop' sign to dart through a gap between cars.

"CIA. I bet you're a secret government project and escaped like the dog in the Dean Koontz book, 'Watchers'. Right!?" Aemea rolled on the throttle to pass a white pickup truck.

"Arrourr!" Trumpet's attention went from Aemea to the SUV behind them.

"Yeah, I see it." Aemea was grinning. "You're not going all backseat driver on me now, are you?"

"Woof!"

A block ahead, amid yet another sounding of horns, they burst out onto the main street near a freeway on-ramp. The rig roared onto the freeway, swinging through traffic with Aemea flattened out on the bike's tank. Following her example, Trumpet ducked behind the low windscreen.

13

Escaping Reno

"This should buy us some time." Still in the fast lane, with the SUV once again closing on them, they were reaching the point where they would overshoot the exit marked Airport Traffic General Aviation. "Here we go!"

As she called out the words, Trumpet looked to their right. There was a small opening between a big tractor-trailer they were overtaking. Gabe wondered just where 'we' planned on going. He felt the bike drop a gear, the engine wind up, and the rig surge forward. They suddenly snapped to the right, zipping between a set of very bright taillights and a looming chrome bumper. Out the other side, they passed what looked to be inches behind a silver van seconds before making a midway entrance to the exit ramp. Peering out from his rearward-facing seat through the rear side window of the van, a small boy stared for a moment, mouthed something, and waved.

"Yeah." Aemea sat up and waved back. "Awesome." She leaned over and gave a quick rub to Trumpet's neck as they slowed for a red light. "And you my weird friend, are an awesome passenger. I haven't felt like this in a very long time."

"Next exit he could make is a mile up the road. I don't see him, maybe we got lucky." At the light she turned right, running along the side of the airport until turning through an open gate bearing a small 'General Aviation' sign.

On a narrow road near a cluster of small hangers, Aemea stopped at a yellow wooden barrier with an electronic locking mechanism. After punching in a series of numbers she turned back to Trumpet. "You're for real, aren't you? Or I'm nuts?" Her eyes were back on his.

"Woof." He first bobbed his nose before shaking it side to side, "arrourr."

"Damn!"

After rolling through the gate, and closing it behind them, they swiftly cruised between hangers until Aemea steered the rig around the front of one displaying an 'Experimental Aviation Member' sign. She stopped at one side of the hanger door and shut off the bike. Before jumping out, Trumpet reached into the nose of the sidecar to where the stuffed bear tumbled during their recent maneuvers.

From next to the sidecar, he watched her use a key from the bike's ring to open the locked cover and again punch in a combination. The hanger door rumbled upward, revealing the sleek powder-blue high-wing monoplane he'd seen among the photos on her wall.

She laughed at the look she got from Trumpet. "You're not the only one with a secret. This is one of those vices I mentioned." She ran a hand over the leading edge of the wing. "As aircraft go, she's not fast, but she can outrun any damn Mercedes." Opening the near door, Aemea instructed him to "get in, right seat," and she winked. "I'm going to be doing a fast preflight. Don't touch anything, okay?"

Trumpet signaled a "yes.' As he settled into the seat Gabe praised him for being a brave smart dog. Carefully, he set the bear to one side.

"Uh, oh." Aemea paused in her checking of the engine oil to look out toward the highway. "I should have pushed the bike in. It looks like we've been spotted." She was looking at something blocked from Trumpet's sight by the hanger. "If he really wants us, the gate won't stop him."

Quickly, she finished her preflight check of the plane. After yanking the blocks from in front of the tires, she pulled the plane out of the hanger, turning it so it was parallel to the opening. After shoving the motorcycle rig inside, she touched the keypad. As the hanger door closed, she climbed into the pilot's seat.

❦

"No." Bunting slapped the palms of his hands on the leather-covered steering wheel. "No, no, no!" A foot away, a red reflector on the splintered yellow wooden barrier shined back at him through the windshield. Bunting jerked his seatbelt loose and poured himself out of his Mercedes. He had intended to nudge the fragile-looking gate, hoping it would simply swing out of his way. That, he thought smugly, was why he spent nine hundred dollars on a heavy chrome brush guard to protect the SUV's grill. Instead, the gate moved partway up in a jerky fashion, snapped, then dropped onto his hood.

Gingerly, he lifted the wooden remains off the shiny black paint. Tossing it aside, he peered hopefully at the hood where several deep scratches and one long gouge down to the bare metal peered back. "That cinches it. Now, it's personal."

Once in the plane, a rapidly spoken checklist was uttered as Aemea slipped on a headset, her hands moving over the controls. "Clear!" The engine roared to life, and she looked behind them. "So far, so good." The plane rolled forward, and they taxied to the end of the hangers where she braked to a stop.

"Here, let's get you buckled in." Aemea quickly adjusted the four-point harness around Trumpet. "It's not perfect, but it'll do."

Gazing between the rows of hangers Aemea confirmed, "He's here." Trumpet looked over to see the SUV pausing as Bunting eyed where the sidecar rig had been parked.

"Reno Tower, Maule November Two Two Eight X-Ray, request taxi to active, over?"

"November Two Two Eight X-Ray, this is Reno Tower. That you, Aemea?"

"Roger that. Randy, can you get me to the active, ASAP? I've got a family emergency in Sonoma County."

The driver of the SUV spotted them and began to turn back in their direction.

"Roger. You are clear to runway Zero Seven, winds zero five at two knots. You've got a heavy twelve miles out, clear to depart west."

"Tango Mike, Reno." The plane surged eagerly forward as she opened the throttle.

"Two Two Eight X-Ray, we have a vehicle on the taxiway, hold your position."

"That's a negative." Trumpet was watching Aemea, who flipped up the boom mike and was staring ahead. "If I had Wartzilla, this would be no problem. Hang on Triumph, we're going to take him." She shoved the throttle full forward. Managing the control yolk with one hand, she reached behind the seat with the other. Finding what she wanted, she popped open her side window.

"Damn!" Gabe stared through Trumpet's eyes as the plane and SUV closed on each other. Trumpet leaned hard against the seat back at Gabe's thoughts.

With only a few car lengths between them, The SUV suddenly braked heavily, swinging to their left. Aemea hauled back on the yoke, at the same time, heaving something out the window as the little plane lurched into the air. Seconds later they were back on the ground, swerving onto the runway.

"Reno Tower, Two Two Eight X-Ray is departing on Zero Seven."

"Two Two Eight X-Ray, go to…." There was a quick pause and Randy gave her a new radio frequency.

"Aemea. You up? Over?"

"Hey, Randy. Thanks much." Aemea eased back the yoke and they were climbing.

"I've got cops on the way. You owe me big time."

"Roger." Aemea smiled into the mike.

"Dinner, next Tuesday. Your treat."

"I'll think about it." Her smile flattened out a little.

"No ma'am. You owe me something serious. Dinner, Tuesday. Over."

Instead of replying, she kept her eyes moving about the outside of the plane and backed off on the throttle slightly.

"I say again. Tuesday. Over?"

"Woof."

Aemea turned her head toward Trumpet. "I don't need advice from you."

Trumpet tucked his chin down, eyed her, and grumbled out a "woof."

Surprised, Gabe looked at her carefully. Trumpet was staring back on his own.

"Okay, okay. Tuesday. Over?"

"Roger. I'll pick you up at your place. Tango Mike, out." The pleasure in the tower operator's voice was obvious.

The plane banked to the west and Aemea gave Trumpet a reproving look. "Don't look so smug. Do you know how to fly a plane?"

The dog cocked his head to one side. "Arrourr."

"See, you're not so smart. For your information, he's been asking me out for quite some time. I might have given in on my own."

Trumpet let out a snort.

"Yes, woof."

They flew in silence for a while. Trumpet leaned back into the seat, his head turned to rest on the seat back. Gabe was content to let his mind become quiet.

"The SUV was heading back through the debris at the entrance when we were leaving the pattern." She grinned.

"I couldn't tell for sure, but I think he took my big flashlight in his windshield."

Trumpet kept his eyes closed.

"You know, as recently as eleven months ago, I would have put you down as a combination of too much alcohol combined with VA-approved drugs." She was quiet for a few moments before asking. "By any chance, do you know how to use a computer?"

Gabe tried to get Trumpet to open his eyes, but the dog ignored him. "Please, boy, come on, this is important." He pictured them playing with a stick out by the cabin.

The dog sighed deeply and blew out through his nose.

"Come on, please. Look, you have a nice new stuffed toy." This elicited another sigh, but Trumpet turned his head toward Aemea and opened his eyes. "Woof."

She eyed him for a moment before looking back out the windscreen. "Why am I not surprised? So, you live in Sonoma County?"

This time he simply dipped his muzzle.

"Is that a yes?"

He gave another nod.

"Cat suddenly got your tongue?"

She saw how his expressive eyebrows narrowed. Apologizing with a tiny smile Aemea opened up a chart book. "I'm not familiar with the area." She held it up and scanned it. "There's a couple of small airports, Cloverdale, Healdsburg. The biggie is Sonoma County Airport."

He let out a last, tired, "Woof."

Aemea looked back at him as if he might evaporate in

a puff of smoke. "Your eyes are really red. I've heard most dogs nap a lot. You've had a big day, want to take a nap?"

Yawning deeply, Trumpet settled into the seat, his chin resting on the armrest of the upholstered panel beneath the window.

Gabe was thrilled that they were returning to Sonoma County, and hopefully to their ranch. He always thought that when he died he would see Sarah again, and live out eternity with her. Perhaps he could connect with Sarah, even while sharing his consciousness with Trumpet; sort of the best of both other worlds. He mused over the possibilities as Trumpet drifted off to sleep.

'Damn, damn, damn!" The SUV slid to a stop outside the airport fence. Apparently, during its recent trip through the passenger side of the windshield, the rugged black aluminum flashlight had switched itself on. Bunting stared angrily at the glass bits glowing against the black leather upholstery backdrop. He gingerly reached over and switched off the light while the plane vanished into the distance. "Okay, Miss Two Two Eight X, whoever you are, you want to play? It's time to call out the big guns."

After the airport security truck headed back to the tower, Bunting drove back through the ruined gate. "Ha!" He pulled up next to the payphone and got out.

"911."

"Please," Bunting spoke quietly through the bandana he held over his mouth, "I'm eight years old and they are abdu, abduct...kidnapping me!"

"Sir, you'll have to speak up, I can't understand you."

Bunting gritted his teeth, took a breath, and raised his voice a bit. "I'm eight years old. Someone at the Reno airport is kidnapping me. Call the FBI!"

"You're being kidnapped? Son, just stay calm. Now, exactly where are you?"

"Oh no, the terrorists have found me! Their airplane has a big number Two Two Eight and an X on the side. I, nooo!" Bunting whipped off the bandana and in a falsetto he hoped sounded feminine, growled, "Come here, kid!" He slammed the phone back in the cradle.

Agent Chuck Sobel listened to the 911 recording for the third time. "Still sounds odd. The kid must be terrified." He sucked at his upper lip, his eyes staring into the distance. "But it just doesn't feel right."

"Sounds like he has a cold." His partner, Ben Washington, held out a sheet of paper. "The tower says this plane took off in a real hurry about forty minutes ago. The pilot is one Aemea Rand, retired U.S. Air Force."

"The last voice was kind of odd. Like the guy from the seventies. Ah, what was his name? Um, small, diminutive...."

"Tiny Tim?"

Sobel snapped his fingers. "Yeah."

Washington shrugged. "One of the guys in the tower knows Rand. He says someone must be yanking our chain."

"Any reports of missing kids?"

"Not yet. The guy in the tower said the plane is on its way to Sonoma County in California."

"I can't put my finger on it. Something just doesn't feel right about this." Sobel nodded to himself. "Okay, we treat this like a kidnapping until things prove otherwise. Do we know where the call originated from?"

"A payphone by the general aviation hangers."

"I didn't know there were still payphones around. Make the calls while I go check out the phone."

At the hanger, Agent Sobel took a small black kit from the car's trunk and headed for the payphone.

After a few minutes of work, he studied the handset. "No prints. Why would they wipe the kid's prints?" His eyes moved to the small chrome change cup at the bottom edge of the phone.

14

DOG IS MY CO-PILOT

"It's beautiful down there." Aemea put the aircraft into a slip allowing her a better view out of her side window. Fifteen hundred feet below, the valley was carpeted in a checkerboard of late summer yellows, reds, and some reluctant greens. "I've read about the wine industry in Sonoma County, but never gave much thought about how lovely vineyards could look from the air at the right time of year."

Ahead to the west she spotted the runways for the Sonoma County airport. "Sonoma County tower, this is 'Maule November Two Two Eight XRay' approaching for landing."

"Maule November Two Two Eight X-Ray this is Sonoma County. Land runway one-four. Wind two six zero at three knots. You are number two behind the Piper."

"Tower, Two Two Eight X-Ray, Roger. I've got a Piper a mile ahead." Aemea rolled the little plane out of a shallow bank and into the downwind leg of the landing pattern.

"Relax. When we get down, we'll rent a car and get this all sorted out." She gave her passenger an encouraging smile.

She throttled back slightly as approaching Sonoma County Airport, they passed over a deep green river winding through the vineyards below. Trumpet let out a wide tongue curling yawn, stretching as best he could against the harness. "Urrr."

"Are you making a comment of some kind?" The smile lingered as she returned her attention to outside the aircraft. "Looks like something going on at a big hanger on the east side of the field." Her eyes narrowed as she studied the airfield with the practiced eye of a former combat pilot.

The airport had expanded since Gabe last flew over the County Airport in a friend's plane years before. There were more hangers at the far end, and the area to the east was built up. The two runways appeared about the same as he recalled, radiating out in a narrow 'V' from their position. He recalled the '14' indicated it lined up a hundred and forty degrees on the compass; the runway to the left had the large white number '19' at its threshold.

The tires chirped, and they were rolling toward the taxiway. "Sonoma County Tower, Maule Two Two Eight X-Ray. Request taxi to the fuel island, over."

Aemea's headset crackled with, "Two Two Eight X-Ray taxi to fuel."

She turned off the runway onto the taxiway when the tower came back. "Two Two Eight X-Ray, proceed directly to the apron of the hanger to your right. I say again, directly to your right."

Aemea could see a pair of patrol cars parked in the hanger, along with a big black late model Ford sedan parked beneath the wings of a large twin-engine plane. A half-dozen men were looking in her direction. "Cops and suits," she muttered and reached over to rest a hand on Trumpet.

"Nuts. First the guy in Reno; now these guys want us to join their party. What happened to 'I'm not part of a government experiment?' Or are they just going to a lot of trouble for a flashlight in a windshield?"

Aemea flipped up her boom mike. "I don't like this. You?"

Gabe suspected somehow Bunting had been up to no good. Trumpet was right with him. "Arrourr."

Feeding in some throttle, Aemea swung the plane back toward the runway. "We have a plane, they don't. I believe we'll pass on this."

"Two Two Eight X-Ray, I say again. Taxi *immediately* to the hanger to your right."

As if anticipating her lack of cooperation, the two patrol cars pulled out, heading in her direction. When Aemea didn't respond, a new voice came over the headset. "Two Two Eight X-Ray, stop at the end of the runway, release the child, and you'll be allowed to depart."

"Child?" Aemea gave a quick puzzled glance toward Trumpet before she spoke back into the mike. "I have no child aboard. Repeat, there is no child aboard. It's just me and my dog." The little plane accelerated forward as she applied more throttle, crossing onto the runway away from the cars. "Alright my friend, we're going to take the runway on the far side and get out of here. Then we'll find a quiet little airport where we'll have a nice long talk." The plane swung onto 19, and Aemea applied full power.

Sure, Gabe mused, I can't wait. Yes, no, yes, no, a few dips of the nose. Oh yeah, it'll be a great little talk.

The patrol cars easily pulled up on either side. The

passenger on Aemea's side slipped a shotgun barrel outside the window. With his free hand, he signaled her to slow down.

"They won't shoot because they think you're a kid, I hope. Triumph, what the hell is going on?"

Gabe was at a complete loss. Aemea's friend in the tower saw Bunting's SUV on the taxiway, even warned them. Maybe there was some obscure law regarding hurling things at cars from airplanes and Bunting, being an attorney, jumped on it.

The deputy driving the car on the right looked up into the passenger side window of the plane.

Trumpet looked back. Seeing a driver in uniform, he snapped his nose forward, urging Aemea on with a string of encouraging barks.

The deputy's radio crackled. "We've got the shotgun on the pilot. Ralston, are you able to ID the passenger?"

"Negative. There's a big red dog in the way."

"Say again?"

"All I can see is a big dog looking back at me."

The radio clicked a time or two, before the confused operator asked him to, "wait one."

On Aemea's side of the plane, the cop gestured with the shotgun.

"Time to go." Aemea pushed slightly on the yoke. When the tail wheel left the runway, she pulled a notch of flaps, added in full power, and eased back on the stick. The little plane stumbled into the air. With a bit of rudder the plane passed over the car with the shotgun. At thirty feet off the ground, she put the nose back down and began to pick up speed. At sixty knots, she retracted the flaps. Their speed went up rapidly to a hundred knots. "They didn't expect that."

While Trumpet watched the vineyards pass quickly beneath them, the plane banked hard to the north.

She listened intently to her headset for a few moments. "It's not over yet. It looks like a pair of the suits have commandeered the Piper that landed ahead of us. They're giving him immediate clearance, and he's a faster aircraft."

"Two Two Eight X-Ray, this is Five Three Nine Three Pop, over."

"Pop, X-Ray, over."

"X-ray, Pop. Give it up lady. I've got the faster plane. Be advised, you're dealing with a former F-16 pilot."

They cleared the tree line along a narrow green river and began to climb. Aemea smiled for a moment. "Roger that, Pop. I flew Warthogs. We had jet jocks on our menu under, 'light snacks.'"

"Uh huh. So, X-ray. It's a long way from Reno. How's your fuel?"

"We fueled on the way. Yours?"

Turning to Trumpet, she shook her head. "He's trying to psyche me. We've got thirty minutes at most. The Piper taxied to the fuel pad but didn't have time to fuel up. So, he's low too."

"Woof."

"Yeah, woof. If you've got a plan, I'd like to hear it."

They were flying up what Gabe recognized as the Dry Creek Valley. Ahead was the dam at the Warm Springs Reservoir.

The name Tom Baxman came to Gabe's mind. Years back, the old friend of his late wife had flown a big Cessna taildragger. On two occasions Tom picked them up at the Healdsburg Airport for a long weekend at his place northwest of the Dry Creek Valley. The so-called runway at Tom's ranch was cut into the side of the hill, nearly hidden among the oak trees. He remembered sucking in his breath when Tom lined the high-winged Cessna up on the narrow dirt runway, which from Gabe's perspective looked to be more of a tree-lined dirt driveway.

"He's faster than I thought. I've got him coming up on our port wing." Aemea scanned the area below. "There's a small runway and hangers down on our right. Must be the Healdsburg airport." The right wing dipped briefly.

Gabe instructed Trumpet to lean across the small cockpit and bob his long nose toward her side. "Woof!"

Aemea leveled the plane, her attention going in the direction Trumpet was indicating. "The chart doesn't show another airport close by." She snatched another quick glance at the chart. "You mean out at the coast?"

"Arrourr."

"Near here?" They continued up the Dry Creek Valley and she peered ahead. "We've got a dam coming up."

The Piper pulled alongside on her left, a couple of wingspans away. Both the pilot and the man in the right seat had their eyes on her. The passenger raised his hand, signaling her with a jerk of his thumb to return to the small airport they had just passed.

"He must be lower on fuel than I hoped. You're sure there's a place to land out this way?"

Something in her tone told Gabe she wasn't going to follow the passenger's suggestion. When he hesitated, Trumpet let off two yeses.

Gabe stared through the retriever's eyes at Aemea and marveled at how often Trumpet was anticipating him.

"Okay then." Just past the dam and on their left, something caught her eye. "You didn't mention a bridge."

The bridge now spanning the opening to the Warm Springs finger of the lake was built long before work on the dam began. Gabe had driven under it when it simply passed over Skaggs Springs Road back in the late seventies. Until construction of the dam was completed, the area filled with water and the road flooded, the structure had been referred to by the locals as "The Bridge to Nowhere." It being a drought year, Gabe could see the water was now within fifty feet of the underside of the span.

Aemea returned the passenger's gesture, frowning at the obvious smirk on the pilot's face. "I hate guys who smirk." She gave him a well-I-guess-you've-won smile. "What do you think, Trumpet?"

For a brief moment, Trumpet stared past her to the other plane. "Aaark!"

"Ooo-kay." Aemea flashed a brilliant smile to the other aircraft. "Hold on. We're going to break hard to the left."

To the left? Gabe stared as Trumpet leaned toward the center of the plane. The area to the 'left' was mostly occupied by the Piper.

In a quick motion, she throttled back. The engine sound suddenly dropped at the same time the right wing came up almost vertically. In a heartbeat, they were flashing under the Piper with Trumpet barking his approval.

"Come on after us you smirking son of a bitch." The engine roared once again as they dove across the main expanse of the lower lake toward the bridge. Aemea threw a quick glance over her right shoulder. "He's got good reactions; he's pulling up on my starboard. I'll just crowd him a bit."

If they kept their present relative positions, there was just enough room for two planes to fly side by side under the span just ahead. Trumpet turned his head toward the Piper allowing Gabe an excellent view of the look on the pilot's face as Aemea banked their plane toward him. As there was no place left for it to go but up, the Piper suddenly stood on its tail. Through Trumpet's eyes, there was a view of the white underside of the other plane, a flash of the underside of the bridge, and just ahead, the masts of a pair of sailboats motoring side by side. Aemea pushed in the throttle. Hauling back on the yoke the nose of the little plane came up hard into a steep climb.

"Did you know while doing a loop, a truly fine pilot can keep a positive 'gee' load so an unsuspecting passenger would never realize he was inverted." Aemea's words were spoken with a trace of a smile and the measured calm of a consummate professional. "Check it out." She tilted her head up, indicating the tinted plastic panels in the headliner above them.

"Uuh." Gabe found he was looking straight 'up' at the bridge, a few hundred feet below. When the retriever swung his head back, Aemea was clicking off a string of shots with her camera.

"Don't give me that worried eyebrow look. I've still got one hand for the controls."

Gabe fervently wished he could close his eyes. Trumpet, on the other hand, was thoroughly enjoying the ride, letting out one of his play barks while he tried to wag his tail.

"I see our F-16 pilot rolled into a classic though somewhat panicky Immelmann maneuver. At the top of the loop, the plane is rolled upright and continues in the opposite direction. We, on the other hand, will continue into the loop to put valuable distance between us." She flashed Trumpet a confidently wicked smile. "First time you've ever looped a bridge, I bet."

"Woof!"

Through the windscreen, the horizon dropped upward. For the second time they plunged toward the water, then the bridge. This time they edged toward the span on the left where there was no boat traffic. With less than a wingspan to spare they again passed under the bridge, while ten feet beneath their tires the surface of the lake streamed by. At the last possible second, they climbed a few feet as they roared over the boats at the floating dock, wriggling between the masts of several sailboats moored there.

Gabe thought he could feel his heart pounding, but it was Trumpet's tail wildly thumping against the seat back. Good god! He thought. The dog likes this.

The little plane banked hard to the left, cleared the low ridge beyond the marina, dropped, leveled slightly over the water beyond then made an equally hard right bank. They were following the narrow winding finger of the lake known as the Warm Springs Branch. Aemea's face was a study of concentration and excitement, for rising from the lake on each side of them were steep brush and tree-covered hills.

~

"Have you spotted her?" The pilot scanned his portion of the sky with no luck.

"Oh yeah," the passenger twisted in his seat to look back toward the dam. "Tell me. How hard is it to loop a bridge?"

"What?"

"I mean, it's easy for a trained professional combat pilot like yourself, right?"

"Damn." The pilot rolled into a tight bank back toward the bridge. "That crazy bitch."

"Yeah, but she can sure fly."

~

Aemea flashed a quick grin at her passenger. "We used to call flying this low 'Nap of the earth' flying. It's handy for evading radar or over-confident fighter jocks." When the branch of the lake split just ahead into two narrower fingers, she made a tight bank to the left.

Still only a wingspan above the water, they flashed past a small sailboat, its main and jib luffing in the uncertain wind of the little canyon. The couple on the boat waved. "Cute. There was a cartoon toucan on the transom, with 'Two Can' painted beneath." Aemea reached over and gave Trumpet's head a quick scratch. "Looks like we're about out of lake."

"Woof." The end of the finger was fast turning to dirt, brush, and trees.

While he watched the shore approach, Gabe again pondered how increasingly often Trumpet was dealing with situations before prompting. *Maybe through the same process I'm using to sense his feelings, he's tapping into a part of my mind.* Not for the first time he wondered if the dog would actually benefit from this shared experience should he leave him.

"Yeah, woof. We're going to pop up and take a peek around. Sing out if you spot anything." Aemea brought the plane up until they were skimming the treetops. Swiveling her head, she spotted the Piper. "Got him. He's still back over the main lake about two miles out."

But Gabe spotted something else. He urged Trumpet to nudge Aemea on the shoulder and nosed to the opposite side.

Aemea looked down in time to see a windsock, its original orange faded to almost white. She banked toward the drooping sock. "Doesn't look like much wind." She slowed the plane and made a low circle over the area around the windsock, her eyes searching both the immediate area and the sky to the east where the Piper had been circling. They were passing what looked to be a section of wide dirt road cut into the sloping wooded hillside. The end vanished under a canopy of oaks. She turned to Trumpet. "Tell me that is not it."

Gabe prompted Trumpet. "Woof. Arrourr."

Aemea put the plane into a gentle bank away from the strip. "Sorry, not a good yes or no question, was it? Okay, is that it?"

His nose ducked several times and he "woofed" softly.

"Woof." Aemea repeated. She gazed toward the east once again. "Our F-16 pilot is heading this way. Once I drop down we'll have a couple of ridges between us." She increased the bank until they were pointed in the direction of the windsock. Throttling back, she began to line up on the dirt strip and started her landing checklist. "Gas. On main tank. Undercarriage. Fixed and down. Mixture. Correct. Prop." She adjusted the pitch of the propeller to its fine setting for their impending landing. "Nice. Your 'runway' slopes up at the end and tilts up on the right." Aemea leaned forward, concentrating on the task at hand. "Flaps." She moved a small lever on the control panel to its first notch. "I'm looking forward to meeting the pilot who flies in and out of here."

There was a light feeling in Trumpet's stomach as the flaps increased the wing's lift, allowing the plane to slow. With Trumpet staring intently ahead, Gabe watched them close in on the strip.

The light feeling came again with Aemea's addition of a second notch of flaps accompanied by her call of, "Flaps." While the engine burbled to an idle, the left wing dipped slightly until matching the sight tilt of the strip.

"This is it." She drew the yolk back slightly; the nose rose a bit and they touched down. The tires rumbled over the slightly uneven ground, while Aemea quickly retracted the flaps.

Trumpet let out an excited yap of pleasure.

"You, my friend, can fly with me anytime." She glanced at him and laughed. "A while back I saw a bumper sticker with, 'Dog is my Co-Pilot' printed on it. I have to get me one of those."

She added a little power, and they taxied up the gentle slope until they were under the trees and passing a weathered old barn, its large open doors beckoning. "Now, that looks like a good place to park."

15

TOM AND JEFFREY

They were both out of the plane and Aemea was pushing it into the barn when the Piper flashed over the hills a mile or so away. "He's going to see the sock, and it won't take him long to figure out where we are."

"Hi there. Plan on staying a while, do you?"

They turned to find an older gentleman standing a few yards away. Snow white hair protruding from under a dark blue baseball cap matched a neatly trimmed mustache. His eyes were set deep in sun-darkened skin. Dressed in faded and mended, but clean jeans, an equally faded work shirt, and well-worn black boots, he looked every inch an old rancher. He was also carrying an ancient Garand Carbine, casually pointed in their direction.

On his right, his intense gaze also on them, sat an older border collie. Mostly black, the dog had a white ruff and matching blaze from his nose to between the eyes. His upper face was marked with tan spots, which added to his look of concentration.

"Tom Baxman." Gabe grinned to himself, recognizing Sarah's old friend.

The four of them paused to watch the Piper as it passed over the trees at a hundred feet or so.

"Sir. I'm Captain Aemea Rand, U.S. Air Force Reserves.

I'm…" She glanced at Trumpet, who wagged his tail and offered a happy dog smile. "We're on the run from terrorists in a matter of national security."

Tom Baxman regarded the two of them for a long moment before replying. "Captain Rand sounds like a kernel of truth buried in a barrel of bullshit." He stared past her at the Maule. "But I like your style."

After another moment of studying Aemea and Trumpet, he ambled over and leaned the rifle against the barn. "Let's get your plane put away from prying eyes."

With the two of them pushing, the plane moved easily and was quickly backed into the barn. Aemea stood to one side as the old man set the hasp on the closed doors. "They'll try to land here."

"This is a strip for a tail dragger. Your pursuer's Piper is too fast to drop in here."

"The pilot said he used to fly fighters."

Sure enough, the Piper was circling out away from them and slowing, the landing gear easing down.

"The guy is pretty sure of himself. Well, we can't have him rolling a perfectly good aircraft into a ball on my little dirt strip." Tom turned to his dog. "Jeffrey, go shut the gates."

Like a shot, the border collie bolted down the strip, Trumpet fast behind him. Gabe could feel Trumpet's joy at running with another of his kind, though the collie was leaving him behind.

At the start of the dirt runway, Jeffrey headed towards one of a pair of gates set on thick posts thirty feet apart and parallel to the strip. Each post supported the hinges of a fifteen-foot wide pipe gate. At the bottom of each gate was a large wheel that supported the expanse and allowed it to roll to the center to meet its partner on the far side. The border collie rose up on his hind legs and caught a rope loop hanging from the center in his teeth. With a deft move, he tugged the gate until it swung into the center of the runway.

Smart guy, Gabe thought. After Trumpet observed the other dog's progress, he eagerly ran to an identical setup across the runway. Without any coaching from Gabe, he duplicated Jeffrey's moves until the ends of the gates latched together at the runway's center.

❦

"You sure you can put us down there?"

"Piece of cake." One hand rested on the flap lever, while the pilot kept his attention on the tiny strip a half-mile ahead.

"Something is going on." The man in the passenger seat leaned forward toward the windscreen.

"It's just a couple of dogs." The pilot was also leaning forward, his eyes on the tiny dirt runway. "The sound of our plane will scare 'em away when we get closer."

"They're doing something by the trees on the right. The red one just crossed to the left side." The passenger squinted. "You know, it looks like…."

"They're swinging a set of gates across the runway!" The pilot added full power. "Damn it!" Hitting the 'gear up' switch he quickly banked hard away from the hillside.

As the Piper flew past, the dogs headed back to the barn. Jeffrey was all business, but Trumpet was determined to make friends.

Relieved to see the Piper heading off to the east, Aemea turned her attention back to the dogs. "What are they doing? Are they going to fight?" She folded her arms across her

chest; her eyes on the two dogs. Trumpet was now sitting very still, his head slightly bowed, while Jeffrey slowly circled him, growling softly and sniffing.

"Your dog's the new guy, so Jeffrey is explaining the rules of the ranch." The rancher gave her a crooked grin. "His ranch."

"Trumpet, say 'hello' to your new buddy." Gabe eyed the border collie as he circled for the second time. Instead of heeding Gabe's advice, Trumpet kept his head low and still. The dog stopped directly in front, their eyes locking. The eyebrows of the collie narrowed, and Jeffrey moved his head until their noses were almost touching.

"Hey, there fella," Gabe thought, "impressive job with the gate."

The border collie's eyebrows rose and his head drew back sharply. He leaned in a second time, the intelligent eyes piercing.

"You can't possibly hear me."

Ears up, Jeffrey tilted his head to one side.

"Jeff, you're a smart guy, aren't you?"

The head tilted sharply the other way. After a long moment, he turned back to where Aemea and the old man stood.

"Jeff, come on old fellow!" The old man slapped the side of his leg for emphasis.

Jeffrey snapped his head back to Trumpet one last time before whipping around to run to his master.

"What a great couple of dogs." Aemea squatted between the two wagging, eager dogs, rubbing their heads, kissing each in turn on the nose.

"Come on, there's coffee on. I've got the makings for sandwiches if you're hungry." He held out his hand. "Captain Rand, I'm Tom Baxman."

"It's Aemea, sir." She returned his firm handshake. "I appreciate the use of your runway."

"Haven't used it myself for a couple of years now, but I keep it up out of habit, I guess. The Doc found out I had a weak ticker and grounded me." He gestured in the direction of a stand of oaks surrounding a comfortable-looking cabin with a wide wrap-around porch.

The dogs ran ahead, and Tom cleared his throat. "How exactly did you find my little dirt strip?"

"That, Mister Baxman, is part of a very interesting story."

He noted her scanning of the sky to the southeast. "Please call me Tom. I'm guessing the guys in the Piper will head for the Healdsburg airport. If they're able to borrow a car, they're in for a good hour and a half drive to get here, *if* they find the right driveway off Skaggs Springs Road. Over coffee and a sandwich, you can tell me your story and we'll see what kind of plan we can come up with."

"You're saying, somehow the Feds think you're a kidnapper, and the dog understands us?" Tom looked doubtful.

Trumpet looked steadily back. "Woof."

"That was a yes." Aemea wiped her mouth with a paper towel.

"And a "no" would be?"

"Arrourr."

With a thoughtful look, Tom asked, "Are you some sort of government experiment?"

Trumpet glanced at Aemea before letting out another negative answer.

"We've been through this, and the yes or no questions are sort of limiting."

"Hmm. Then, let's try something a little different." Tom went to a drawer in a kitchen cabinet and returned with a thick stick of blue carpenter's chalk. He rolled the rug back, then on the clean wooden plank floor he quickly wrote out the letters of the alphabet. When he was through he smiled at Aemea's look of concern. "A damp mop will take it right off."

Tom moved his chair, turning his attention back to the retriever. "Now then, do you know what this is?"

Gabe was beside himself with excitement. Trumpet was getting better at following his directions, and now they finally had a way to communicate.

"Woof."

"Is your name, Triumph?"

Instead of answering with his usual yes or no answer, Trumpet trotted over to the line of letters. Slowly, he placed his right paw on one, then carefully went to the next. When he was finished with 'T R U M P E T' he returned to Aemea's side.

"Damn." The old rancher dropped his hands to his lap. "Damn."

"Trumpet?" Aemea rested a hand on his neck. "Funny, I

didn't know what else to call him, so I went with the brand of my motorcycle. I was close since Trumpet is a nickname for a Triumph motorcycle."

While his friend appeared calm and settled, Gabe asked him to spell out more. Trumpet moved back into the middle of the alphabet, and placed his paw on a letter, then another.

Tom found a pad to write on and handed it to Aemea. The two people leaned forward in their chairs, and even Jeffrey got up from beside Tom's chair to watch.

'G A B E   P I C K E T.'

"I, I don't understand." His eyes fixed on the letters, the old rancher got to his feet. Reading the letters again he suddenly recognized the name. "This isn't possible." A few moments passed before he sat back heavily into the wooden kitchen chair. "Gabe Picket is the husband of a dear old friend. She passed on almost two years ago. They owned a small ranch outside of Cazadero, a small town near the coast. Sarah is buried at their ranch."

Trumpet walked over, sat in front of Tom, and looked up at him expectantly.

"At her funeral, Gabe had a young golden retriever with him." His hand went to the side of the dog's head. "That was you, wasn't it?"

"Woof." Trumpet turned away and went back to the letters. This time it took longer.

"L I G H T N I N G H I T U S B O T H I N D O G." Aemea looked up from the writing pad where she jotted down the letters Trumpet had indicated.

Tired from his efforts, Trumpet flopped down on the

floor next to Jeffrey.

Together Aemea and Tom took turns looking at the letters, constructing them into words. Tom finally read them out loud, "Lightning hit us both in dog." He muttered. "This is…it's unbelievable."

"There is still a small bare spot next to his left ear." With a slow shake of her head, Aemea continued. "It looked like some sort of a burn. I put salve on it when I first found him."

Tom rose shakily to his feet. "I'm going to make a phone call." From the wall, he took a portable phone, studied a list of phone numbers pinned next to it, and dialed a number. After a few moments, he dialed again.

He smiled thinly at Aemea. "Gabe's cell phone at his cabin is out of service. I'm trying the town's store." He held up his hand. "Yes, I'm a friend looking to talk to Gabe Picket. I'm afraid his cell is out and I'd…" The skin beneath Tom's tanned face paled. After listening for an interminable amount of time, he made some small talk before hanging up.

"Are you alright?" Aemea went over to where the rancher sat slouched back on the wooden chair, his eyes on Trumpet. She rested a hand on his shoulder until he slowly drew himself back up, shaking off the obvious shock of the phone call.

"Gabe and Trumpet were caught in a thunderstorm last week while walking on a road west of his cabin, which is where Gabe's body was found. The local sheriff who found him thinks judging from a tuft of singed fur on a couple of Gabe's fingers, they were apparently both struck by light-ning. Trumpet still hasn't been located."

"But how did he…" Aemea stopped and turned to

Trumpet, who ignoring Gabe's urging, lay with his eyes closed. "How did you get to Nevada?"

Gabe pictured a series of images beginning with the cage. Then the attorney shooting at them; his face sneering at them through the louvers of the dog shelter's truck. Finally, he pictured the shelter accompanied by the despairing howls of the other dogs held there. The last image brought Trumpet to his feet.

'B U N T I N G.' Aemea read the word out loud. "What does 'bunting' mean?"

Tom looked thoughtful but said nothing.

Hearing the name Trumpet began barking furiously. When he calmed down, he rushed back to the letters on the floor. 'M A N I N S U V.' Satisfied that his work was done, he returned to his spot next to Jeffrey and laid down with his chin on his front paws.

This one took Aemea and Tom a bit longer to figure out. 'Man in SUV.' Once Aemea identified the words she instantly made the connection to the jerk at the airport. "The guy chasing us in the SUV didn't look like a cop, or a Fed." She thought for a moment before adding. "He wasn't in an official car either; it was a big Mercedes SUV. We took my plane to escape. But I don't understand why he was chasing us?"

It was becoming more difficult to get Trumpet to engage in this game. Gabe promised him that if he would cooperate one more time it would be the last. Reluctantly Trumpet trudged over to the letters. 'N E W W I L L N O T S E L L.'

Aemea quickly deciphered the letters, and read out loud,

"New Will. Not Sell."

"Well, this all seems to fit." Tom pushed to his feet. "Gabe brought Trumpet home for Sarah when she was ill, and now she is gone." He smiled at Jeffrey who was sitting off to one side watching the whole thing. "My own Will states if I pass on before Jeffrey, he will be allowed to live out his life here with an assigned caregiver. My heirs can't sell the ranch until after his death. I bet because of Trumpet, Gabe made out a similar new Will no one knows about. Except us."

Gabe's elation caused Trumpet to dance with a wagging tail around their chairs.

"Except, maybe, Bunting. But why should he care?" Tom blew his breath out through his lips. "Now what?"

"What if Gabe has a copy of the Will at his cabin?" Once again facing the dog, Aemea asked, "Is there a copy at your cabin?"

Trumpet sat in front of her, pawed her knee, dipping his nose several times in a definite, "yes, yes, yes!"

Gabe could hardly believe things were going their way. All they needed to do was get to the cabin. The addressed envelopes were gone, but there was a signed copy in the filing cabinet, and they could look in the computer. But, like the two envelopes, Bunting could have found the third copy in the files. The one in the computer would not be a signed copy. Now that he had a way to communicate they would think of something.

The phone rang and Tom answered it. "Baxman Ranch," was followed by, "Oh, hello Phil, how's airport life?" He listened for a time, at one point replying he'd been out fishing and hadn't seen anyone. Finally, he thanked the caller and hung up.

"Phil's an old friend who runs a small machine shop out at the Healdsburg airport. The Piper's pilot was an FBI agent, and you're wanted for kidnapping an eight-year-old boy in Reno and escaping by plane. The agents gave Phil a description of my little runway here. After drawing them a map he reluctantly loaned the agents his truck. I have the distinct suspicion your friend Bunting could be the concerned *father* of the missing boy."

"Do you believe them?"

"Did you swap the boy for a golden retriever who claims to carry the consciousness of a family friend?"

A few moments passed before they broke into laughter.

"Do you have any aircraft fuel here? My tanks are about dry."

Tom shook his head. "After the Cessna sold, I dumped the last into my ranch vehicles. Besides, there's no place near Gabe's ranch to land." He went over and took his hat from the hook by the door. "My truck is at the dealer in town, I'm afraid, and hanging around here doesn't appear to be a sound plan. I'll show you what I've got for wheels."

The double garage door slowly rose, revealing a well-used and cared-for Kawasaki KLR dual-purpose bike. Behind it was an old three-wheeled All-Terrain Vehicle and several dirt bikes.

"Me and lot of my pilot friends ride motorcycles. I may not fly anymore, but I still like to get around. I think I have just the ticket. You mentioned a Triumph. I take it you can ride a bike." Tom walked into the darkened garage to find the light switch.

"I can manage." A smile accompanied her modest words. "But Trumpet is too big to stay on the back of the seat of your Kawasaki. Same with the ATV."

"I was thinking more of this." With a flourish, he pulled a blue tarp from a large object in the corner.

16

BACK ON THREE WHEELS

"A Ural sidecar rig." Aemea circled the rugged-looking Russian-built motorcycle sporting a camouflage paint scheme. Fastened to the top of the motorcycle's fuel tank was a dark gray tank bag with a clear map pocket on top. A spare wheel and tire were mounted at the back of the car and at the front an extra fuel can was strapped into a bracket to the right side of the car's nose. "The shaft from the rear wheel to the sidecar wheel can be locked in, right?"

"You certainly know your bikes." Tom smiled as he tapped the headlight. "This is the Sportsman model. The back wheel of the bike and the sidecar wheel can be locked together for steep climbs or seriously rugged spots. She won't quite climb a tree, but she can handle all the fire roads around here."

"Back home, I have a 1960 Jawa sidecar fitted to a two-year-old Bonneville. I was on my way home from work in Reno when Trumpet flagged me down."

"Why am I not surprised?" Smiling, he shook his head as he reached into a side pocket in the nose. He slipped a map into the top of the tank bag. "Once you make it to Cazadero you can ask for directions to the Picket ranch from the clerk at the general store."

"Good idea, I'm not familiar with this area."

Tom pointed on the map, "You can take Skaggs Springs Road all the way out to Stewart's Point at the coast, then head down the coast from there. Just south of the little town of Jenner cut back inland on River Road to Cazadero Road. Or, if things get dicey, you can pick up the fire roads all the way to Cazadero. You'll notice that besides the county roads, there are also fire roads indicated on this map. The closest access to one is a few miles west on this road, hidden behind a big rock covered with lots of kid's graffiti. I am a volunteer firefighter and have a master key to the fire road gates in this area. You'll find the key in the side pouch of the tank bag."

Tom gestured to a closet nearby. "There are jackets and helmets hanging in there, take whatever fits you." He tapped the back of the sidecar. "Survival kit, emergency rations and a sleeping bag are in the back compartment." At a nearby worktable, he picked up a chromed part. "I had to do a little welding on the kickstart lever. It attaches here." Tom explained as he pointed to a splined shaft protruding from the side of the gearbox. "I haven't gotten around to bolting it back on, and since time is a little tight right now, you should keep it with the rig until you get her back." After quickly showing her where the lever fit on the bike, he placed the part in the nose of the sidecar. A few minutes later a small battery charger gave enough life to the battery to get the bike started.

The rig sat idling while Tom was explaining the control for reverse and the locking shaft drive when they heard the sound of an approaching vehicle. "I'd recognize the pipes on Phil's truck anywhere." Tom glanced at his watch as he jogged to the open door. "Those guys made damn good time."

Aemea rapidly pulled on a jacket and helmet while Trumpet leaped into the car.

Here we go again, thought Gabe; while Trumpet was reflecting on his Sonoma Bear, left sitting on the seat of the plane. Gabe wasn't very consoling. "Well, you should have remembered it earlier."

"They're stopping in front of the barn." Tom hurried back into the garage.

"To the right of the house take the gravel road out to the main road, turn right, and follow the map. The truck may look old, but Phil dropped a late V8 into it. Good luck."

He patted Aemea on the helmet, then bent to Trumpet. "Trumpet, you and uh, Gabe, take care. I'll see what I can do from my end to get over there as soon as I can." He shook the offered paw and went back to the door.

Aemea gave a quick dip of her head, opened the throttle, and eased out the clutch. She had a brief glimpse of two men in dark blue suits turning toward her as she burst from the garage and accelerated toward the house. At the house, she slid the rig out onto the drive and made her escape.

"The dog!" The driver yelled. "That's her!" Both men sprinted for the truck. The front of the barn vanished in a billowing cloud of dust, as the old red Ford truck spun in a half circle before rocketing toward the driveway. Strange, Tom thought, the passenger was smiling slightly, his hand up in a kind of half wave at him as they swept by.

The old rancher waved back. When they disappeared after Aemea, Tom smiled down at Jeffrey. "You know, a smart man would have stopped and asked where they were going."

He returned to the garage, a thoughtful look on his face. "It might be a good idea if we're not available for a while. How 'bout you and I go for a ride?"

Jeffrey made a soft grumbling noise as he looked to where the Ural had been parked.

"Sure, that ride's gone, but remember what we used to do before I brought it home?" Jeffrey's head snapped toward the dual sport bike. Punctuated by a series of encouraging barks, he dashed around Tom in happy circles while they headed to the back of the garage.

A few minutes later a cut-down plastic crate was securely strapped to the metal rack at the rear of the KLR. With the garage door behind him closed, Tom straddled the bike, adjusting his goggles on the open-face helmet. On the second kick, he brought the engine to life, looked over his shoulder, and called, "Jeff!"

The border collie was patiently waiting a few feet away. Hearing his name, he launched forward. Springing up the side of the bike, he dropped hind feet first into the crate. A sharp bark let Tom know he was ready to go.

"Yeah, I can see him," Aemea answered the urgent bark of her passenger, who was looking back over his shoulder. "This thing isn't as fast as my Bonneville." The Ural she was driving was more of a three-wheeled ATV than a road bike. It sat lower than her own rig, with a heavy front suspension and knobby tires all around. The Russian-built bike was also a good twenty miles per hour slower than her Triumph. When they crested a small rise in the narrow road, the bike hung in the air for a few moments before thudding down which allowed her time to set up for the next turn.

One advantage they had over Phil's hot-rodded old truck was that he chose to lower it within a few inches of the pavement. The modern V8 gave it lots of power in the straight parts and wider turns of the nicely paved road. But just over a mile from Tom's ranch, the tarmac narrowed back down to the old dirt and gravel road to the coast, dotted with potholes and the occasional tight, gravel-strewn corners. In the straight sections the truck would gain ground, but in corners she could easily slide the rear tire on the bike, allowing set up for the turn's exit. While the pickup braked hard and wallowed, Aemea used the torque of the bike's engine to launch them smoothly toward the next turn. Through one particularly gravelly right-hand hairpin turn, she slid the rig sideways on all three wheels. Leaning hard toward Trumpet, who also leaned deep into the turn to keep the weight to that side, she shouted, "Three-wheel drift!" Trumpet barked his approval.

Whatever happened to my mild-mannered dog, Gabe wondered, wishing he could close his eyes. Instead, Trumpet looked behind them in time to see a clear view of the truck barreling uncontrollably toward a small stand of young redwood trees. Aemea gave a quick glance in the mirror before shooting a grin at her passenger. "Ooh, now that's too bad!"

"I got it, I got it." Back in the truck, the driver twisted the wheel harder to the right, but they continued to plow toward the redwoods. "Ahhh, man…" The passenger pushed back into the seat as the trees closed in on the front of the truck in slow motion. The hood eased a bit more to the right as the front tires bit, then the left fender brushed through several small ferns before thudding heavily into the trunk of the nearest redwood.

"The big heavy engine up front gives this thing a bad tendency to understeer." The driver was able to speak quietly, the engine having died with the abrupt stop.

"Yeah, and back in the plane it was, 'she'll never be able to get away in a slow little high wing tail dragger.'" The passenger eyed the damaged fender. With a slow shake of his head, he mimicked the pilot's last words to the truck's owner. "Don't worry, sir, I'll treat your truck as if it were my own."

The driver ignored the slandering of his slight southern accent and tried the starter. The second try brought the engine back to life. "Still runs." His confident smile was not returned. As he backed the pickup onto the road they were greeted by the loud blare of a truck horn.

"Nice." The passenger watched a large bright yellow bread truck pass by within inches of his door.

"What did he say?" The pickup was back on the road and was rapidly gaining on the delivery truck.

"Something about your mother."

They caught up to the larger truck, following it through a set of tight turns. "The guy must know the road. I couldn't get around these any faster than he is."

"Maybe, he used to be a fighter jock."

The driver flashed his passenger a nasty look.

❧

Slowing down, Aemea spotted a turn-out on the opposite side of the road with large graffiti-covered boulder. Behind the boulder was a rutted dirt track leading up an incline with the gate Tom predicted at the top. At the gate, she killed the engine but left the transmission in gear so the rig wouldn't roll. She tossed a glance back the way they had come and swung off the bike. "I hope that turn bought us some time."

With Tom's key in hand, she and Trumpet approached the faded yellow metal pipe gate. There was a length of chain securing the gate to the post. The chain was connected by 4 different padlocks linked together. This allowed ranchers to access the gate with their individual keys, by unlocking their own lock. It took her a moment to find the lock that opened with Tom's key. Meanwhile, Trumpet paused to mark the post. Aemea fumbled the lock open, slipped the chain free, and gave the gate a shove. For a moment, she stared across the opening at the rugged fire road which was level for about twenty feet before dropping away severely as it vanished into the scrub a hundred feet ahead. "Boy, it gets seriously steep here."

As they turned back to the rig the sound of the approaching trucks grew in intensity. Trumpet was in the car and Aemea astride the bike when the pickup and the bread truck passed by on the main road. When she hit the starter there was a quiet mechanical clicking down near the engine. "Uh, oh."

At a somewhat straight and wide stretch of the road the pick-up driver drew up next to the bread truck, barely passing it, as he cut in front of the larger truck. "Anything else?"

"Let's see; the truck driver gave me the finger, mouthed something about your mother, again. Oh, and Phil will be pissed when he sees his truck."

After passing the bread truck, the driver accelerated looking ahead for motorcycle rig.

"That's them." The passenger turned his head as the pickup flew by the turn-out and distinctive boulder. "Must be nice to have time to stop and enjoy the view."

A short distance ahead the tires squealed as the pickup slued off the opposite side of the road, sliding back around to the left in a rooster tail of dirt and rock. "Perfect, another turnout."

The delivery truck hurtled by and continued down the road.

"Now, that wasn't nice." The passenger watched the paper coffee cup roll across the pick-up's hood. Coffee splattered across the hood and up his side of the windshield. "Now, we'll have to wash Phil's truck before we return it."

In seconds they were back on the road heading toward their prey.

"You know, there's something here I can't understand?" The driver peered through the dirty windshield. "Why is she running?"

The passenger braced his feet against the floorboards as they closed on the graffiti-covered boulder. "She's running because we're chasing her. Like a dog chasing a cat. The cat sees the dog, the cat starts to move, dog sees the cat move, starts to run, and the chase is on. It's a kind of Catch-22."

"I see you're moving from agent comedian to agent philosopher."

"There's another thing."

The driver nodded for him to go on.

"How was the truck driver going so fast and drinking coffee at the same time." The passenger suddenly smacked his palm against his forehead. "I'll bet his truck doesn't understeer!"

Aemea was off the bike and pushing the heavy rig through the open gate. Trumpet piled out and took a loose end of the strap securing the spare fuel can to the sidecar at the front in his teeth, tugged and pulled. The rig was clearing the gate when they heard the sound of the returning pickup. "Just a little more," she groaned, her boots slipping in the dirt. She dug in, slipping again as the pickup was braking to a hard stop. From the slight elevation gained by the incline she was able to see the truck as the doors swung open. "Ah damn."

Trumpet continued to jerk on the strap. The ground leveled, and rig rolled easily on the other side of the gate.

"Hold it!" The passenger was reaching into his coat.

Trumpet barked.

"Get in!" Aemea pushed the rig the last few feet before the road began its descent.

Gabe cheered as Trumpet leaped into the sidecar.

Aemea was barely back in the saddle as they picked up speed, plunging down the track. She switched on the ignition, at the same time toeing the gearbox into second. Easing out the clutch, she jumped the engine to life.

The two men ran up the incline, stopping at the open gate in time to see the rig vanish into the cover of the scrub. An exuberant "yeah!" and a bark carried over the sound of the engine as the rider and her passenger disappeared.

The passenger holstered his weapon. "I think what passes for a road here is way too narrow for this truck and probably beyond its capabilities."

"I agree." The driver put his weapon back. "I guess the least we can do is relock the gate. Then let's head back and talk to the old guy at the dirt airstrip. I'm betting he knows where they're off to."

"Pretty amazing."

"Yeah, she managed to outrun us."

The passenger gave him a long look. "Us? Right." He returned his attention to the disappearing Ural. "I was just thinking she was pretty cute. Tall, too. I wonder if she's single."

"What does it say?" The driver jogged back from the locked garage and found the passenger reading a note tacked to the edge of the wooden screen door.

"Jeff and I are bored and decided to get out and about for a while. We'll most likely be back tomorrow. The door is unlocked. There's coffee by the microwave." He checked the back of the note. "That's nice of him."

Back at the Healdsburg Airport, the two FBI men faced the irate owner of their pirated truck. The driver held out a card in his hand, "If you submit a bill to this address, they'll see about compensating you for the damage to your truck."

Phil Stirling, the fifty-year-old owner of Phil's Machine Shop and Fabrication, stood an easy six feet and carried just over two hundred pounds. Partially owing to his profession, not much of it was fat.

When the passenger first met him, he'd seen past the friendly demeanor and calm brown eyes, sizing him up as someone who was plenty tough in his youth. The passing years, he guessed, by the rough hands and easy confidence, probably made him tougher.

"I worked on her for five years to get her the way I wanted. It took me four months to find a straight, original, driver-side fender on eBay." Phil rose from where he'd been examining the damage to the fender and suspension, ignoring the card offered by the driver. When he tried to open the hood, it groaned a bit but refused to budge. He ran a finger along the far side and up the windshield. "Stop for coffee, did you?"

Through their mirrored sunglasses, the agents held Phil's stare. The usual easy-going look of the machine shop owner's eyes had vanished when his truck lurched to a stop in front of the shop's big double doors.

The tense silence was broken by the ringtone of a cell phone. A third agent, who had been waiting at the small country airport with an agency sedan, slipped his phone from his coat pocket. For better reception, he walked out onto the airport's concrete apron while pressing a finger against his ear,

The driver started to speak but Phil cut him off with a raised finger. "Excuse me." He turned, and walked past one of the shop's big metal lathes and out the back door.

The passenger observed, "I think he took it pretty well."

"What else could he do?" The driver smirked.

"Did you hear something?" The agent with the cell phone paused in his conversation. The airport office obscured the view of the gravel parking area. With a shrug, he returned to his conversation.

"Sounded like a car door." The driver reached in and tossed his card onto the borrowed truck's front seat. "Let's go."

Reappearing through the back door, Phil ignored the three men. Rolling a blue Yamaha dual sport bike out of his shop, he kicked it to life. While fastening his helmet, he glared at the driver and passenger. "If you don't mind, I'm going for a ride to calm down. Sort of keep the anger at bay." With that, he roared off across the tie-down area.

"Nice wheelie." The passenger raised his sunglasses as he watched the rider cross the runway and swing onto the access road running along the far side.

"Okay. We head back to the County Airport." Placing his cell phone in his pocket, the third man returned to the other two.

"What about the plane?" The passenger nodded to where the Piper sat parked near the fuel pumps.

"She's about out of fuel." The driver shrugged.

The third man replied. "The agency will send someone from the County Airport to retrieve it. At least you two didn't damage it."

The three rounded the corner of the office together and stopped.

"Shit!" The driver swore as he ran with the other two to their agency car.

"It's an old pickaxe." The passenger tugged at the weathered wooden handle of the tool embedded in the center of the car's hood. It held fast.

The driver slammed his fist down on the hood, ignoring the furious gaze from the third man.

"There's a note." The passenger slipped a small, ragged piece of paper from the north end of the pick. "It's kind of hard to read." He raised his sunglasses. "Anger and haste will do that to one's handwriting."

"Alright, alright. What does it say?" The third agent slid behind the wheel and tried the starter. There was only an ugly grinding sound from beneath the hood and the smell of gasoline.

The passenger's eyes went back to the note. "It says, 'If you wish to submit a bill to this address, you can kiss my...'" He turned the note over. "Hmm. No name or address."

17

—

A PREMONITION

"Tom, good to see you." A lean and tanned man in his mid-forties, Gary McNeil of, McNeil and Associates, shook Tom's hand with genuine fondness. Tom Baxman had been one of his clients since he'd hung out his shingle some fifteen years back.

"Thanks for seeing me, Gary." He smiled as the attorney dropped down to take the border collie's offered paw. "Jeffrey, careful with the nice suit."

"A little dog hair never hurt anybody. Hey, Jeffrey, how you doing?" He scratched the friendly animal at the base of his neck, causing him to wriggle with pleasure.

With the dog greeted, McNeil gestured to the open door of his corner office. "Come on in. May I offer you coffee?"

"Sure, offer away."

Chuckling at their old joke the attorney called to the young woman at the receptionist's area. "Sienna, if you have a moment, would you please bring two coffees?"

They settled across from each other into comfortable chairs at a small coffee table near the corner windows. The arrangement of dark wood furniture and filled bookshelves backing McNeil's large desk in the corner gave the room a personable, airy feel. Tom thought having a large family portrait on the wall near the door and several smaller framed photos of his family near his desk added some warmth. It pleased him to see the expressions on the faces of Gary, his wife and two pre-teen children showing genuine affection toward each other. He also noticed the portrait and most of the photos included a pair of sleek black and tan Dachshunds.

They exchanged a few more pleasantries while Sienna brought their coffee. After placing the hot drinks on the table, the young woman paused to offer an appreciative Jeffrey a treat.

When the receptionist closed the office door behind her, Gary settled back in his chair. "Now, what has brought you off the ranch today?"

"You heard about Gabe Picket?"

"Of course. Sarah, and now Gabe. Lightning, who would have thought?" His mood turned somber. "I wonder if he had a premonition."

"A premonition?"

"Last week he called and left a message on my office phone. It must have been the day before it happened."

"It involved his Will?"

"As a matter of fact, it did. Gabe didn't say much. But he mentioned a change, and someone named B.P. He said he would drop a copy in the mail, and stop by when he could make an appointment."

"Hmm." Tom searched his memory, but no B.P. came to mind. "I take it a new Will did not show up in the mail?"

"As of today's mail, nothing. Mail from Gabe's place would take two days to arrive here." The attorney was curious about the rancher's interest. He was aware of Tom and Sarah growing up on neighboring ranches, and remaining close friends after she married Gabe Picket. He also knew the man well enough not to hurry him.

"Your partner, Bunting, does he stand to gain anything from the old Will?"

The abruptness of Tom's question and its subject caught the attorney off guard. "Warren, well, no." He thought for a few moments. "At any rate, not directly."

Tom simply sipped his coffee, waiting for him to go on.

"Warren has been interested in purchasing Gabe's property for some time. After Sarah was diagnosed, they sold their house here in Santa Rosa, moving onto the ranch full time. Gabe wasn't inclined to sell. He told me once there were too many memories of Sarah there for him to let the place go. I guess you know her ashes are up there, along with a bronze plaque; soon Gabe's will join hers. The local church is putting together a memorial service." The attorney sighed softly. "I'll be having Gabe's date added to the plaque."

Staring out his window, Gary swirled his coffee before continuing. "After Gabe's death I reviewed the existing Will. Warren has already made an offer, a reasonable one. As the executor, I'm obligated to consider it."

"Where does the money go?"

"Charities, the local fire department, sort of thing. As you know, neither of them had anyone close."

There was a light rap on the door. It opened slightly and Sienna poked her head in. "Excuse me, Mister Fields is here." She offered Tom an apologetic smile.

Gary made no move to usher Tom out.

Tom set his cup aside. "No mention of Trumpet?"

"His retriever?" Gary nodded his head slowly. "Trumpet is supposed to go to one of their relatives. I presume when he turns up, if they don't want him, one of the neighbors or someone in town might adopt him. He'd be good company for Jeffrey there."

"Yeah, he might just be." Tom smiled. "I'm glad you haven't given up on him."

Gary returned the smile, "Never happen." He cleared his throat. "At any rate, Gabe and Sarah would have wanted Trumpet to go to a loving home. I will make certain he gets one."

❧

"You hungry?" The dog tilted his head to one side, his ears up and alert. They stood out in the attorney's parking lot, Tom with his helmet in his hand, Jeff making muttering noises indicating he was anxious to get back into the crate and on the road.

"I'm thinking some pie at the Caza Café sounds like a pretty good idea."

Jeff barked his approval.

The Caza Café was a small folksy diner a half mile south of Cazadero proper. The diner offered good basic cooking and a variety of homemade pies, including an award-winning strawberry rhubarb. A favorite among the locals, and the only place to eat in the village, the café was also popular with motorcyclists and bicyclists who chose the long but scenic way to the coast.

In a little while they left the freeway in Santa Rosa for River Road going west. "I'm thinking maybe we can find out something about this B.P. fella. If the folks at the Café don't know him, he probably doesn't exist." Tom didn't have to shout, because Jeff was leaning forward in the crate, his chin resting on his friend's shoulder.

By the odometer on the Ural, Aemea and Trumpet had gone a few tenths over four miles since leaving the two agents behind. The fire road, a wide dirt path cut through the woods and hills, digressed from being passable by a two-wheel drive vehicle, to the four-wheel-drive-is-the-only-way-go stage; the kind of terrain for which the Ural had been designed. Just past the crest of a small hill, Aemea parked the rig to get out for a quick stretch. Her own rig was lighter than the Ural and she generally kept to the paved roads. The last half hour left her shoulders sore from steering the Ural through heavily rutted portions of the lightly maintained fire road. After checking out several interesting tree trunks, Trumpet joined her at the high point in the road.

"Except for the wind in the trees, there's just a serene quiet. Judging by what we've just driven through, those guys in their little hot rod truck would be stuck about three and a half miles back." She shaded her eyes with a hand to watch a hawk hunting as it slowly circled the rising air of a small thermal.

"You know, since you've entered my life, things have..." With a soft sigh, she stared out across the hills for a time.

"I get things done, you know. But it almost feels as if for the last couple of years, I've been, well, coasting along. I mean, sometimes I push the limits on the sidecar, maybe a few tricks in the Maule to keep myself on top of things." Aemea smiled at the look Trumpet gave her. "So when the need arises, I can confidently loop the occasional bridge. But now, now I feel like I'm getting myself back." She bent and hugged him. "Thank you."

Trumpet replied with several "you're welcome" licks to her chin.

"This area is so green, so peaceful." Aemea let out a soft chuckle. "When we're not eluding the FBI."

"Woof!"

"Yeah, 'woof.'" She rubbed his neck. "The solitude, and tranquility, reminds me of what I love about the place where I live. When I first found you I started thinking about the two of us living together, just a girl and her dog. Just when I hope, 'well this time the whole situation will be settled for sure,' something comes up. I have to say I didn't consider the last 'something' would be so, so…" Aemea held her arms out in front of her with her palms up. At a loss for words, she simply shook her head. "I wish I knew what was going to happen to us." She pushed to her feet.

Although she had been speaking to the dog as if he were a person since they met, Aemea now realized that the conversations could be more meaningful, and should perhaps include Gabe. "Before I get going again, I need to ask you something. I was getting used to 'Triumph.' So, now what do I call you? Is it Trumpet? Is it Gabe?"

The sound of her voice saying his name brought a huge sense of relief to Gabe. For the first time, because she and Tom knew about him, he felt there was real hope in dealing with Bunting.

Trumpet turned away from Aemea and flopped down in the dirt with a sigh.

Aemea began to laugh. "Gabe's Trumpet?" Suddenly it occurred to her the irony of Gabe's relationship with Trumpet. "Gabriel's Trumpet!" She reflected on her Sunday school lessons about Gabriel as an archangel who accompanied God when he appeared before humans. Instead, Gabe is accompanying a dog (God spelled backward). Gabriel was also known to blow his trumpet on the judgement day to announce the raising of the dead when the temporal minds were released from their earthly binds; while Gabe is maintaining his earthly attachment in a dog's mind. "I have no idea what this means, but it just all seems to somehow fit."

"Come on Trumpet," Gabe pleaded; "it's just a name." He tried to think of how to explain why he wanted her to use his name. From somewhere, his own voice, but not *his* voice came back with, "Gabe no. Trumpet, yes." Gabe was momentarily stunned. Previously, the dog thought in feelings and then images. Now he was thinking his voice back at him.

"Trumpet?" Aemea squatted down next to him. "This is a little confusing. Actually, a lot confusing. Which of you is, ah, in charge?" She shrugged.

"You're right my friend." Gabe relented. "She sees you, she touches you."

Trumpet began to thump his tail in the dirt, encouraging Aemea to lean over so he could tilt his head up and give her a quick lick on the chin. Sitting down on the edge of the road next to him, her arm went over his back. They sat quietly for a long while.

Aemea finally broke the silence. "From what I've seen of the way you do things I think you're Trumpet the dog." She smiled down at him. "No offense. And part of you is Gabe, who is somehow able to talk to you, help you understand things."

Yeah. Gabe stared through the retriever's eyes out toward the distant hills. His thoughts went back to just before the lightning, to the regret he felt that he hadn't done more. Then, to the first realization of his current condition and how he had been given a second chance to help him.

"I believe we'll stick with Trumpet. Sound good to you?" After hugging him, Aemea got to her feet.

Gabe felt a growing sense of peace within himself. Sounds okay to me. The happy feeling from his friend was accompanied by some serious tail wagging.

Feeling somewhat rested, they loaded back up and resumed their trek. When they arrived at the next gate Aemea reached for the gate key. "Nuts" After running her hands through her pockets one last time, she shrugged helplessly at her passenger waiting patiently in the side car. "I must have left the key in the lock at the first gate."

The gate blocked the way where the road was cut into a steep brush-covered hillside. The terrain to the left was a nearly vertical climb. To the right was an imposing drop down to a wide, though shallow-looking, stream. With Trumpet happily trotting alongside, Aemea left the idling motorcycle and jogged back down the road, pausing several times to look over the terrain. A few hundred feet from the gate, she found what she was looking for. The way down to the creek was steep but passable. On the far side there appeared to be an old road. "All we have to do is get down there, cross the creek, run parallel to the road past the gate, then find a way back up."

Trumpet, in his usual fashion, shared her optimism, while Gabe thought the grade a challenge for even a regular four-wheel drive.

"Okay, we've got both rear wheels engaged. Let's see what this baby can do." The rear wheels bit and slipped in the packed dirt as she angled the rig toward the edge. "Steering might be a little tough. Ready?" She smiled at Trumpet, who peered over the front of the car, then quickly leaned back as they rolled over the edge.

Keeping the rig at a slight angle to the hill, Aemea began a bumpy descent toward the creek. A few yards from the road, the incline increased. The rear tires slipped then gripped as she dodged a thick bush and grinned. "We're good!"

A large rock appeared in the weeds in her path, catching the sidecar wheel, jerking them sideways pointing down at a right angle to the hill. Instead of the gradual sloped route she'd chosen, the rig was forced down a steeper grade. It was about a good fifty feet before it flattened out, followed by a second and steeper drop into the creek. The rig began to slide.

Trumpet pressed back in his seat as they accelerated down the hillside. Aemea yelled to, "hang on!" Gabe thought she'd try to brake to a stop. Instead, she rolled on the throttle while letting out an enthusiastic, "Yee haw!"

When they hit the flat part they bounced before being launched downward. For a moment they were airborne until the sidecar slammed mercifully into a shallow part of the creek. A ragged curtain of water cascaded over the front of the bike and car. When the tires bit into the gravel bottom, Aemea, still on the gas, managed to direct the rig over to a gentle slope leading out of the creek. They rolled to a stop on the old road with steam rising off the engine and pipes of the idling Ural. A drenched and dripping Aemea grinned at Trumpet. "What a great bike. That was fun, wasn't it?"

Trumpet gave her a long look before he hopped out and began to shake the water from his coat.

"I hear you, buddy." Gabe could see the still-smiling Aemea peeling off the wet riding jacket. "Aemea considers anything where we don't quite die as, 'Fun.'"

18

B.P. Pfeifer

"Here you go. Our multi-berry pie under a scoop of homemade vanilla ice cream." Milly, waitress and co-owner of the Caza Cafe, slid the plate down next to Tom's coffee. "Your friend looks like he loves to ride with you."

Tom followed her smile to the gravel parking lot in front of the window where he was seated. Jeff's intelligent gaze was on him. "Yup. These days I have to hide the keys so he doesn't go riding without me."

"I'm sure he'd come back."

"When he was hungry, I suppose." He noted a Sheriff's four-wheel drive backed into a space a couple of cars over from his Kawasaki.

"Anything else I can get you?"

His attention went back to the server. "I have a question, if you don't mind?"

"Shoot."

"A friend of mine told me I could find 'B.P.' around town."

"You don't know him, do you?" She shook her head in a friendly way and pointed out the front window. "He's right outside talking to your riding companion."

A deputy was standing next to his bike, shaking Jeffrey's offered paw. After giving the happy dog a final scratch of the ears, he looked toward the front window. Tom's easy wave was acknowledged by a friendly nod.

Tom further observed the deputy as he entered the café. He was probably about 30 something, an easy six feet tall with broad shoulders. His dark blond hair was cut conservatively, but without the sidewalls he'd noted on some of the younger officers. He wore what was likely a longer than approved moustache. There was a casual authority about the man, and the posture of ex-military. He noted that the deputy did not seem to be wearing a bulletproof vest.

"Nice dog."

"Jeff's a good one, all right." Tom stood and offered his hand. "Tom Baxman." He saw the deputy's name tag read, 'Pfeifer.'

Deputy Pfeifer introduced himself simply as, "B.P."

At first the deputy declined Tom's invitation to join him. Then the older man dropped Gabe's name. "I am an old friend of Gabe and Sarah Picket. I've known Sarah since we were kids. She and Gabe came out to my ranch on a few occasions."

B.P. sized Tom up through steady hazel eyes. Apparently not finding him lacking, he pulled out the chair across the table. "That pie looks pretty good."

They made small talk about dogs and motorcycles through most of their pie, until Tom figured he'd done almost enough sizing up of his own. "By any chance, does the 'B,' stand for Barney?"

The deputy gave him a long slow smile, followed by an easy shrug of the broad shoulders. "My folks watched a little too much of the Andy Griffith Show, I guess. My dad loves Johnny Cash and was partial to the lesson the guy learns in 'A Boy Named Sue'." He made a 'go figure' raise of his eyebrows. "At least I didn't get 'Sue.' After the Army, the guys at the Police Academy tried to give me some grief. I've learned you have to keep your sense of humor. Anyway, around here I've been known as B.P. for as long as I can recall."

During their conversation and B.P.'s explanation, Tom watched the younger man carefully, and he began to understand why Gabe liked him.

"How well did you know Gabe Picket?" Tom observed an expression of wariness moving into the deputy's eyes as he asked the question.

"Like I said, Sarah and I were childhood friends. I hadn't seen him since she passed, and well, I just heard about his accident."

Somewhere out in the mountains, Aemea and Trumpet were making their way to the Picket Ranch on his Ural. When Tom last saw them, there had been a pair of FBI agents in hot pursuit, but he doubted the resourceful Aemea would allow herself to be caught. With Bunting in the somewhat fuzzy picture, Tom decided she and her companion, or companions, he reminded himself, might be able to use some help.

"A few hours ago, a young woman, an Air Force Captain, I might add, flew into my ranch from Reno. Her name is Aemea Rand, her passenger was Gabe's dog, Trumpet. I'm not exactly clear on the reason, but the FBI is chasing her.

In addition, an attorney named Warren Bunting is somehow involved."

The mention of Trumpet caused B.P. to lower his coffee cup to the tabletop. At Bunting's name he sat up straight, his look even more attentive. "Trumpet's alive?" How the hell did he end up in Reno?" The deputy's eyes narrowed. "Bunting."

The waitress stopped at their table with a coffee pot. Both men slid their cups toward her. When she'd gone on to another table, they picked up their conversation. Tom filled in a few more details about Aemea and Trumpet, their escapades with Bunting, the fake kidnapping, and the FBI. He described how she showed up at the little airstrip at his ranch, but carefully left out the part about Gabe residing in Trumpet. Fortunately, B.P. didn't ask how Tom knew the dog with Aemea was Trumpet.

Perhaps B.P. was distracted by the next part of the conversation. Tom continued by relating his recent discussion with his attorney, Gary McNeil, whom he long ago recommended to Sarah and Gabe. "According to Gary, Bunting is putting together an offer on Gabe's ranch."

"It's only just been a few days."

"Yes." Tom took a short sip from his cup, his eyes steady on B.P.'s. "There's more. The old Will allows for the sale of Gabe's ranch upon his death."

"You said 'old.'"

Tom smiled at the deputy's quick take. "When I spoke with Gary, he mentioned that Gabe may have written a new Will, but he hasn't seen it. We're thinking Gabe may have written one so the ranch wouldn't be sold during Trumpet's lifetime." He could see the wheels were turning in B.P.'s head, so he laid all the rest out. "Bunting is a partner at Gary McNeil's law firm where I stopped in a little while ago to see how things stood. So far, the old Will is still valid."

"You don't think your attorney buddy is somehow in it with Bunting for a piece of the ranch?"

"Not a chance." The force behind the words served to end any discussion in that direction.

B.P. kept his eyes on the older man, but there was no hint of doubt at Tom's faith in McNeil's integrity. "Okay. So, where is the new Will?" He glanced at his watch.

Tom spread his hands on the table. "Right now, we don't know. I planned to run up to Gabe's place and see if I can find it."

B.P. leaned back in his chair. "Interesting story. Where are Rand and Trumpet, and how exactly do I fit into all of this?"

"Aemea and Trumpet are most likely running the fire trails in my Ural motorcycle and sidecar to get to the ranch. I think if Bunting was smart enough to get the FBI involved, he may know Aemea and Trumpet are on the way here." He gave B.P. a meaningful look, then took a folded sheet of paper from his back pocket, unfolded it, and slid it across to the deputy.

"What's this?"

"A map of the fire trails. The ones you have to take to get there from my place are marked with the penciled arrows."

"It would have been a lot easier if she followed you or rode out to the coast and headed south."

"The FBI showed up a little sooner than we anticipated. They kind of put the main roads out of the picture."

The deputy looked thoughtfully at the map. "If there was no kidnapping, why didn't she just turn herself in, and straighten the whole thing out?"

"From my conversation with Aemea, she served in Iraq. For some reason she developed a deep suspicion of authority."

The deputy chuckled. "You realize because there doesn't seem to be a crime involved, I can't do much in an official capacity."

Tom shrugged as B.P. again checked his watch before tossing down the last of his coffee. "Well, what do you know? I'm off duty as of right now, so why don't we head up to Gabe's and check things out?"

At the cabin, while B.P. checked the file cabinet, Tom found himself drawn to the large oval-framed photograph of Gabe, Sarah, and Trumpet. The three of them were seated on the grass at the far edge of a small pond. Sarah leaned slightly into Gabe and Trumpet sat next to Sarah, who rested a hand on his shoulder. "They all look so content."

B.P. came over carrying a manila folder. "Yeah. I remember Gabe telling me Sarah wanted to have a portrait made so Gabe would have a slice of time capturing their happiness together. A professional photographer came up here, and the picture was taken down by their little spring fed pond. Gabe told me the photographer took three rolls of film, and he and Sarah picked out the one where Trumpet looked the best. See how he's looking into the camera and his ears are perked up and slightly forward. Sarah just adored Trumpet."

Tom recalled something Sarah told him when she was a young woman and lived near him. "She used to say dogs were a vessel you poured love into, and they were always there for you to tap into when you needed them. Unlike people, they don't measure or bargain their love, but gave it freely." He reached out and ran his fingers over the edge of the smooth oval redwood frame. "That's how she and Gabe lived their lives."

B.P. broke the short silence with a wave of the manila folder. "This is marked, 'New Will' but it's empty." He set it aside. With Tom looking anxiously over his shoulder and Jeff watching from the front door, he booted up the laptop. Fortunately, or perhaps unfortunately, the computer wasn't password protected. "Uh oh. Here's a file under 'Gabe's Important Documents' with the same title as on the folder, but it's empty too."

"I noticed the door was unlocked when we arrived." Tom sat back on the arm of the couch.

"That was my fault." B.P. checked a few more places before shutting down the computer. "Right after Gabe was struck, I came over, looking for Trumpet. He can open the door and come and go on his own. I didn't want him to get here and find himself locked out. I left some food in his dish and the door unlocked. Looking back, I guess it wasn't such a great idea."

"I'm hoping maybe Trumpet can find something when they get here." Tom stepped off the porch and watched B.P. lock the front door.

"Pull a Lassie, you mean?" The deputy smiled. "It's a nice thought, I guess. Against impossible odds, the dog returns to save the ranch from the bad guy."

"You never know; Trumpet might surprise you." He took out his wallet and pulled out a card. "My sister's kids are showing up at my place tomorrow, but, if you find anything, good or bad, I'd appreciate a call from you."

In a few minutes B.P. watched Tom and Jeff get settled on the bike and ride off. Just as they passed through the gate, Jeff turned to look back over his shoulder.

B.P. waved. "Huh." He lowered his arm. "I'd swear that old dog thinks he knows something I don't."

As he drove to the substation to swap his Sheriff's vehicle for his own, he thought about Trumpet. "He'd be a great dog to have with me." He glanced over at the passenger seat, picturing Trumpet sitting there as they patrolled the area. The image brought out a smile. "Totally against regulations." The deputy shook his head and sighed, but the smile remained.

19
—

Camping Out

Aemea and her companions made a few more miles with the track finally breaking off to the West, away from the creek. Along the way, she hadn't seen a spot remotely suitable for recrossing, and the fire road on the opposite bank was out of sight. The warm air dried them both but was cooling quickly when Aemea steered the rig from the track into a small inviting meadow. To one side, near a stand of young oaks, a tiny bubbly flow of water was making its way along a thin, rocky channel.

"It's getting late. I say we set up camp while there's still light." To one side of the clearing Aemea engaged the reverse gear and backed the bike up the slope. "Now that would be a handy gear to have on my Triumph."

With the rig parked, she got off the bike and circled the area while Trumpet went to the stream for a serious drink of water. After sniffing around a bit, he followed Aemea across the meadow. Under an oak near the little stream, she dropped her jacket. "This looks good. We have a bare spot for a fire ring; the ground isn't too hard." She headed back up to the sidecar.

In the back compartment, she found the sleeping bag was wrapped in a small plastic tarp, which could serve as a ground cloth. A waterproof bag held Tom's 'survival kit.'

"Okay, we have an Emergency Medical kit in a lovely red box, a bundle of small hand flares, a Mylar survival blanket, and a small plastic box of food." She offered each up for Trumpet's approval. "And finally...ooh, a 'don't leave home without it' item." She held up a black plastic rifle stock, which Trumpet dutifully leaned forward to sniff.

Gabe recognized the item for what it was.

"One AR-7 survival rifle. A couple of the pilots I flew with carried these." Aemea opened the butt of the stock. Removing the barrel and receiver, she quickly assembled the pieces into a small lightweight rifle. With a frown, she held up the rifle's clip. "Only two bullets. I guess we won't be shooting our way out of any roadblocks." Noting the way Trumpet's eyebrows narrowed, she gave his head a reassuring rub. "Ah come on, guys, I'm kidding. When have I put you in any kind of danger?" As if reading their thoughts she added. "The loop at the bridge was completely under my control, I could have done it with my eyes closed."

Trumpet made a small grumbling sound, and Gabe agreed.

Aemea got to her feet. "Okay, but let's remember, if it weren't for a certain dog and his, um, friend, I'd be home getting ready for another spectacular sunset."

After lifting out the plastic food container, she flipped up the lid to inspect the contents. Inside were various rations consisting of assorted cans of chili, tuna fish, peaches, a small jar of peanut butter, and a box of crackers. Aemea held up one at a time for Trumpet to sniff. "Tom must have put the food together with Jeffrey in mind, 'because we have three cans of lamb and rice dog food." She held out one of the cans as she had the others. After his wag of approval, she shook her head as she read the can's label. "Do you realize this looks better than some Air Force food I've eaten?"

Trumpet helped Aemea collect some sticks and wood for a fire. After the fire was glowing sufficiently she placed some rocks into the center to balance an aluminum pan with water. "Cold or heated?" Aemea held the can of dog food out toward Trumpet, who examined it for a moment before looking up at her expectantly.

"Okay, because of our little talk earlier, I'm thinking room temperature will suffice." She finished opening the can, dumped the contents onto one of the plastic plates and set it in front of him.

She placed an open can of chili into the aluminum pan to heat for herself. When it was sufficiently warmed she began eating from the can. Trumpet was watching her and hadn't touched his meal. He looked from his plate to her food. "Come on." She gestured with her plastic fork. "It smelled pretty good to me."

He continued to look at her, his eyes flicking from her face to the fork, until she set her meal aside. Then they both looked at the can-shaped blob of dog food on his plate.

"Okay, I admit the presentation isn't the best, but it is *dog food.*"

Trumpet nudged the hand holding the fork.

"I didn't spoon-feed you at my trailer; I am not doing it now. You just, just eat it like a…Oh, no. Not the sad, sad eye-browed look of disappointment." She wasn't sure if it was Gabe or Trumpet who was messing with her, but she folded her arms and continued to eat her chili. Eventually, she knew she'd have to give in to something. "Okay, I'll cut it up for you, but that's it." Using the camp knife, she carefully cut the lamb and rice meal lengthwise, then sliced sideways until the meal was in six fairly even pieces. In the middle, she placed two of the crackers on edge. "There you go."

After a grumbling that she took to be a thank you, Trumpet began to eat.

"Just remember you're the one with the nice fur coat, and there is only one sleeping bag."

The sun was down behind the mountains and B.P. sat in the driveway of his cabin in his thirty-eight-year-old Toyota Land Cruiser. He owned the rugged old four-wheel drive since high school, leaving her sitting under a tarp at his folks during his time in college, the Army, and the Police Academy. During the previous summer, he brought her back to life for some backcountry exploration and spent a large number of hours doing just that.

In a waterproof metal box in the back, he kept a small survival kit, complete with an emergency medical kit. There were also two gallons of water, a down mummy bag, and a tarp large enough to cover the vehicle. A plastic box contained four extra seven-round clips, plus a hundred rounds of ammunition for the British Royal Enfield clipped next to the driver's seat. The World War Two era .303 rifle had also been his since high school. Since his return from the Army, his dad kidded him about carting around so much ammunition; surviving an ambush in Iraq by virtue of superior and sustained firepower taught B.P. you could never have too many bullets.

From his past conversations with Gabe, he knew the old veteran was of the same belief. His thoughts of Gabe brought him forward to his recent conversation with Tom. That he and Miss Rand thought Bunting was involved in Trumpet's disappearance didn't surprise him. Bunting and his new wife purchased their summer place next to Gabe's without understanding all the surrounding trees could not simply be cut down to improve their view. In addition to all the permits required by the Department of Forestry, there was the huge cost of County permits. It long puzzled him how once people bought places in the woods, they were surprised to find trees.

B.P. carried a measure of guilt about Trumpet. He was fairly sure Bunting knew the dog survived. He thought back to when he found Gabe's body. Because of their social contact, Gabe's death closed the professional distance he was normally able to maintain while doing his job, allowing Bunting to play him at the site.

At first, he considered running the fire trails indicated by Tom on his map and intercepting Aemea and Trumpet. But through his knowledge of the area, he knew there were several sections of the dirt roads left in poor shape by the heavy rains of the past winter. If she encountered one or more of these, she wouldn't be taking the most direct route. Instead, he chose to wait the night at home and head out in the morning.

B.P. went inside to make a semi-official phone call to the FBI's Santa Rosa office, mentioning his understanding of a fugitive who might possibly be heading in his direction with a kidnapped child. He was put on hold for several minutes before being asked about his source of information. Relying on his discussion with Tom, he made up a simple story about a friend being at the airport and hearing a rumor to that effect. He was then told an initial investigation ended when the whole thing turned out to be a hoax, which the Bureau was now looking into. After being thanked for his offer of help, the agent hung up.

Darkness was closing in and B.P. went outside to stack up wood for a small fire in a circle of stones. He always did his best thinking outdoors. With the wood ready to go, he struck a small flare. Sliding it into the stack, the wood quickly ignited from the intense heat. Watching the flames, he wondered how Aemea and Trumpet were doing, though he wasn't too worried. In their conversation, Tom didn't say much about what Aemea Rand was like. They were equally impressed with the risk she took to bring Trumpet home. If Aemea was an experienced Air Force fighter pilot, as Tom mentioned, she would have attended a survival school. He tried to picture her as a jet pilot, which for some reason didn't come easily. In fact, since Tom hadn't given him a physical description of her, he was having trouble picturing her at all.

He easily recalled taking heavy weapons and machine gun fire while doing convoy escort duty in Iraq with the

101ˢᵗ, and having a Thunderbolt, or called affectionately by the troops, Warthogs, come hurtling out of the sky to their aid. Most of the bad guys opened up on the 'Hog,' yet, like an angry dragon attacking rats, the plane flew right into the thick of it. He couldn't read the lettering on the plane's nose, as it roared over the convoy in a victory roll, but he could still vividly recall an odd red design and bright yellow letters. If Aemea Rand was anything like that pilot, he just had to meet her. Any way he looked at it, she was one gutsy lady.

～

"Hard to believe just this morning we were at the 'Retriever Rendezvous'." Aemea let out a quiet sigh. "You were going to be all mine." She lay on her back, her head resting on the folded motorcycle jacket, her eyes watching the gentle wind push at the treetops brushing across the stars. The sleeping bag was unzipped, and Trumpet lay partially covered, his back pressed against her. The moon was nearly full and well above the surrounding mountains. "You know, this reminds me of my dad and me, and our camping trips. My mom and sister were never the outdoor types. So it was just Major Rand and his 'Loopy' daughter." She rested an arm on the dog's side, and he let out a contented sigh.

"I always wanted to fly. I used to draw pictures of me with wings. My mom thought I wanted to be an angel, but I just wanted the wings. I never built model planes or anything like that. One day, it was almost my twelfth birthday, and my dad came home at lunch and asked me if I wanted to 'go up' with him. He flew Hueys in Vietnam and had been checked out in fixed-wing aircraft for quite a while. The base had a flying club, and one of the planes was a Citabria, a little high-wing aerobatic plane. We flew out over the desert, where he showed me how the controls worked while we did some turns and stalls. A couple of times he asked how my stomach was doing." Aemea chuckled. "I never gave my stomach a thought because I was flying, actually *flying*. Pretty soon he wiggled the stick and told me to 'take it.' It was a tandem seat plane, with me in the front seat. Suddenly I felt like it was just me, all mine."

She began to move her hands as if they were the little high wing plane. "First, I climbed and got into a stall like my dad showed me, then stood on the rudder and we went over on one wing. We were heading straight down. I throttled back, started easing back on the stick, bringing the nose up, fed in power, and eased back more until she needed some forward stick to keep from dropping her nose. I knew exactly what I wanted to do. When my dad started whooping and clapping at the top of the loop, I just knew he did too."

"What he didn't know was every time he brought a pilot buddy home, I was listening to everything they said. I would write down everything I could remember and make little diagrams. That morning, Dad had no idea he was taking me out of the classroom and into practical application. Anyway, from then on he called me his 'Loopy Girl'."

Trumpet rolled upright to rearrange himself so his head lay across her stomach, his eyes on her face. Even Gabe could sense the damp gray feeling of approaching sadness.

"I just wanted to fly, I got into ROTC in college, got my degree, joined the Air Force, and worked my butt off in flight school. My dad told me it would be tough, being a woman and of mixed race, but at each step of the way, I couldn't wait to get to the next. I received my commission and earned my wings. Then we went to Iraq." Her voice broke, and she shivered slightly under the cover of the sleeping bag.

Trumpet moved so his chin was on her shoulder, allowing Aemea to wrap an arm around him.

"Mostly, it's this one thing." She drew in a deep breath and slowly let it out. "Near the end of my deployment, there was a convoy getting hit, and I went in to take out the enemy positions. Things happen pretty fast in situations like that; your body and mind can go their own way. It's an odd thing, a kind of dual consciousness where you're thinking on two levels. One is on self-preservation auto-pilot, directing the body to get the job done, while the other contemplative mind sits back behind your eyes and observes."

She took a deep gulping breath, swallowing hard before she went on. "There were several emplacements, with most of them turning their fire on me when I came in. I lit 'em up right back, blew right over them, and came back around for a second pass. In all the dust and confusion, there was a clear area, and a couple of people." She paused to take a few more measured breaths as if the telling of the story was stealing her air.

Gabe looked into her eyes and saw they were focused on something far, far away.

"They were side by side. The woman was in the

traditional long black robe. She must have expended her ammo because she lowered her rifle. The man was firing at me with a light machine gun. It stopped too. I was too far away to make out their faces, but she just stood there in this defiant pose while he was reloading. I thought I was going to let them slide, but my fingers let a pair of rockets off and the whole area just went to bits. Afterward, I did a victory roll over the convoy."

"Up until then, it hadn't been so damn personal. But the scene kept playing over and over in my dreams and wore away my edge. In that kind of business, you need an edge. I was about through my tour, saw it out, went home, and ended up seeing a VA shrink. It was war, right? That's what I was trained to do." Pulling Trumpet tightly against her, she began to sob. "I just wanted to fly."

Gabe knew from his own military experience how she felt. Listening to her sobs and sighs, Gabe lamented his helplessness.

"I'm sorry. I just can't seem to get past this. It's always with me and won't go away. Most of the time I can push the scene back into some little corner, but then…the dream comes again." She was dabbing at her eyes with the back of her sleeve when Trumpet's head came up and swiveled toward the sidecar. With a deep growl, he was on his feet.

"What is it?" Aemea stared out into the moonlight, her hand going for the smooth plastic of the rifle's stock. "Coyotes? A bear? What is it Trumpet?"

While Gabe tried to feel what his friend was sensing, he was coming up with nothing. I'm trying too hard to focus.

He tried to relax his mind.

"Trumpet?"

He responded to his name with a sharp "aark!" Then he was bounding across the little meadow, his red coat glowing in the moonlight.

She threw the top of the sleeping bag aside and was on her feet, the rifle at a loose port arms. Trumpet let out a 'hurry' bark, and she was running barefoot to him. She stopped next to him, breathlessly searching the wooded shadows, when he bounded back toward the fire. When Aemea was part way back, he charged toward her, whirling and loping in a circle, making her turn after him.

"What? I don't... Trumpet, what are you doing?"

His response to her and Gabe's confusion was a slapping of his forelegs in the dewy grass. He romped just ahead of her, not quite letting her touch him. When she stopped, he sidled over, leaping away when she reached out.

"You. You set me up." Aemea stopped and brushed a strand of hair from her face. "There's nothing out there, is there?" She let the rifle slip to the ground.

Trumpet stood a few feet away. Tail snapping, he lifted his chin and let out several playful growls.

"I, am going to get you." She turned away, then went for him, her fingers just brushing his fur as he danced away. They chased across and around the little meadow, dodging and then lunging. The red dog just a happy bit away.

"Oww!" Aemea stumbled, clutched at her foot, and went down. Trumpet was at once at her side, his tail stopped while he brushed his concerned face near hers.

"Gotcha!" She threw her arms around him. Trumpet, panting hard and tail happily smacking the grass again, was easily pulled down next to her.

"God, it's beautiful out here." Her eyes on the star-filled night sky, Aemea let out a quiet sigh, which grew into a throaty laugh as she came to a realization. "You. You chased away my nightmare the first night you stayed with me. Three, four nights a week I have this repetitive nightmare. There are one or two variations, but it just won't go away. I remember now, I was at the bad part. And you showed up." She scratched his ribs. "When I woke up I didn't remember, but I felt a sort of peace." Nodding to herself, she smiled. "I remember now. You disrupted my nightmare, you big handsome guy."

Trumpet tipped his nose up, licking her face.

"I have to let go of at least the bad parts, don't I?" She patted his hip.

"You're such a good listener. If my shrink at the VA was able to get that out of me, she'd probably call it a 'breakthrough.'"

Returning to the sleeping bag, she settled back in on her side, an arm across the big red dog who snuggled tightly against her.

In the moonlight, B.P. stood on the hood of the Land Cruiser, hands cupping his ears. He heard something, but whatever it was, was too far away, too indistinct to make out. Now he couldn't hear anything but the wind in the trees. It didn't strike him as a fearful sound which was some comfort.

20

BOAR ATTACK

"Today, we make your ranch. I've topped off the bike from the spare gas tank, and we, my big red friend, are ready to ride." Aemea smiled at Trumpet, who had been out sniffing around while she packed everything into the sidecar. The only thing she kept out of the back was the AR-7 which she left assembled and in the sidecar's nose. He stopped next to the car as she mounted the Ural. "Come on. If we're going to jump start her, I'll need your weight."

Trumpet jumped in, settling quickly into place. Accompanied by a nod of his head, he gave her a 'ready to go,' "wuuf!"

"Yeah, woof. I bet in the Ukraine where they build these things, they offer optional dog harnesses for when the battery is low." Like the prior day at the gate, there was only a click of the starter's solenoid from somewhere beneath the seat. "Okay, 'Plan B' it is." She released the brake and the rig began to roll forward. When they were nearly out of downhill momentum she toed the gearbox into second. This time when she let out the clutch the rig's tires slid in the grass enough to slow the bike, however when they caught the engine didn't turn over fast enough to start. Now sitting in the flat part of the little clearing, she knew she couldn't push the heavy rig fast enough to start it on her own. "Nuts. Well, I guess we'll see how 'Plan C,' pans out."

Trumpet and Gabe watched her get off the bike. She reached past him into the nose of the sidecar. "Kick starter." She held up the chromed part Tom repaired. "I've never used one, but once I've bolted it on, it can't be much harder than hand-propping my Maule."

Trumpet jumped out of the sidecar to watch her work.

"Let's see. Pull the bolt, slide the kicker onto the splines. Eyeball, to see if it looks right." She smiled at her friend, who leaned forward to offer an encouraging nudge. With his approval she slipped the bolt in place, spun on the nut and tightened it down.

With the wrenches back in the car she shrugged. "I guess it's time to see if we ride or hike." She brought the lever up, putting her boot on the flat part. "I'll just get her some compression, I hope." She pressed part way down a couple of times. "Okay. I'll switch the key on and see how things go." She rose up, put her weight on the lever, and then quickly brought it down. To their mutual surprise and delight, the engine rumbled to life, quickly settling into a fast burbling idle. It was time to ride!

While the track continued winding along the rise and fall of the land, it also began to deteriorate to the point where Aemea thought a machete and possibly a pick and shovel might soon come in handy.

In the years Gabe visited and then lived in the area, he never ventured out in this direction. The large redwoods and stands of madrone were interspersed with reminders of past logging operations in the form of huge redwood stumps. Some were three to four feet high and nearly that in diameter. He surmised the primitive old road they were following had been used to skid the fallen giants to a better road, and from there they were hauled to a mill.

As the rig bounced and jerked over the rough terrain, Trumpet did his best to stay steady on the sidecar's seat, though at times he bumped his nose against the windscreen as he swung side to side.

Aemea instructed her companion to 'hold on.' They began to move up a grade steep enough to require her to stand on the Ural's foot pegs while leaning forward over the front of the bike. At another incline she fought the rig into a sharp turn; finally bursting out onto a flat section of fire trail. A hundred feet ahead another one of the gates beckoned. "Damn, without a key, we are going to need to find a way around that gate."

About forty feet from the gate, Aemea stopped the rig on a level section of road, set the brake and shut off the engine. Jumping off the bike she started toward the gate. Trumpet lost no time in exiting the sidecar to join her. About twenty feet from the rig, Trumpet halted and growled at something hidden in the brush across the road. Two little animals suddenly broke cover and rushed across the road between him and Aemea, followed by their mother. Their appearance brought a bark of warning from Trumpet and got Gabe's attention. Wild Pigs! He watched them disappear into the trees on the far side.

"Hey." Aemea called, "did you see that?"

Gabe was familiar, as were all the local ranchers, with

the wild hogs and the damage they caused to the meadows with their constant rooting. The little piglets and their sow didn't worry him, but from the area where they made their break there was a crash of branches, then a real reason for concern. A brutish boar at an easy two hundred pounds of ugly fury burst onto the road. His dark eyes spotted Aemea, and he charged. She ran for the gate and dodged behind the minimal protection of the post, barely missed by the angry swipes of his deadly curved yellow tusks. Aemea sprinted back for the rig, her adversary following in hot pursuit, squealing his challenge.

Gabe could only observe as Trumpet issued warning barks, rushing to intercept the attacking beast. The boar diverted his wrath in their direction, plowing headfirst into Trumpet. The squeals and barks ended with a searing pain in his left shoulder, the impact knocking him off his feet. A dusty view of dirt and sky passed across Gabe's view, and Trumpet struggled back to his feet. The swine then focused his attention on the Ural a few yards away, turning his back to them.

Aemea made it to the sidecar and reached for the rifle. On the far side of the rig, she yelled for Trumpet to stay away while trying to get a clear shot with the AR-7. Her shot seemed to glance off the tough hide of the boar, failing to slow his charge. Maneuvering to the front of the rig, she fired a second shot which didn't do much more than the first.

From Gabe's perspective it seemed they were moving in slow motion. Trumpet went for his enemy's hind leg, biting hard and holding on. However the boar managed to use his other foot to deliver a blow to his head. He glimpsed Aemea swinging the empty weapon by the barrel, using it as a club to beat the brute with the stock when a third and much louder shot interrupted their battle. A heartbeat later, the boar shook his ugly head, staggered backward, and dropped to the dirt.

The world quieted while a breathless Aemea lowered the rifle. Trumpet limped over to sniff the dead animal. Gabe heard a familiar voice.

"Captain Rand, I presume?" Having made his way down from a hillside near the gate, B.P. was jogging over to them.

Taking note of his rifle and Sheriff's ball cap, Aemea let the AR-7 slide to the ground. "Am I under arrest?"

B.P. held the Enfield out to one side, a soldier's way of indicating he meant no harm. Damn, he thought as he shook his head, she may have dropped her weapon, but her eyes met his with the steady gaze of a lioness ready to protect her own. "No, ma'am. I'm off duty and here to help."

Though immediately in front of him, the image of the boar blurred to a vague dark shape. There was a throbbing above one eye, along with a deep pulsing pain in Trumpet's shoulder. Hang on, Gabe coaxed him as the view continued to dim. From a distance, he heard both B.P. and Aemea calling Trumpet's name. Feeling the heavy panting, he willed his wounded friend to open his eyes as he dropped to the ground.

Gabe thought of the times when he'd been in pain, and it came to him. "Trumpet," he called, "I can take it! I'll take your pain." He pictured a sunny spot on the ranch where he and Trumpet sat side by side. In his mind, Gabe placed his hand over the dog's torn and bleeding shoulder. As he gently touched the wounded area, he spoke calm encouraging words until the area began to glow with a soft vibrating blue radiance. A heartbeat at a time, the glow gradually enveloped his hand, then began to ease up to his envisioned arm. He continued to speak until the wound closed itself, and his own shoulder throbbed.

"Trumpet!" Aemea's fingers moved around the long, ragged wound.

"I've got an emergency kit in my truck." B.P. got to his feet. "I'm parked on the other side of the gate, just past a slide, down on the road below." In moments, the deputy was back and opening the plastic box. While Aemea cradled Trumpet's head, she watched B.P. use the cotton pads to clean around the wound.

B.P. tried to sound reassuring. "It's not as bad as it looks. I've dealt with worse. The tusk just opened the skin up and grazed the muscle, probably bruising him too. It's the chance of an infection we need to worry about. We'll clean him up as best we can and get him to a vet."

"When the pig came after me, Trumpet tried to defend me." Aemea could feel tears welling up. "Why doesn't he open his eyes?"

"Shock maybe. When he was going for the boar's leg I saw him take a pretty good kick in the head."

"You seem to know what you're doing."

"We get some basic first aid at the Police Academy. Before that, there was the Army. With some pretty intense times over in 'The Sandbox'."

"Iraq?"

"Two deployments." The deputy continued to work carefully, cleaning away the dirt and tossing used pads for fresh ones.

Aemea spoke quietly to Trumpet while she stroked his face, saying encouraging things. She looked up at the deputy as a thought occurred to her. "You know who I am."

Without pausing, he answered her. "A character named Tom Baxman cornered me at the local café. He told me quite a story."

"The FBI is after me."

"Not anymore." B.P. grimaced as he began to dab some salve into the wound. "I wish I had something to give him for the pain." With the salve in place, he carefully folded over the flaps of skin. Aemea helped him run a length of the bandage around Trumpet's chest and shoulder, covering the wound. "We need a way to move him."

"There's a tarp in the sidecar we can use." Aemea swiftly returned with it. Working together, they quietly but quickly placed it on the ground then gently slid Trumpet onto it.

"There isn't enough room in the sidecar to lay Trumpet out comfortably." B.P. suggested, "You stay with him while I shove it back by the trees, then we'll carry him to my truck. We can be at the vet in a little over an hour." With one of them on either side, they used the tarp like a stretcher and headed for the gate.

"How are we going to get the gate open? I lost my key."

"In my rush to help you I climbed around the gate by going up the hillside earlier. But I have a better solution for us now. Fortunately deputies have a master key for most of these back country gates." B.P. smiled as he produced the key from his pocket.

After setting their patient down, B.P. unlocked the gate and swung it open. Once they were through the opening, they set Trumpet down again. B.P. quickly closed the gate and relocked it. Picking up the stretcher again, they cautiously navigated the gravel and dirt from the slide that littered the incline down the road to B.P.'s vehicle.

Trumpet was stunned by the kick in the head from the boar, allowing Gabe to absorb the pain in his shoulder. With the jostling of the move to the Land Cruiser, he began to regain consciousness. Briefly, eyes closed, he raised his head trying to focus on the reassuring words from B.P. and Aemea. Comforted that Gabe and the others were caring for him, he drifted back to oblivion.

At the Cruiser, they placed Trumpet carefully on the backseat, with Aemea sitting sideways in the front seat to steady him. "He's unconscious and shivering."

"I'd guess he's in shock. My coat is rolled up behind my seat. Tuck it around him to keep him warm."

With the jacket over Trumpet, Aemea rested her hand on his still form, as much to comfort him should he again awaken, as herself. "All set." She suddenly thrust out her hand, "I'm Aemea Rand."

"B.P. to the locals, and all my friends."

His grip was firm, warm, bloody and dirty, but she didn't mind. "You, you are a deputy?"

"Yup, but currently off duty. Yesterday, I started a week of time off. Good behavior." He winked.

On the fire road, the deputy kept his speed down, taking care to keep the bouncing of his wounded passenger to a minimum. "We're thirty minutes out of Cazadero. When we get to the pavement, we'll make some time. But it will be at least another thirty minutes to Santa Rosa and the emergency vet."

When they made the main road, B.P. put his foot in it. "In the glove box is an emergency light. Clip it to the top of the windshield frame and plug it into the lighter socket. The switch is at the base of the light."

Aemea quickly did as she was instructed. With the rotating light flashing alternately red and blue they reached Cazadero. As they sped through the little town, well over the 25-mph limit, a couple reading the display board in front of the general store turned in surprise as they flew by.

"Sometimes, it's good to be a cop." B.P. grinned.

"You said the FBI wasn't after me anymore."

"Apparently some new evidence came to light, which pretty much took you out of the picture."

"Were you working with them?"

"Ah, no. Mister Baxman told me about you, Trumpet, and about a possible second Will. I called the FBI before I came looking for you two. The agent I spoke with treated me like a country bumpkin, saying you were no longer a 'person of interest,' and new evidence altered the 'focus of the investigation.' He pretty much hung up without exactly telling me to get lost. Tom provided a map, then we figured a possible route you'd take." He dipped his chin. "And here we are."

Aemea watched the deputy's face carefully. "How much did he tell you about Gabe and Trumpet?"

Since they were running down a winding narrow road, still well over the limit, the deputy kept his eyes on the road. "Tell me? It's not like Trumpet being Gabe's dog was a state secret. With Gabe gone, a lawyer named Bunting is trying to buy the ranch to build himself a fancy home and hunting lodge. Tom thinks there was a second Will to take care of Trumpet and keep the place from selling. Which, could be the reason why he ended up in Reno." He risked a quick look at Aemea, who he decided, besides being a woman who would take on a wounded boar with a rifle butt to save a dog, was extremely nice looking. "That's pretty much it."

"Tom knew Bunting was a lawyer."

"Bunting is an associate of Tom's attorney." He shook his head. "One of them at any rate."

"Then that son of a bitch dumped Trumpet out in the desert." Her voice showed an angry edge. "Bunting may have been the one who shot him."

"What?"

"Trumpet has a grazed spot on his other hip. I thought maybe someone mistook him for a coyote."

"Damn." He slowed slightly at the stop sign on River Road before making a left turn. On the first straight stretch, he accelerated to overtake a Sheriff's vehicle heading in the same direction. B.P. instructed Aemea to roll down the passenger window as they swung out to pull alongside the deputy. When the deputy rolled down his window too, B.P. called over to him, "Hey Paul, got a hurt dog here!"

The driver nodded his understanding, motioning for them to drop in behind. The vehicle's emergency lights and siren came on.

"Paul's covering for me. Like I said, sometimes it's good to be a cop."

21

A Hero's Welcome

The young dark-haired woman in blue scrubs at the Redwood Animal Clinic came to her feet from behind the counter, calling for a doctor almost as soon as Paul opened the front door with Aemea and B.P. close behind him carrying Trumpet. Moments later, a slightly older brunette woman also in light blue scrubs wheeled a gurney through the doors from the back room. The four of them gently moved the red dog from the tarp.

"He isn't opening his eyes, and he keeps shivering." Aemea explained to the vet, whose nametag read 'Patricia Poul DVM.'

"He tangled with a big old boar." B.P. rested a hand on Aemea's shoulder. "I cleaned the shoulder wound as best I could, and used some salve with an antibiotic. He also was kicked in the head. It's been just over an hour." He gestured to the bloody spot on the bandage.

"Let's get him into the surgery." The vet motioned to her assistant. "Anne, get a drip ready." She rattled off the contents for the drip's bag as they pushed the gurney through the doorway. Aemea followed close behind.

"I just got a call." Paul stopped next to B.P. "Hell of a way to start your vacation."

"Yeah." B.P. clutched the jacket which had been keeping

Trumpet warm. "Well, I wanted to meet her. It looks like I got my wish." He noted the other deputy's puzzled look. "I'll explain later."

❧

After more than an hour of pacing the waiting room and examining the large framed cork board covered in photos of patients ranging from bunnies, cats and dogs, to horses, and one tortoise, Aemea and B.P stood across the table from the vet. Trumpet lay between them on a soft blue blanket. From a chromed stand hung a fluid-filled plastic bag from which a small tube ran to a catheter taped in place in his foreleg.

"He's not opening his eyes." Aemea gingerly ran the backs of her fingers over the side of Trumpet's face.

The vet removed her glasses and offered a reassuring smile. "As you can see, we have shaved, cleaned, and sutured his shoulder wound with fourteen stitches. He is loaded up with antibiotics, and we gave him something for the pain; we're also re-hydrating him. Although the injury was painful, he'll be fine. His pulse is strong, his breathing is normal. Luckily you got him here quickly." She eyed the couple. "I'm a little concerned about the possible head injury B.P mentioned. I think he'll be okay, but I want him to stay here tonight where we can keep an eye on him."

"Do you want us to contact Mister Picket about Trumpet?" Anne looked up from the vet's notes she was entering into the computer.

"Um." Aemea looked at B.P., who cleared his throat.

"Mister Picket passed away a few days ago. Trumpet has been in Ms. Rand's care."

"Oh." She turned her attention to Aemea. "I see."

The tone of Anne's voice caused the deputy to say more. "Look, it's a long, complicated story, but someone kidnapped Trumpet, eventually dumping him in the Nevada desert where Ms. Rand rescued him. At great personal risk to herself, she was bringing him back home when they were attacked by a wild boar. I arrived at the scene in time to witness Trumpet saving her from the beast's charge. In turn, she retrieved a small caliber weapon from her sidecar, getting two shots off, which expended her ammunition. Ms. Rand then defended an injured Trumpet by taking on the animal with the butt of the empty rifle." B.P. realized both women were now staring at him. "I, ah, managed to get in a lucky shot, which killed the boar." He cleared his throat again, "Is that about it, Ms. Rand?"

Ms. Rand smiled up at him. "It's, Aemea." She turned back to Anne. "Yes. That's pretty much it."

"Wow." Anne looked them over, especially Aemea, with a new respect. "You guys are awesome." She asked Aemea more questions about the fight with the wild pig while B.P. signed the paperwork, slipping her his credit card to secure the bill. With the promise they would be called as soon as Trumpet was awake, they finally left the office.

"I feel guilty, leaving him by himself." Leaning back into the Land Cruiser's seat, Aemea tilted her head back and closed her eyes.

"By the looks of things, I'd say he is in very good hands."

"Yeah, you're right." Aemea suddenly sat up, wrinkled her nose, and sighed. She cleaned the dirt and blood from her hands and arms while they waited during Trumpet's surgery, but her clothes still bore traces of their recent adventure. "I definitely need a shower."

"What do you think of this plan? I'm about half-starved, and you must be pretty hungry after wrestling with a wild boar. How about we get something to eat here in town. Then we can go back to my place for a shower." He noted her look. "There's a grill joint nearby where we can eat outside. If there's a breeze we can sit downwind from the other customers. The vet has my cell number if they need us. After our meal, we can stop by and make sure he's okay, then we can head back to Cazadero."

Aemea replied with an affirmative shake of her head, while giving her stomach a pat.

Their meal was quite pleasant; the conversation leaned toward Sonoma County. This was Aemea's first time to the Russian River and she was impressed with B.P.'s knowledge of the area. As the child of a military man, her life consisted of one move after another. The last eighteen months at her trailer while working in Reno was the longest time she ever stayed in one place. On the other hand, B.P. had been raised in this area, left for college, the Army, and returned. She wondered what it would be like to be so comfortably familiar with a place.

After lunch they stopped back by the animal hospital to check on Trumpet. He was still in recovery and they were told to go home, and expect a call later with his prognosis.

At first, Gabe could only hear the muffled sound of voices. When Trumpet's eyes slowly opened, there was the face of a pretty young woman in scrubs peering anxiously down at him. "Hi there, I'm glad to see you're awake." She said something to someone out of his sight and came back to him with a smile. "I'm Anne. I hear you're quite a hero."

I'm in a hospital at Danang, Gabe thought, I was Medivacked to the hospital. He wanted to ask how his buddies were doing, but couldn't quite get his mouth to work. Something else wasn't quite right, something about this Army nurse; he didn't recall ever seeing a female soldier with a small jewel set in the side of her nose.

His mind tumbled. He concentrated for a few moments on the memories slowly emerging. The recollections came faster and time skipped ahead at a pace almost too furious to follow. He listened to the sound of a heart beating in a loud but steady rhythm. Finally, the events of the prior week came to him. He tried to focus on the last 24 hours when he realized: Trumpet had been hurt, and they were at a veterinary hospital. Something was nagging him in his slightly woozy state that took a minute to sort out. "I'm still here!" The trauma of the injury and surgery hadn't sent him out of the retriever's consciousness. "I'm not that easy to lose, Trumpet, I'm still here for you."

"What do you think of this?" The woman was holding a star shaped medallion near his face. "Hero" was neatly printed in large block letters diagonally across the star. "We made this for you to wear home."

Another face joined hers, a slightly older woman wearing glasses, her dark hair pulled back into a ponytail. "You've been asleep a while, welcome back."

Trumpet thumped his tail against the bed. His show of happiness was not as much for the two women, but for the sound of his best friend's words. In his grogginess, he raised his head, peering around the small room for the source of Gabe's voice.

The second face glanced at her watch. "You have two very concerned people who came in to check on you a while ago."

Trumpet lifted his head so he could look back at the shaved area.

"Careful, it's going to be tender." I'll just check you over and see about getting you on your feet, if you think you're up to it?"

Trumpet dipped his muzzle, "Woof."

The older woman stared at him for a moment, then began carefully examining the dressing. In a familiar manner from years of conversing with her pet patients she continued. "You were so lucky. That pig could have seriously hurt you. I've seen some awfully bad cases, but you're going to be just fine, aren't you?" She moved her hand to his head, carefully running her fingers along the area just behind his left eye. "We also cleaned up a small cut right here. It's still a bit swollen." While moving a finger side to side a few inches from his nose, she watched his eyes follow her move. "Good."

Stretching carefully, Trumpet snuffled out another "woof."

"How's he doing?" Anne was back. She bent to rest a hand on Trumpet's hip.

"For a moment, I had the feeling he was answering me." Doctor Poul shook her head. "I guess that's from being around these guys all day. Let's see how he does."

They unhooked the tube. Carefully lifting him from the table, they set him on his feet. After Trumpet once again checked the wound, he looked around, his tail slowly swishing side to side.

"He doesn't appear unsteady on his feet." She put her hands on each side of the retriever, giving him a light sideways nudge. Trumpet lifted his head, offering a wide gold-dog smile. When she straightened up, he headed awkwardly for the room's door.

"Hey, wait." She dropped down in front of him. "Where do you think you're going, huh?"

Trumpet pointed his nose toward the door.

"You need to stay here until tomorrow, understand?" She motioned toward a second open door leading to a series of cages containing thick pads with blankets. "We have a nice comfortable bed for you."

He gave her a longing look. Finally, head drooped, he padded toward the cages.

"See what I mean?"

Her eyes on Trumpet, the assistant shrugged, "He's a smart guy."

"Yeah. It's been a long day. I guess I'm just tired."

When the vet left the room, the assistant guided Trumpet to a cage where he stretched out on his uninjured side. "You're a pretty smart fella, aren't you?"

Trumpet lowered his head as she closed the door to the cage.

"I'll be right out there, so, if you need me, just bark." She filled the water container hanging from the side of the cage, offering a few more encouraging words before leaving him alone.

22

GETTING TO KNOW YOU

They pulled into B.P.'s gravel driveway and parked in front of a two-car garage. Aemea climbed out and stretched. Next to the garage was a small cabin with an inviting wrap-around porch. When she looked more carefully, she noted the cabin had a second story, with the second floor being smaller, a sort of large cupola with windows on the two sides she could see. The cabin stood in a cleared area surrounded by redwoods, but with gaps allowing the late afternoon sun to cast the structures in a warm golden light. Somewhere in the background she could hear the gentle sound of moving water. B.P. had mentioned earlier that Austin Creek bordered the property on one side.

When his cell phone went off, he slipped it from his shirt pocket, flipped it open and answered, "Pfeifer." After listening to the caller a few minutes B.P. smiled at Aemea standing a few feet away. "He's awake."

The smile blew away most of her fears about the retriever's fate. "He's okay?"

"Doctor Poul said he's making an 'amazing,' recovery. He came out of it a little bit ago, was able to walk around. She doesn't think the head injury is serious." At her unspoken question, he added, "Trumpet's sleeping now. She said we can pick him up in the morning."

"Thank God. The whole time we were at the restaurant, I felt guilty about not being with him. When we stopped by and he was still out, I was really worried."

"I know the feeling." He watched her mostly pick at her food and didn't eat much himself. At their stop to check on Trumpet, she reminded him of a little girl whose puppy was sick. He gestured toward the porch entrance.

She stopped at the steps. "What about Tom's Ural? There's enough light to go back and get it."

"I thought you could take it easy tonight. After we pick up Trumpet tomorrow, I can get Paul to run me out there." He saw her doubtful look. "You saw how little the roads are used; it'll be fine. Plus, I know three words that will make you see things my way."

She folded her arms across her chest, her eyes suspicious.

"Clawfoot bath tub." He drew the last word into two.

She visibly relaxed. "I believe that's actually two words, but you win." He opened the door for her, allowing her to step into a spacious room smelling of pine and varnish. At the far end was a kitchen with an island. The Formica covered countertop was laid out in an 'L' shape to break up the space. At the back and flanking the kitchen, there appeared to be a small bedroom. "Nice."

"The landlord has been letting me remodel the place in my spare time. You're my first, um, guest." He slipped by her to open the bedroom door the rest of the way. "There's a robe and slippers in the closet; they might be a bit large but should be comfortable. The bath is to the rear of the kitchen. The washer and dryer are on the back porch."

In the awkward silence which followed, he found she was staring at him. He stared back. "What?"

"You're just a, a nice guy."

"For a cop, you mean?" He instantly knew he'd said the wrong thing. But her words about being a 'nice guy' were pretty much the same as those of a young woman in the not-so-distant past.

"Feeling a little defensive, are we?"

She raised her eyebrows in a way he found incredibly attractive, causing him to be at a loss for words. He gestured to the front door with a thumb and finished with a clumsy, "I'll just put the Cruiser away, and stuff."

Once outside, he hurried to the garage where he opened the double door, stepped inside, and leaned heavily against his workbench. "What the hell was that?" He went over the scene, wondering at his reaction to her words. Aemea was nothing like the woman he briefly dated the previous summer. Though she spoke of the personal courage of keeping to one's convictions, she hadn't been able to get around the fact he was a cop, and liked being a cop.

But, Aemea. "Wow." He straightened and let out a breath. When he came upon her and Trumpet fighting off the boar, he intuitively knew there was something special about her. He felt a powerful attraction like the opposite poles of two magnets. It was that power which was turning his brain to mush.

He consoled himself that their meal had gone well. They kept their conversation in a low-key, safe mode, mostly talking about the local scenery and the weather. Having both served in Iraq provided a common ground, though they didn't bring it up. What little he knew of her was she had warrior's heart and loved Trumpet, which was enough for now. One thing for sure, he mused, Tom's brief description of Captain Aemea Rand did not do her justice.

He ran the Land Rover into the garage next to his Sheriff's four-by, then came back to the cabin, built a fire, and put some music on, when she appeared in the kitchen. Her wavy chestnut brown hair was no longer in the short braid but fell just past her shoulders. He knew she was tall, but while the old work shirt and jeans did little to compliment her figure, the oversized robe accomplished the opposite. Something about the way the terrycloth fabric crossed in the front accentuated her breasts, and how it was tied and cinched at her waist, brought out an appreciative, "Wow!"

She was pleasantly surprised at the compliment, but pretended otherwise to see how he'd react. "Sorry?"

"Um, I have brandy. It's Korbel, locally made." B.P. mentally slowed himself down, determined just to take things easy. He smiled, meeting the unwavering gaze of her deep brown eyes with his own. "What I meant to say, Ms. Rand, um, Aemea, is you clean up really well."

After she accepted his offer for a brandy, he decided to give her some alone time, and went out to the garage to do some work on the Cruiser. Aemea loaded her clothes into the washer, then poked about the living room. There was a small flat screen TV, but she usually didn't watch much. She sat on the couch with a wooden coffee table in front of it. She picked up a soft bound book on deck planning from the table, then exchanged it for a 'Rod & Custom' magazine. Absent-mindedly she thumbed through the magazine while her thoughts went back to B.P..

Something between them changed from the time they arrived at the cabin. Up until then, they were both in 'warrior mode' as her mother once defined her condition, concentrating on saving Trumpet. When the deputy arrived on the scene, he hadn't taken control of the situation, so much as joined her and Trumpet in their battle with the wild pig. He treated her with respect, as an equal, a characteristic she found attractive in a man. Knowing he'd once been a soldier only added to the attraction she was feeling. She set the magazine on the table. Getting up, she retied the robe's belt and headed out to the garage.

"What are you doing to her?"

B.P. straightened from where he'd been leaning into the engine compartment. His elbow caught the tray resting on the fender, sending a small assortment of wrenches and sockets clanging to the floor. When they both bent to pick them up, he found he was staring through the open front of his old robe. His eyes quickly went up to hers. He noted she was smiling.

Aemea chuckled softly. "Are those coveralls clean?"

"What?" He looked up to see she was pointing to the far wall by the back door. "Coveralls. Oh, yeah. They came with the place. They're, ah, too small for me."

She went over, took them off the hook and made a 'turn around' motion with her free hand.

He faced the far wall. "I'm giving her a tune up. Plugs, points; she's old enough so she still runs points and …" Realizing he was beginning to babble, B.P. was relieved when she announced she was, "decent."

When B.P. turned back around he found her filling out the old coveralls in a truly decent manner.

"There. These should cut down on the number of awkward moments."

He was beginning to regain his feet and grinned, "Ms. Rand, I've been told I thrive on awkward moments."

Offering him a dazzling smile, she agreed. "Yes, I'm sure. Would it be awkward if I hung out here with you?" Without waiting for an answer, Aemea peered into the engine compartment. "Wow, a Chevy V8. You do this yourself?"

"Most of the parts, the adapters, you can buy these days. I welded up the odd bracket and wired her up." Pleased to be on somewhat common ground, he rested an elbow on the fender, staring at her openly. "Your, ah, boyfriend have something like this?"

"My dad was always tinkering on old cars and trucks. Every time he was reassigned, he was towing something out of the base hobby shop and dragging it along." Almost as an afterthought she added, "I don't have a boyfriend, a husband, or a significant other, and I see the hopeful look from your face." She looked up at him and smiled.

"I was not looking, hopeful."

"Deputy Pfeifer, that was one of the most hopeful looks I've ever seen. I might remind you I have been around a lot of men in the military. Some very hopeful."

B.P. sucked in a breath and blew it out noisily through his lips. "Is there a chance we can go back to awkward? I was a lot more comfortable with awkward."

"Sure." She returned her attention to the engine compartment. "If you want, after I check on my clothes, I can put in the plugs while you finish up with the points." She motioned to his workbench where there was a new oil filter sitting on an unopened case of oil. "Were you planning on changing the oil too?"

"I wasn't sure if I'd have time."

"There's two of us now." She gave him a cheerful smile. "I'll be right back."

As she hurried out of the garage, B.P. continued to stare after her. "I thrive on awkward moments?" His hand went to his forehead. "Yup, that's me, Ms. Rand, 'awkwardness' is my middle name." He understood she was teasing him, but it had been a while since he found a woman he felt so attracted to. He wasn't sure exactly what was happening between them, though it didn't seem to be going too bad. He tapped a finger on the fender. "I think, we're flirting. Or at least I am. And that smile!" He finally turned back to the Cruiser.

With the two of them working, the tune-up went quickly. Aemea was happy to get the coveralls dirty by sliding under the truck to drain the oil. With everything finally connected, drained and refilled, B.P. hooked up his timing light and dwell meter. As he clipped the instruments in place, Aemea commented she couldn't recall how to use either tool.

"Why don't you show me," she gave him a demure look. "It'll help with your masculine ego."

"Well, I thank you for that." He made a small bow.

With the engine idling smoothly and there appeared to be no oil leaks, B.P. suggested a test drive. When she readily agreed, he added, "We didn't have much for lunch. There's the Caza Café in town. The food is good and it's only ten minutes from here."

They cleaned up and Aemea changed back into her jeans. As her shirt had sustained a tear or three, she borrowed one of B.P.'s sport shirts.

After they ordered, B.P. had been given a wink or two by the locals, along with a nod of approval from the waitress. Pretending not to notice, Aemea asked, "How soon can we get up to the Gabe's cabin?"

"We pick up Trumpet tomorrow, see how he is. Afterwards I'll bring in Tom's rig. We could go late in the afternoon, or the following day."

"How fast is Bunting moving?"

"I would guess he's moving as fast as he can. Though, according to Tom, an offer may be submitted, but not accepted for another twenty-six days." B.P. thought for a moment. "Are you always like this?"

Seated across the table, Aemea set her iced tea aside and rested her hands in her lap. "Like what?"

"So, um." He groped for the words, and she let him. "I

mean, you've just been through quite a bit, with Bunting, the FBI, Trumpet. You, you're taking what would stress out a lot of folks, incredibly well." He leaned forward. "I like being with you."

She surprised him by reaching across and taking his hand. "I've had my moments. It's funny in a way, but, since Trumpet came into my life, things have changed in a good way. I lived alone and never pictured myself having a dog. Now, I don't know what I'd do without him. Knowing Trumpet is going to be okay means a lot to me." She saw he was waiting for something else, his hopeful look was back. "Taking everything into consideration, this has actually been one of the best days I've had in a long, long time." She squeezed his hand. "Thank you."

The sun was down when they left the Café. She put on the extra jacket he'd brought while he fished in his pocket for the keys. She gave him a grin. "How about letting me drive?"

She deftly caught the keys and dropped into the driver's seat.

They were easing out of the parking lot, when B.P. told her, "She's doesn't weigh much and has a lot more power than with the little six she came with, so just take it easy at first."

"No problem." She brought the engine rpms up, then snapped out the clutch. The rear tires instantly spun, and the Cruiser slued sideways. Instead of letting off, Aemea banged second, sending the vehicle hurtling forward down the road. She hit third at almost sixty. "You know, if you were driving like this, I'd be terrified." She gave him a sweet sidelong smile.

"Yeah, I know what you mean." Loosening his grip on the dash and windshield frame, he smiled back.

Back at his place, he offered Aemea use of the upstairs bedroom. She readily accepted. Following a "goodnight and thanks," she gave him a quick kiss on the cheek before heading upstairs.

"Well," he said to no one in particular as he was alone in the downstairs bedroom. "At least she didn't tell me I was sweet." That phrase was the kiss of death when he had been in high school and college. In his experience, a "sweet" guy was destined to be a friend of the non-romantic variety.

"He's so sweet." Aemea lay on her back on the bed, the covers drawn up to her chin. As her mind wondered back through the day, and the last few months, she decided the last few days were better than anything in over a year. She liked his sense of humor, and he wasn't some smooth-talking dude trying to get her into bed. He's at ease with his life, she thought, a trait I'd like to learn. Like most nights, sleep didn't come easily. But this time, though she worried about Trumpet, most of her thoughts were of her good fortune.

23

ARE YOU STILL THERE?

"Hey Trumpet." Aemea smiled as she squatted down in front of him. If it weren't for the shaved area around the long-sutured shoulder wound, and the plastic cone-shaped device he wore fastened at his neck, she wouldn't have known he had been injured. With his tail snapping from side to side he appeared to be ready to go.

"He looks as good as new." B.P. grinned at Dr. Poul. "You did a fantastic job."

"He's been a good patient." She handed him a small bag. "An antibiotic and some doggie downers to keep him from being too active. We don't want him to pull out those stitches."

"Why this?" Aemea tapped the lampshade. When she saw the 'Hero' medal attached to his red bandana, her smile broadened. "Nice touch."

"Thanks." The smile was returned. "The collar is to keep your friend from licking at the wound. He'll need to wear it for a few days." Dr. Poul bent down and rubbed Trumpet's nose. "You don't mind, do you?"

Trumpet stopped his wagging and sat. His head dropped down in a sudden picture of dejection.

"I think he minds," B.P. observed dryly.

When they arrived back at B.P.'s place, Paul's official four-by was parked out front, the deputy sitting on the porch, a paper coffee cup in hand. He got to his feet and came down the steps as B.P. eased the retriever from the Land Cruiser and set him on his feet on the ground.

Paul was older than B.P., with a slightly shorter and stockier build. His short graying hair capped a friendly tanned face. He looked like he smiled a lot.

"Paul, this is Aemea. We didn't have time for introductions yesterday, but Aemea found Trumpet in Reno and brought him back."

Over the phone, B.P. had filled him in a little bit on what was going on, but left him wondering why she chose the route she did. He figured he'd find out more when they went back for the Ural. After a few pleasantries were exchanged, Paul knelt next to Trumpet. "Hey fella, you sure don't look like the same pup I helped carry into the vet's yesterday." He fingered the plastic cone. "You don't like this much, do you?"

Trumpet shook his head side to side, looking from him to the others expectantly.

Paul gave Trumpet's nose a gentle rub. "I bet you want it off, don't you fella?" When Trumpet immediately bobbed his head, Paul looked up at the other two. "I swear he understands me."

"He's a pretty smart guy." Aemea decided it prudent to avoid the subject. She wanted to know B.P. a little better before she brought Gabe to his attention. Also, though she couldn't put her finger on it, there was also something about

Trumpet that seemed a little different. Maybe, she thought, it might be the wound and drugs. After offering B.P. a warm smile, she deftly changed the subject. "You never said you could drive a sidecar."

The deputy smiled back. "You never asked."

Paul chuckled. He liked what he saw was going on between the two. "B.P. grew up on dirt bikes. We have a couple of ATVs out here for Search and Rescue. If he gets stuck, I'll come back for you so we can embarrass the hell out of him."

After the two men drove off in Paul's Sheriff cruiser, Aemea followed Trumpet, who cautiously made his way up onto the porch. "We picked up dog food yesterday. You hungry?"

He looked back over his shoulder, then, with a deep sigh, dropped down next to the top of the steps.

She sat on the steps next to him. "Would you like this off?"

The expressive eyebrows flicked up.

"You have to promise not to lick or scratch your wound."

The eyebrows went up again. He lifted a paw.

"Okay, but one scratch and its back to lampshade city."

The tail thumped as he got up so she could remove the protective collar. When she set it aside, she bent so she could look into his eyes. "Gabe? Are you still there?" The tail stopped and he lowered his head. Trumpet was aware Gabe had been quiet for some time.

Gabe could hear someone calling his name as if from a great distance. His shoulder didn't hurt as much as before, but now he was having trouble concentrating. He recalled the hospital and a young woman talking to Trumpet. There was light and he could see, but not clearly. Besides taking on the pain from the injury, he also absorbed most of the effect of the painkillers. He wanted to find out what was happening, but he was so sleepy. The tractor seat by the valley eased into view, and he moved toward it.

Concerned by the lack of a reaction, Aemea rubbed the retriever's face. "Okay, you just rest for now. We'll try again later." Trumpet's eyes came back to her, and, mindful of his stitches, she carefully laid her arm across his back. "I can't say I understand what's going on, but that was you who kept the boar from hurting me, wasn't it Trumpet?" Seeing his eyes brighten, she gave him a careful hug. "You're a brave guy, my big red friend."

She sat there thinking for a while, with her 'big red friend' leaning contentedly into her. "What do you think of B.P.?"

The tail thumped a few times.

"Yeah." She sighed. "Me too."

They hadn't said much since leaving B.P.'s cabin, but when they were passing the Caza Café, Paul suddenly gave the younger man a playful punch on the shoulder. "Good lord, B.P., she's gorgeous. Is she smart too?"

"Ex-Air Force pilot." He glanced over at his buddy. "Yesterday, she helped me tune up the Cruiser."

Paul shot him an 'I am impressed' look.

"I suppose you'd like to know what's going on?"

"Just the good stuff."

Returning his friend's punch, he began to explain.

When they neared their destination, B.P. suggested that Paul park the Sheriff's four-wheel drive in a wide spot below the gated fire road. They walked up the steep incline, careful not to slip on the dirt and loose gravel across road, before reaching the gate. Still carrying his gate key, B.P. unlocked the gate and swung it open. He and Paul walked over to the remains of the wild boar, which had provided an overnight feast for the area scavengers. There were a pair of vultures pulling at the carcass when they arrived, but they could still tell he'd been a sizeable animal.

"Damn, Aemea was taking *that* on with an empty rifle?" He let out an appreciative whistle as he toed one of the crooked yellow tusks with his boot.

"He caught Aemea between the bike and the gate. Aemea left the little survival rifle in the sidecar. When she ran for it, Trumpet stopped the boar from catching her. The rifle only had two shots in the clip. They slowed it a bit but mostly made it angry."

"Luckily, you came along."

"I climbed that hill to get a look around, when I heard the barking, then the shots. I didn't have time to open the gate but climbed around it instead." B.P. pointed up between a pair of small firs.

"An easy thirty, forty yards... Nice shot, considering."

They rolled the rig back onto the road. After trying the starter, B.P. kick-started it to life. He eased it forward, motioning Paul to get in the sidecar.

Paul looked doubtfully at the Ural. "It's a short walk; I'll close the gate behind you."

By the time Paul was locking the gate, B.P. began slowly traversing the slide littering the road. With the bike on the downside of the slope his friend appeared to be having an interesting time of it.

When Paul reached his Sheriff's four-wheel drive, he gave the younger man a big grin. "Didn't quite flip it over, did you?"

"Oh, you mean back at the steep part of the slide. I was just getting a feel for having the sidecar's wheel off the ground."

"Which, was why you were laying way off the bike, across the sidecar and screaming for mercy."

"I was leaning over to keep it down. And, I was not screaming, it was more of a 'yee haw,' thing."

"Right. So you want me to follow you?"

B.P. rubbed a forearm, which was sore from only the hundred yards he just traversed. He wondered how Aemea managed the rig and hoped it was just a matter of him trying to over-control the bike. "Naw. I know you're anxious to get back on the job. You go on ahead. I'll just poke along home."

"I could go get Aemea to help you out." At his buddy's chagrined look, Paul laughed. "See you later."

☙

When he rolled up to his house, B.P. had gained a whole new respect for his houseguest. Having never ridden a rig before, he assumed it would be like riding something between a bike and an ATV; but he had been wrong. It didn't lean like a bike, handle like a four-wheel ATV, or anything else he'd ever ridden or driven. Left turns weren't too bad as the sidecar wheel just dug in. Right turns were a whole different matter, causing the sidecar to lift with speed. On his first tight turn in that direction, the car came up far more than he anticipated. He made the turn with the Ural wobbling all over the road, the car's wheel kissing the pavement when it wasn't lurching back into the air. Thankfully, no one was coming from the other direction. He was pleased that she had covered most of the distance on the fire roads leaving him only a few miles to go before reaching a County road.

Through the glass in the front door, B.P. could see Aemea and Trumpet sleeping on the rug in front of the wood stove. The red dog was stretched out full length on his side, feet toward the stove, with Aemea snuggled tightly against his back, her head on a pillow from the couch, an arm across Trumpet's neck. He noted the red bandana had been washed and was back on him, with his 'Hero' star reattached. The 'lampshade' was lying near the door.

When he tiptoed in, Trumpet's snoring stopped. He briefly lifted his head. His tail made a couple of thumps before he settled back, making a contented smacking-of-his-lips sound. For a minute or two, B.P watched them. Great, he smiled to himself. I'm envious of the dog.

24

HANGING OUT

"How long have you been here?" Aemea stepped lightly off the porch and stretched. She smiled at B.P., adding, "you didn't have to do that."

The deputy was nearly through washing the Ural. He raised the chamois from the bike's fuel tank and began to wring it out. "It's no trouble, and Tom will probably appreciate getting a clean rig returned to him." The battery is on the workbench with my charger hooked to it." He found himself admiring her, wearing his clean shirt with her jeans. Well, he decided, they may not flatter her, but she sure flatters them. He realized he was staring, and from the way she was smiling, thought she might be enjoying it.

Trumpet came onto the porch, yawning broadly as he limped down toward them.

"Hey, Trumpet." When he came over, B.P. set the chamois aside and sat next to him, nodding at the 'medal' hanging from the bandana. "You're a brave guy all right."

Trumpet gave him a retriever grin and licked his face.

They decided to just hang out for the rest of the day. While Trumpet, still recovering from the effects of the anesthesia and pain pills, settled in for another nap on the porch. B.P. took Aemea for a walk along Austin Creek, which flowed along the west edge of his property. They found a large rock in the sun where she took off her boots and socks.

Leaning back, she sighed contentedly as she dipped her feet in the cool water.

"How long have you lived in Reno?"

"Actually, I have a place in the mountains, about thirty miles from the city." She told him about her Airstream, the fantastic view, her job as a bartender, about how she found Trumpet waiting along the side of the road.

By a silent mutual agreement, neither spoke of their service in Iraq except in general terms, as in, "Just before I was deployed," or, "after I got home."

When they returned to the cabin Trumpet was waiting for them. B.P. and Aemea sat on the step to the porch, and Trumpet stretched out next to B.P. The deputy rested his hand on the dog's hip while he told Aemea some of what he knew about Gabe. He noticed the way she kept stealing glances at Trumpet, finally asking if she was worried about him.

"He's *different* from before he was hurt." She leaned down to look into his eyes. "Are you okay in there?" Trumpet closed his eyes, happy to lie in the soft warmth of the sun, listening to the two people talking.

B.P. could sense something was bothering Aemea about Trumpet, which he was missing, and she wasn't revealing it to him. He tried to put her mind at ease. "He is doing quite well. If it weren't for the wound and all those stitches, I'd say he is the same as when he was with Gabe." He decided to change the subject. "I'd like to know more about your plane. Tom told me his little airstrip was pretty tricky to get into."

A light came on in Aemea's eyes. "Well, she's a nineteen

seventy-four Maule I bought from an old guy who re-builds them as a hobby. He'll fix one up, fly her for a while then sell her off to start another. This was his seventh plane, a lucky seven. Since he's ex-Air Force, he made me a pretty sweet deal."

Surprisingly, he wasn't taken aback from a law enforcement perspective when she was telling him how she had outflown the FBI jet jock. He also loved the way she moved her hands as she described flying under the bridge, with the Piper breaking away.

She was completely lost in the memory, laughing about how, during the loop, she told Trumpet to look up at the bridge. "He looked and barked, a kind of happy 'aark, aark' he makes."

"You looped the 'Bridge to Nowhere'?"

"If that's what they call it, then yes." She was flattered by the genuine admiration in his voice and his interest in her passion of flying. "When this is all settled, we can go back to Tom's to retrieve my plane. I'll take you up, and we'll have some fun."

He assumed his cop-on-duty voice. "But nothing, *illegal*, right?"

"Oh no, sir. Of course not." She crossed her heart while making sure he could see the fingers of her other hand were crossed.

They were getting hungry so B.P. made a run to the store in town to pick up sandwiches for lunch and something to barbecue for dinner. While he was gone, Aemea tried to elicit a response from Gabe, but only got a wag from the retriever. The temptation was strong to call Tom and ask if she just imagined the whole thing.

At B.P.'s suggestion, she slept in the downstairs bedroom so Trumpet wouldn't have to climb the stairs. He was content to sleep on a spare blanket folded on the floor at the foot of her bed. The next morning, after a lazy breakfast, they helped Trumpet into the back seat of the Cruiser.

B.P. pointed over the hood of the Land Cruiser. "The coast is just a few miles beyond those hills." On the way to Gabe's ranch, he pulled off the dirt road and onto a section of pasture, which fell away toward a view of the fog cascading over a ridge to the west. A pair of liquid ambers framed the view, some of their fire red and orange leaves carpeting the short pasture grass. "I'll take you there sometime." He tried to make his offer sound as casual as possible.

"I'd like that," she smiled. "During my stint as a fugitive I may have been a little too preoccupied to fully appreciate the local scenery. I can see why Trumpet wanted so badly to get home. It's beautiful up here." B.P. gave her a quizzical side glance in response to Trumpet's desire to get home.

"Almost there." As they drove by, B.P. pointed out a large weathered stump surrounded by small groups of wildflowers poking their heads above the deep grass. Beyond, the hill dropped away to reveal a pretty little valley. Fastened near one edge of the stump was an old tractor seat. "Gabe and his late wife, Sarah, used to sit there with their morning coffee. 'Used to be a pair of the seats, but after she died, he took away the other one. Since then, it's been just him and Trumpet."

Smiling her understanding, Aemea reached back to give Trumpet a pat.

"You're home Trumpet." She and B.P. lifted Trumpet from the rear seat to the ground. Soon he was happily sniffing at the porch. The breeze was blowing from the west, sighing in the trees. Trumpet took in the smells of home. Sarah's fragrance lingered even after all this time: the sweet aroma of rosemary and roses, but also the disturbing odor of acid and sulfur caused by her cancer treatments. There was of course Gabe's scent everywhere, but a new smell of something burned was part of the mix. He noticed his beloved Yogi bear on the little wooden table next to the old couch. Grabbing it in his mouth he settled onto the sofa and watched to see what B.P. and Aemea were doing.

Aemea took in a deep breath and exhaled slowly. "For some reason I expected something a little more on the drab side, maybe a brown or dark green." Instead, the board and batten sides of the cabin were a vivid yellow, with the trim bright white. Pale green curtains drawn across the large front window prevented her from seeing inside. Hanging from the front of the porch cover were a trio of hummingbird feeders. Two pairs of the little green birds darted in and around them, the males flaring their tails and flashing their luminous red necks when Aemea drew close.

B.P. noted, "It takes 'em about a week to go through all three. I made sure they were topped off."

He tried the front door, then snapped his fingers, and stepped back. "I forgot, I locked it after Tom and I were here. There may be a key under the flowerpot, or if all else fails, Gabe told me he kept one in the barn down below where I parked his truck." After looking under the flowerpot to no avail B.P. set off on foot for the barn.

25

BUNTING RETURNS

Aemea was admiring the flowers in the little garden and observing the bees busily making their rounds and B.P. was barely out of sight when a black SUV made its way in through the gate. With a low growl Trumpet came to his feet. Aemea also immediately recognized the driver. Moving toward the cabin she reassured her protector. "Yeah, we both know who that is."

On the other hand, Bunting didn't recognize either the old four-wheel drive, or the tall young woman staring in his direction.

"Now that's a very nice looking caretaker." His passenger and potential investor in the proposed hunting lodge, Howard Ledging, leaned forward with a smile.

"I had no idea there was a caretaker." Bunting muttered.

He drove past and halted near the garden.

"I assume you are aware you're trespassing," were the first words out of Bunting's mouth when he got out.

Aemea confronted him, ignoring the friendly greeting from Ledging, when Trumpet appeared at her side. "Bunting!" She spat at the attorney; Trumpet adding a deep growl with his lips pulled back to reveal his intentions.

The sound of the name brought Gabe back awake, and he realized a long time must have passed. Around him, the retriever's innocent warmth melted away into the emotion he expressed at T-Top.

"If anyone is trespassing, you son-of-a-bitch, it's you."

"Warren? I believe I'll just take in the view from over there." Without waiting for a reply, Ledging hurried toward the gate.

The attorney's eyes narrowed as he realized who she was. "Did you bring the damn dog back here in your plane?"

"Damn straight. After you shot him and dumped him in the desert."

"I dumped him?" Bunting was suddenly overcome with a rage of his own. "He locked me out of my Mercedes. He made me break my window. Do you know how much that cost? He's damn lucky I, I..." Bunting abruptly caught himself. "I have no idea what you're talking about."

Bunting, Gabe thought tiredly, you're a complete idiot. He struggled to keep Trumpet from launching at the attorney by picturing the tractor seat and valley, which had become a calming point for both of them. The scene kept fading into a collage of images of the terrible things from the last few days. Aemea's palpable anger wasn't helping. Though only seconds passed, Gabe was feeling the strain.

"Now, would you please restrain, your animal?" His words were not in the form of a question.

"Trumpet." Aemea's voice became hard and icy. "After I'm finished, you may have the pieces." She took a step toward Bunting.

Bunting took a step back. "I don't think you want to make threats to an attorney."

"I don't think you want to tangle with an angry American combat vet."

When she took another step toward him, he reached out, grabbing her hard by the shoulder. His other hand became a fist "I'm warning you!"

The next thing Bunting knew, he was flat on his back, the wind knocked out of him, the clear blue sky partially obscured by the muzzle and bared fangs of an angry Trumpet.

"I'm going to sue," he wheezed. "I'll…"

"Trumpet! Aemea!" A man's voice called. "Let him up."

"Howard. Thank God. You're a witness to all this."

"Trumpet." The voice softened. "It's okay fella. Let him up."

Bunting realized it wasn't his investor intervening.

Accompanied by a growl coming from deep within his chest, Trumpet leaned in closer for a moment before abruptly pulling away.

When Bunting shakily regained his footing he was relieved to find Deputy Pfeifer standing next to the woman, whose hand rested on Trumpet's head.

"Deputy, you witnessed the attack, I want you to do your duty."

"You're asking me to arrest you?"

"What? No! Her!" He pointed an angry finger in Aemea's direction. "You witnessed her assault, and that vicious dog nearly ripped out my throat." He stared incredulously. "I'm telling you to arrest her!"

The look the deputy was returning was one of a hunter

with a small rodent in the sights of a very large weapon. "Mister Bunting, I witnessed your assault of Ms. Rand, who I must say used commendable restraint while defending herself."

Shocked but undeterred, Bunting charged ahead. "I want this woman, this 'Ms. Rand,' arrested, or I'll have your badge!"

B.P. folded his arms across his chest. "Not a good move, making threats to an officer of the law. Mister Bunting, if I wasn't off duty, I'd be hauling you in."

"You're taking her side?"

"Ms. Rand, at great personal risk to herself, brought Trumpet back to his home. Besides, I believe she happens to be the niece of the late Gabe and Sarah Picket. She has every right to be here."

"His niece?" Bunting frowned. "I wasn't aware of a niece."

"Warren?" Ledging called from over by the gate, where he was casting anxious glances at his watch. "I'm afraid I have another appointment. Perhaps we could continue this at another time."

Bunting slapped the dirt from his suit as he tried to stare down Aemea, which did not go well for him. "This isn't over," he finally blurted, painfully aware it was yet another line from some movie where the bad guy gets thumped by the end of the flick.

"I certainly hope not," Aemea shot back. She would have gone after the attorney a second time, but B.P. rested his hand on her shoulder, giving it a gentle squeeze.

They watched the SUV stop at the gate, pick up Bunting's passenger, and drive out down the road. When the vehicle was out of sight, Aemea turned to B.P. "His niece?"

"Technically, yes."

"Technically?" She shifted into an 'I'm waiting' posture. Beside her, Trumpet sat, his head cocked to one side, his eyebrows giving him an expectant expression.

"Ah, well." B.P. rubbed his chin. "One time Gabe referred to Trumpet as the child he never had. Then, Trumpet found you while he was exploring the desert, um, adopting you. As I see it, that makes you Gabe's niece, on the canine side of the family."

Aemea shook her head at B.P.'s 'not bad huh?' grin.

"Hmm." She turned to the object of their discussion. "What do you think Trumpet?"

Gabe looked wearily out through the happy eyes of his friend, who was barking his pleasure at the young couple laughing. "Looks like you have a family. I'm amazed B.P. recalled me telling him that; I thought mostly he was just listening to be polite."

"Isn't this where you throw your arms around me and tell me I'm brilliant?"

"I don't think so. You lied."

"I'd like to think I just exaggerated in the direction of truth." He grinned at her. "And I just wanted to shake him up a bit."

"Well, I'm glad you didn't arrive a few moments earlier, or you would have stopped me from nailing him."

"Yeah, I guess I shouldn't have waited."

"What?"

B.P. dropped down on one knee. "Hey, Trumpet, you could have hurt him badly, but you didn't. You're a fine guy." He rubbed the retriever's neck until Trumpet tilted his head up and licked his friend's face. "If he shot me, I would have gone for him too."

"You heard?" Aemea

"Every word." B.P. got back to his feet. "I always thought the thug only spit out a confession in the movies, or on television." He pointed to the side of his head with one finger extended. "Fortunately, in this case, my memory is 'on duty'."

❧

"Who exactly were those people?" Ledging looked back in the rear-view mirror in case the young woman and her dog changed their minds and were chasing after them.

Bunting thought not mentioning the off-duty deputy might be the most prudent move. "Just the delusional niece of the late owner, her boyfriend, and their dog."

"Not a problem then?"

"A problem?" Bunting pretended to be surprised by the question. "Of course not, Howard. There is no mention of her in the Will."

"She can't sue, or something like that?"

"I suppose she could sue the estate for part of the funds from the sale, but it won't prevent the sale of the property."

The rest of the trip back to Howard's office in Santa Rosa was made in relative silence, while Bunting's thoughts bounced furiously around. Where the hell did the niece come from, and how did she hook up with the dog? She was definitely the woman in the sidecar and the pilot of the plane. Of all the places he could have dumped the dog, he left him virtually in her lap. What a stupid coincidence. And why couldn't he come up with movie lines from the good guys for pity sake? He'd have to work on that too.

26

Where There's a Will

Aemea stepped inside the front door and stopped. "Oh."

"If this was a car, I'd call it a 'sleeper'." B.P. grinned at her look of pleasant surprise at the cabin's interior. "Clean, not much to look at on the outside. But, under the hood, built to the hilt."

"Like your Cruiser." She smiled at him. "I expected something more widower-like."

"Widower-like?" A puzzled look crossed the deputy's face.

"Um, more stark, I guess." She reached out and ran her fingers over one of the curtains by the front window as B.P. pulled a small cord at one side of the window. The curtains drifted open, immediately brightening the interior. "This is just such a lovely surprise." She looked up at the open beam ceiling to where a large centrally placed skylight allowed the sun to cast a warm glow about the living room.

"Sarah sewed the curtains." B.P. nodded toward the ceiling. "Gabe added the skylight. It cranks open, and he even installed blinds for the sizzling summer afternoons." He placed his hands on his hips, surveying the room. "Over the years they cleaned up, painted the board and batten walls. Gabe even had the windows replaced with dual paned ones."

Besides the large fixed window on her right, a second large window ran from the corner toward the wood stove, which was placed near the wall's center. A well-filled bookshelf stood on the far side, with a gray filing cabinet beside it. To the left near the kitchen door, stood a pine dining table with four matching chairs, and butting together in the corner were a pair of cabinets with cut glass upper doors. Reading lamps were placed around the room and next to the two comfortable-looking chairs angled toward the wood stove. When B.P finished pulling the curtains back from all the windows, the entire room glowed. "It is so warm and..."

"Homey?"

He gestured to the ceiling. "The pine planks covering the ceiling are from the local mill. Here, check this out." B.P. touched a light switch by the front door. Light shown upward to the ceiling from inside the long pair of wooden box-like pieces connecting the walls. "They boxed the crossties to keep the walls together, left the tops open and added recessed lights."

Aemea moved past a couch tastefully placed against the wall, with a coffee table in front of it, facing the front window. Her eyes went to the walls, which were filled with framed photos or drawings. "There are so many pictures."

"Yeah. The first time Gabe invited me up here after Sarah passed away it seemed a little like a mausoleum, but..."

"It's a celebration."

"Of their life. Yeah, that's what I figured out."

"Wow." Aemea smiled as Trumpet ambled past her to climb carefully up onto the couch. Among other smaller framed photos over couch, hung a large oval-framed portrait. Like Tom a few days before, Aemea was drawn to it. "So, this is you and Sarah." She reached down to stroke the side of Trumpet's face.

"How much did Tom tell you about Sarah?" B.P. turned to her from in front of the metal file cabinet.

"Not much, I'm afraid."

The smiling woman in the portrait stared back through sea green eyes well placed over high cheekbones. The sun on her long medium brown hair brought out auburn highlights.

"According to Gabe, she was quite a woman, smart as well as pretty."

"You never met her?"

"Oh, I'd see her around town, she was tall, with a nice figure. One time she bought me a soda when I came up short at the store. Her eyes were clear and bright, like yours."

There were smaller photos flanking the portrait. In one, both smiling, arms around each other, the couple stood in front of the cabin. In another, Sarah sat on the couch, a small red puppy on her lap. The puppy was stretching up to lick her chin. Aemea turned to Trumpet, he moved so he could rest his chin on the arm. With a contented sigh he closed his eyes.

B.P. motioned toward the file cabinet. "I'm just going to take another look around here. When Tom and I came up here a few days back, we took a quick perusal and I found a folder." B.P. dug into the third drawer down in the file cabinet and straightened up waving the manila folder in Aemea's general direction. "It has 'New Will' printed on the top. It is empty but maybe he dropped the document into the wrong file."

"Did you check the laptop?"

"Yeah. I checked it right after I found the empty folder. If Bunting took the copy, he probably also deleted the file."

"We're still hoping Bunting didn't take all the copies, aren't we?"

B.P set the folder on the top of the table. "You betcha. Why don't you check the little desk in the bedroom while I keep poking around out here?"

Above the bed on wooden racks were several antique rifles, along with two modern ones. She called into the next room. "Was Gabe much of a hunter?"

"Nope. I think they had to do with his time in Vietnam. Guys with that sort of experience tend to pick up the odd weapon here and there."

"You don't seem to have any. Except for your official issues." She thought for a moment. "And your Enfield, thank God."

As metal drawer banged shut, he answered, "You didn't look in my upstairs closet, did you?"

On the wall over the desk hung several small, framed photos. In most, a happy looking Gabe and Sarah stood with scenery from Mexico, Europe, or with the ranch in the background at various stages of their life. Some of the more recent ones included Trumpet. In one there was only Trumpet and Gabe.

Held by a pushpin in one corner was an unframed photo of a young soldier. A rifle by his side, he sat on the ground slouched back against a heavy looking pack. His jungle boots were scuffed and worn, his uniform sun bleached, the brim of his boonie hat turned up. He wore a broad smile on his tanned face. On his lap was a small notepad. But it was what was in his hand that caught Aemea's eye. He was holding up a small photo of a young woman.

"Sarah," Aemea breathed and bent for a closer look. In faded blue ink on the edge of the photo of Gabe was written, 'Ashau 1971.' "B.P. how long were they together?"

"Sarah and Gabe? About forever, I guess." B.P. paused in his search and came over to the bedroom door. "They met in Vietnam where she was a Red Cross Girl; Gabe said the soldiers called them 'Doughnut Dollies'." The girls went from base to base visiting the troops, playing games, bringing doughnuts and sodas, sometimes just hanging out. Anyway, Sarah and another girl managed to get a trash can full of ice and sodas out to an Observation Post where Gabe was, as he put it, 'stuck for almost two miserable months.' Afterward, he wrote her, she wrote back; they ended up sharing his R&R in Hawaii. A huge flaunting of both Army policy and Red Cross regulations, as I recall him telling me. Gabe referred to her as his 'adventuress'."

While Aemea continued to look over the photos, he returned to the living room. The small wooden desk in the bedroom held mostly small bundles of old Christmas and birthday cards, held together with rubber bands. There were a few computer supplies, which was about it. On an impulse, she felt along the underside of the drawers, before sliding them back in.

Aemea was going through the few boxes on the closet shelf when she realized Trumpet stood watching her from the doorway. She felt suddenly awkward at searching through Gabe's possessions. "Come on, Trumpet, aren't you going to help us look?" Aemea gave him an expectant look. "There *is* a copy of the Will here, isn't there?"

B.P. called back from the other room. "He may be smart dog, Aemea, but he's still just a dog."

The room appeared out of focus to Gabe. He wondered if there was something wrong with Trumpet. Besides the trouble he was having concentrating, simply keeping awake was becoming a problem. Gabe was about to direct Trumpet to the file cabinet when he went over on his own and nudged the second cabinet drawer from the bottom. Fortunately Trumpet could still anticipate some of his thoughts, and he also understood more of Aemea's words.

"I've already looked there." B.P. squatted down next to the retriever. "If you saw Gabe put something there, it isn't there now." When the move was repeated, B.P. eyed him curiously for a few moments before relenting. "Okay I'll look again."

Trumpet watched closely as he looked through each file folder until there were none left to open. When the retriever nudged his hand, he took the empty folder from the top of the cabinet and showed it to him.

"See?"

Gabe stared dumbly at the empty file. So, Bunting took them all. At least they made it back. A while back living with Aemea seemed to be a pleasant fate, and overall things could have turned out a lot worse. "Well my friend, Gabe thought hazily, want to go live with Aemea?"

With that, Trumpet turned away to sit by Aemea, who had come back into the living room.

"I checked the underside of the drawers in the desk," Aemea offered.

"A little farfetched, but not a bad idea." B.P. opened each drawer checking them carefully, even going so far as to check out the backs before pulling out the bottom one to inspect the floor beneath. He also investigated the underside of the dining table, and for good measure, all the chairs. "I honestly don't know what else to do. Bunting has made an offer on the place. It looks like he's going to get it." The tone of his words carried his discouragement.

"Somehow, using 'honestly' and 'Bunting' in the same breath doesn't sound right." Aemea scratched Trumpet's head. "How about we take a break? I could fix us some coffee?"

She was filling a blue enameled pot, when there was a sound by the kitchen's back door. Setting the pot aside, Aemea stepped back from the sink in time to see the handle to the door jiggle. She reached over and unlocked it, as the handle jiggled again, moved down, and the door eased open.

The masked face of a large raccoon poked through the gap until the door swung far enough to let him in. His intelligent eyes went to the old aluminum pie pan on the floor. Seeing Aemea, he began to back away.

"Well, hello little guy." Aemea slowly squatted down and smiled at Reggie, who looked from her to the pan. "I'd guess you've been here before." Her gentle words brought him the rest of the way into the kitchen. After peering around a bit more, he chittered at her, again peering down at his empty dish. "B.P., look who knows how to open doors."

The deputy leaned against the doorframe leading to the living room. "This must be Reggie, and he's come for his meal."

"I didn't know Gabe had a pet raccoon." She held out a piece of the dry dog food from a bag on the counter.

After a moment's hesitation, Reggie approached her, shyly took the dog food with a front paw then backed away toward the water bowl. Before eating it, he dipped and rubbed the food in the water.

"He's not really a pet. Gabe told me he just shows up for meals and brings something in payment."

"He is really cute. What kind of something?"

"About anything, I guess."

Aemea picked up the pie pan, filling it from the dogfood dispenser. "So, Reggie, what do you plan to pay us with?" She held the pan out for him to examine before placing it on the floor.

After Reggie carefully studied the pan, he sat back and looked up at Aemea for a few moments. Without touching the food, he hustled back out the kitchen door.

B.P. forced a chuckle. "Maybe, he didn't like your presentation."

"Maybe, he's going for his check book."

B.P moved back into the living room for more searching, and Aemea prepared their coffee, when Reggie reappeared at the backdoor. This time, in his teeth he carried a dirty envelope by its edge. He came directly to Aemea. Rising up on his hind legs, he took the envelope from his mouth, holding out his 'payment' for her to take.

"Ah, well, thanks." Puzzled, she set the coffee on the counter and accepted the envelope.

His task accomplished, the raccoon scuttled over to his pan of food.

Aemea turned over the envelope; Trumpet raised his head from the arm of the couch.

"What is it?" B.P. replaced a cushion on the couch facing the front window.

"A letter." She held it out. "Addressed to you."

B.P. stared at the letter in Aemea's hand. "To me?"

"You. With Gabe's name and return address."

"Reggie had it? How did he get it?" The deputy came over, hesitating briefly before taking the envelope. When it was in his hand, the hair on the back of his neck stood up. He read the front of the envelope carefully then shook his head. "It is to me."

"Well, Gabe obviously trusted you." Aemea glanced down at Trumpet who dropped down off the couch and stood watching them. "Okay then." She tapped the envelope with the tip of a finger. "Are you going to open it anytime soon?"

27

ASKING FOR IT

"Damn." B.P. grinned when they read the signed copy of the Will carefully for the second time.

Aemea flashed the deputy a brilliant smile. "Bunting's going to be pissed."

"Yeah. Bunting." B.P. got to his feet. At the table, he ran his fingers thoughtfully over the laptop's case. "At the county office, there's a guy who can retrieve deleted files from computers. It won't matter now with a signed copy."

"Take a look Trumpet." Taking the letter from the table Aemea held it open in front of the dog's face while B.P. gave her an indulgent smile.

"Thank God." Gabe quit reading after the first few lines as the urge to sleep nearly overwhelmed him. Their adventure seemed to be coming to an end, and more and more he just wanted to drift off and rest.

"I guess all this is yours." Folding the copy of the Will, she handed it to the deputy. "It states you'll be Trumpet's guardian for the rest of his life."

Something in her tone changed, and B.P. could see sadness creeping into her eyes. He tried to tease her into a smile. "I guess he is."

"You guess?"

"I suppose we could work something out." His casual

words didn't have the expected effect. He'd thought their earlier playfulness would come back and then he'd suggest they could both take care of Trumpet.

"You suppose?" A flash of anger drove the sadness from her eyes. "You think we're just discussing some old dog, a simple piece of property, don't you?" She reached out and poked him in the chest. "Don't you!"

Baffled by her sudden rage, he found himself turning to Trumpet for support; a wag of the tail or, something. Instead, the retriever tucked in behind her, looking up at him as if he were now the enemy. "I was just…"

"Out!"

"What?"

"You're as bad as Bunting. You see everything as property, as something to take over, a conquest."

"That's not…"

"Get out of here!"

B.P. was going to say "fair," to try to explain he was only kidding, but realized he must have touched some nerve which pushed her way beyond listening to his explanations. He also began to feel angry himself, nearly pointing out he shouldn't have to leave since the cabin was now his. Instead, he thought about the woman who fought off a wild pig with an empty rifle to save the dog she loved. Some part of his mind told him he just blew it. The best thing he could do was leave and think things out before he said something so stupid he could never fix things between them. Without another word, he turned and left.

❧

As B.P.'s Land Cruiser passed through the gate, Aemea left the porch for the kitchen to fix a fresh cup of coffee. Reggie had long departed and she turned to where Trumpet stood in the kitchen doorway watching her.

She refilled the pot, and with the flow of the warm water her anger subsided, leaving her feeling shaky and tired. Turning towards Trumpet she sought his response, "When I get angry or threatened, I just react. Ok, sometimes overact, and direct my rage at the wrong person if they happen to be near-by, kind-of collateral damage. My counselor at the V.A. thinks things I've suppressed in the past finally come out. Would you please tell me what you think?"

"Wuuf." Trumpet backed into the living room, lifted his nose and 'wuffed' again.

"Is this Trumpet, or Gabe talking?" As he slowly circled the room, pausing here and there, she followed and was soon examining the walls more closely. The photos didn't seem as randomly placed as when she first looked.

"It's their life story, and it starts here." She touched a photo of a twenty-something Gabe and Sarah hugging under a palm tree. "Hawaii, I bet; when they first got together." In the next there was an old Triumph motorcycle where Sarah sat behind Gabe, her hair in a long braid draping over her shoulder, a hand resting on his hip. A few photos down Sarah sat astride a Yamaha twin parked next to Gabe's Triumph. There were mountains in the background and both his gold bike and her red motorcycle sported saddlebags, with sleeping bags strapped to the rear racks. "Well, how about that, you didn't settle for just being hauled around like common baggage, did you Sarah? You had your own bike."

She moved along the walls, pausing to touch several of the pictures with the couple standing next to a white and blue sailboat on a trailer, or on the boat. There was one with Sarah wearing a big grin and a ball-cap pulled low over her forehead at the tiller of the small white wooden sailboat with teak trim. Aemea stopped at a large photo in a dark frame, staring for a long time before taking it down and returning to the couch by the front window, where she sat hugging it to her chest.

This time she was addressing Gabe, "You loved each other so much. I can feel it everywhere in the cabin. I want that. I want a love like my parents."

Trumpet carefully climbed up next to her and rested his chin on her knee. The sun pouring through the window warmed his fur. With a soft umph, he closed his eyes.

"Trumpet, I don't know exactly who or what you are, but you're very special and dear to me. I will not give you up." Aemea leaned down and kissed him on the nose.

Gabe slowly opened his eyes and could see the little garden with its high fence to keep the deer out. With the pain nearly gone, he felt a floating sensation similar to the one after the lightning strike. "We had some great times here, didn't we, Trumpet? What we need is someone who will appreciate the ranch and the cabin. Aemea and B.P. would be perfect, wouldn't they? They would love this place, and you, as Sarah and I did. I don't think Aemea quite sees it yet, so you must tell her how good she and B.P. would be for each other. They just need a little push, and you have to be the one."

Trumpet sighed his agreement.

"Come on." Aemea gently moved his chin aside and got to her feet. "If you two were out walking and were struck near here, then your car must be around." She headed to the door. "We'll go find it, and run back to Tom's. I could use the time to think of how to deal with B.P."

Trumpet merely stared at her.

"I'm sorry. I guess I'm forgetting you're still hurt. You rest here while I check the barn."

Trumpet climbed off the couch and limped past her. At the front door he settled down in front of it, blocking her exit. Making a soft 'snorting' sound, he tilted his head up so his eyes could meet hers.

They stared at each other for long time before she dropped down next to him and sat so she faced into the room. "Okay, you're right. We're not leaving." She draped an arm across him. "I suppose he was just trying to be funny. But I didn't want funny. I wanted serious and I couldn't bear the thought of losing you. When he said you were his, something just snapped and I fought with my heart, not my head." Aemea rested her head back against the wall, sighed deeply and closed her eyes. "How bad do you think I've screwed up?"

Trumpet rested his head across her leg, making a soft grumbling noise she found to be oddly soothing.

28

TIFFANY-JEAN

After building a small fire in the wood stove, she was staring despondently into the dancing flames, Trumpet snuggled beside her, when his head came up.

A bright yellow convertible sports car with its top down was pulling into the yard. Following close behind came a leaf green commercial van with large black spots painted at odd intervals. Mounted to the roof, a giant replica of a cockroach with long waving antenna appeared to be ready to charge some unseen foe. On the side, a painted logo of the same creature was circled in red with the type of cross hairs in a hunting rifle's scope in the center. Beneath the logo, red block letters spelled out KILL ZONE EXTERMINATORS.

Behind the van, a black full sized four-door pickup riding on large off-road wheels and tires appeared. Above the sides of the bed were mounted shiny diamond plate aluminum toolboxes. Lettering on the door proclaimed, David 'Bear' Punket, Contractor.

Aemea and Trumpet watched as the three vehicles stopped side by side on the far side of the little garden. "Wonderful." She pushed to her feet, a less than wonderful expression on her face. "More company. Is there something you haven't told me?"

From the window they observed a top-heavy looking blond woman exit the car. Wearing a snug fitting designer denim pants suit with an open plunging top, her look was completed by medium blue shoes with stiletto heels.

"Hmm." Aemea nibbled at her lower lip.

A low growl came from Trumpet.

"Me too. Oddly enough, I think I know her."

By then two men climbed out from each vehicle and were standing to each side of the woman. As she began to speak, making sweeping arm gestures in the direction of the cabin, at least three of the men were glancing appreciatively in the direction of the substantial cleavage flaunted by the pantsuit's plunging neckline.

Aemea turned for the front door, but Trumpet beat her to it, tugged at the handle until it opened wide enough, then dodged through the opening. By the time Aemea made it outside, he was standing at the edge of the porch, a stiff ridge of fur up along his back. A low growl complemented the way his lips pulled back to reveal a surprising number of sharp white teeth.

Noticing Aemea and Trumpet watching them, the woman's hands stopped in mid-air.

"Trumpet, easy. We don't want you to pull your stitches." Aemea and the little group eyed each other.

The familiar scent of the woman's perfume confirmed to Trumpet she was the one who helped put him in the crate. The growls increased.

The men from the van each wore white coveralls with the bug logo over the left chest pocket, their names stenciled over the right. From their similar slight builds and reddish hair and glasses, Aemea surmised they were brothers, probably in their early thirties and well suited for getting into places to deal with various pests. Despite the growling dog, one smiled at her. She smiled back.

Well-worn denim, scuffed work boots and T-shirts appeared to be the uniform of choice for the pair from the pickup. The larger of the two sported a thin scruffy beard. The sleeves from his T-shirt had apparently been removed to accentuate arms, which Aemea guessed, a few years back were quite muscular. Changing, she mused, as the man's gut grew over his belt. Unlike the others, the younger man with straight longish hair and a thin mustache moved away slightly, his eyes locked on Trumpet.

"How did he get back?" Folding her arms across her chest, the blond glared accusingly at Aemea.

"Tiffany-Jean Blunk. As sure as bad nails on a blackboard, I'd know that voice anywhere." Aemea chuckled. "I see you're still trolling for attention with your boobs."

Shading her eyes and mindful of Trumpet's warning growls, T.J. took a step toward the cabin. Warren assured her the cabin was as good as theirs already, though he cautioned her to stay away until the place was legally in their name. However, not wanting to waste any time, she contacted the bug company and carpenters about cleaning up and then creating her new country home with its lovely Tucsony garden. In fact, in her car were several magazines on country living with a number of the pages marked with colorful Post-it page markers. Now the damn dog was back and some horrible dark-skinned woman with him. Not, she reminded herself, that she had anything against dark skinned people. "Who, are you?"

"You may remember me from the 'T-Top.' I tended bar while you, ah, entertained."

T.J.'s eyes narrowed while her mind raced. She only worked at the T-Top for a few weeks, quitting after meeting her current husband at another Reno bar. But even if they had met, what the hell was she doing here, and, how did the dog manage to return from Nevada? Well, she reassured herself, Warren was an attorney, and he would straighten the whole thing out.

She raised her chin. "I don't have the least idea of what you're talking about. I have the contractor and the, the terminator here." She indicated to the men around her in case Aemea hadn't noticed them or their vehicles.

"This isn't your place to 'terminate'." Aemea smiled while giving her friend a reassuring ear rub. "It belongs to Trumpet."

"It can't belong to him because, the Will, um, the Will..." She suddenly realized it probably wasn't a good idea to mention the earlier visit to the cabin. "My husband and myself are buying this," she gestured around her, "this place."

"You can't buy something if it's not for sale." Aemea leaned against one of the porch posts supporting the roof. "You're trespassing, and Trumpet would like you to leave his home. Right Trumpet?"

"That dog does not belong here." T.J. motioned to the

larger of the two men from the pickup. "Bear, tell them to go away."

Standing next to Aemea during the short conversation, Trumpet had calmed enough for his fur to smooth out along his back. At T.J.'s words, the teeth reappeared with a growled warning.

"Sure, we can handle this for you." Bear motioned to the younger man. "Zeke?" The two men headed back to the truck. When they quickly returned, each carried a sizeable crowbar. Besides the crowbar, Aemea noticed something else about Bear. On his right hip, a black holster, its safety strap still in place, held a pistol she took to be a Glock.

"We ain't afraid of your dog." Bear tapped the curved end of the crowbar in his palm for emphasis. "Now, Miss T.J. wants you outta here."

Trumpet's growl deepened. Putting himself between Aemea and the others, the ridge on his back was at full attention. "Easy, Trumpet." Aemea's eyes narrowed as a familiar chill of anger washed over her. She pointed to the weapon on the contractor's hip. "You brought a gun with you. To chase off an unarmed woman and her injured dog?"

"If I have to." Bear smirked. "Miss T.J. is going to own this place; she makes the rules here."

"Huh." She spoke quietly to Trumpet. "I've always hated people who smirk."

She held Bear's eyes until he glanced over to T.J., who unfortunately for the situation, wore her own little smirk.

"Okay, okay." Aemea held up her hands. "Just let me get his leash. Then we'll continue our little discussion."

She reached down, tapped Trumpet on the shoulder and spoke in her best Air Force officer's command voice. "You. Wait right here."

Once in the cabin, Aemea stormed through the living room for the bedroom. "I'll show you, you smirking son of a bitch. Think you can threaten me and my dog." She was still saying unkind things about the contractor when she found what she wanted in the rack above the bed. Back on the porch when she stepped out next to Trumpet, she cradled an old bolt action rifle at the position of port arms. "Couldn't find the leash."

A low conversation between the five other people ceased.

"I bet you don't even know how to use that thing."

Aemea simply smiled at Bear and the others.

The exterminator crew eyed Aemea for a moment before the driver suggested T.J. call them, 'when things have settled down a bit.' A minute later the van was heading out through the gate.

As the exterminator crew left, a light of recognition came on in T.J.'s eyes. "I know her. She's one of those crazy people they sent over to Iraq. She worked behind the bar because the club manager thought she was too old for the, the, um, stage."

Aemea nodded coolly. "And you worked the stage because you were young, pretty, and lots of men go for a set of silicone filled boobs."

The attention of the two carpenters moved to the low-cut top.

T.J.'s eyebrows went up and her eyes widened. "That's just not true. These, are all natural." She turned to Bear and Zeke. "Everybody knows saline is natural."

They nodded.

"Good." She gestured in the direction of the porch. "Now make her and that dog leave."

"You heard her." Bear's attention was back on Aemea and Trumpet. He took a step forward, a grin spreading across his face when Aemea took a small step back. "Thought so."

Lips pulled back again; Trumpet let out warning barks.

Still approaching the porch, the two carpenters moved slightly apart, crowbars ready. "Now why don't you just make this easy and take a hike out of here."

Aemea responded to Bear's suggestion by snapping the rifle bolt back. After a quick glance into the action, she shoved the bolt forward, swung the barrel around and squeezed the trigger. The rifle spoke and the glass of the passenger side truck mirror blew out.

Aemea's demonstration caused three reactions. The crowbar of Bear's assistant thumped to the ground as he sprinted for the gate. Bear turned to see the damage to his truck. T.J. peed in her pantsuit.

"At the Air Force Academy, the instructors thought I had 'an affinity for weapons'." She ran the bolt a second time. The spent brass shell spun in the air and she smiled. "This lovely old rifle is a vintage World War II M-1. The stock is what is referred to as 'sportified,' plus she carries a *seven*-round clip."

"Ahhh, I'm wet!" T.J. screamed. "Get rid of her!"

Bear turned back to Aemea to find the rifle pointed at his ample midsection.

"My dad, a two-tour Vietnam combat vet, I might add, used to say, 'if you carry a weapon, you'd better be damned ready to use it'." Her eyes went icy. "I suppose you know a gut shot usually passes through the body, taking out the spine, should the target possess one." She motioned toward the holster. "Left hand, slip it off."

His hands still held the crowbar. Bear fumbled for a moment before carefully lifting the holstered pistol until the belt clip was clear. "If I ever get..."

The driver's mirror blew to pieces with Aemea's second shot. "Little man, don't you even threaten me or mine."

But he wasn't listening. The pistol and the bar hit the ground next to each other. Moving surprisingly fast for a man his size, Bear reached the truck, was inside and backing up while T.J. stood screeching and waving her arms.

"Look what you made me do! I'll get you. My husband is an attorney who will sue you! He'll have you and that dog put away." She pointed a well-manicured finger at Aemea. "I'll have my Tucsony garden while you'll be in jail. And him," the finger went to Trumpet. "I'll be no more missus nice person. No more Nevada for you. No...no, ack!" A spiked heel sank into the dirt causing her to topple over backward.

After setting the rifle aside, Aemea once again disappeared into the cabin. In a few moments she returned with a towel. Bending down next to a wailing T.J. she held it out. "So, I gather you're Bunting's wife. I suppose we all get what we deserve."

Sensing the major portion of the threat had passed, Trumpet moved back on to the porch and made himself comfortable on the couch.

"I don't want a dirty old towel, or anything else from you," T.J. snarled as she pushed herself upright. "Unlike you, I've got a man who can take anything he wants, and give it to me." She suddenly snatched the towel from Aemea's hand. "I have a life! A beautiful life."

"You think he's going to steal the ranch from Trumpet and then give it to you?"

"Warren won't have to steal the ranch." The smirk returned. "It's for sale, and we're buying it."

"It isn't for sale. The Will states the ranch was left to someone who will care for Trumpet for the rest of his life."

"That's not true!" T.J. pushed herself to her feet. "The copies of *that* Will are, are all, all... Well, it's just not true."

Aemea tried to correct her. "There is a copy of the new Will. We..."

Pulling the towel up around her hips, T.J. cut her off. "You're just saying this out of spite. Because the men wanted me and the other dancers but ignored you. All the girls said you were damaged goods. If a man did look at you, you'd chase him away."

"Maybe, I was just being selective." But because the other woman's words rang a little too close to the truth, she sounded doubtful.

Seeing she had an effect on Aemea, T.J. pushed on. "Well, look what that's got you. You're here all by yourself with just a dog to keep you company. When the sale goes through the two of you can move back to wherever you came from. I, will have a beautiful country home with a Tucsony garden."

Staring into T.J.'s eyes, it was Aemea's turn to smirk. "We have a copy of the new Will."

T.J. stared back. "I happen to know that is not true."

"A little raccoon brought it to me."

"That filthy creature? "Her eyes widened. "But, but…"

"Right now, my boyfriend is on his way to deliver it to the law firm representing Trumpet."

Her mouth moving soundlessly, T.J. slowly turned. This time mindful of the heels and soft spots, she tiptoed to her convertible. Opening the door, she suddenly called to Aemea. "I bet he never gives you a Mercedes."

"Some of us don't need a Mercedes." Aemea smiled as the other woman snugged the towel around her waist before dropping into the driver's seat.

"Aha." T.J. made a face as she jerked the door shut. The engine started and she backed around until she was facing the gate. "The trouble with you is unlike me, you don't know what you want. And I'm just the one to take it from you." She pointed to Trumpet. "And him. He's, he's. Well, I'm going to take it from him too." Having said her piece, she eased the bright yellow Mercedes forward to leave.

As an afterthought, Aemea shouted after her. "Tucson is a town in Arizona. You meant Tuscany, you dumb ditz!"

Though he'd witnessed most of the confrontation, Gabe was seeing everything through a fuzzy sort of light. Even the sounds were distorted as if he were dipping his head in water. While he pondered this, he wondered if she actually would have shot the man.

Aemea moved back to the porch and sat on an arm of the couch. "You know, somewhere in her somewhat odd choice of words, there might exist a modicum of truth." With that, she got up and retrieved the rifle. "Good thing 'Bear' took off, I used the only two rounds in the clip on his truck's mirrors. That's the second time. I guess if I'm going to protect us properly, I'd better prepare a bit better." She dropped back down next to him.

"Woof!"

"What?"

The tip of Trumpet's tail began to flick side to side. "Woof." He nudged her hand.

"You don't miss much, do you?" Aemea sighed as she leaned back and stared off across the yard. "Yeah. You heard correctly. I said, 'boyfriend'."

B.P.'s mind ran through the recent scene with Aemea for the hundredth time or so as he drove toward Santa Rosa to deliver the Will. 'Well, damn.' He thumped his fist on the steering wheel, condemning himself for being so stupid. Not only did she love the dog more than life and logic itself, but he made light of the situation. 'Mister Awkward strikes again.' The wheel took another heartfelt thump.

Burned vividly into the loop playing through his mind was the image of Aemea, standing on the porch with her arms folded, chin up, daring him to come between her and

Trumpet. He definitely liked the big red dog and admired his courage and heart. He didn't have the chance to suggest they could share him, and maybe the ranch too. Now he may have lost both of them. B.P. pulled over to the side of the road and rested his head against the steering wheel. 'I've only known her for three days, never even kissed her. And now, I can't picture my life without her.'

He was still parked by the road when Paul swung his Sheriff's four-wheel drive over behind him, switched on his warning lights and walked up to the passenger side of the Land Cruiser. Without a word he opened the passenger door and climbed into the seat.

"Didn't find the Will?" Paul asked at last.

"Oh, I found the darn Will. I've got it right here in my shirt pocket." B.P. gave a casual slap to the pocket.

"Bad news?"

"Nope, the best. I get Trumpet and the ranch, but it came with a curse."

"A curse?"

"The recipient would be cursed with gross stupidity."

"Ah. Trouble in paradise."

"Gee, why do you say that?" B.P. sucked in a breath, then blew it out noisily between his lips.

"You're sitting by the road, the engine running, as you're banging your head on the steering wheel."

"That's because all on my own, I managed to boot myself out of paradise." He shut off the engine. "Somehow in my own charming way, I said something so far beyond dumb that I can hardly believe it." He trailed off morosely.

"What did she say when you told her?"

"Told her what?"

Paul chuckled. "Don't you ever read those articles in woman's magazines?"

B.P gave him a withering sidelong look. "Oh sure, besides Rod & Custom, and Hot Rod Bikes, I subscribe to Women's Day and a few more. I just hide them when you come by."

This time Paul laughed outright. "Okay, fair enough. My wife subscribes to a couple, and I check 'em out sometimes."

"I don't want to look sexier, younger, or to drop those extra pounds."

The other officer laughed again. "You know what a woman wants to hear?"

"No, please enlighten me, oh guru of women's publications."

"The same thing a man wants to hear. If you truly want a happy ending, you're going to have to do something about it." Paul checked the radio at his belt. "Got to go." He placed a hand on the younger man's shoulder. "Two things. First, wipe that pathetic look of despair off your face, 'cause it is not you. And next time pull a little further off the road, I don't want some inattentive motorist driving into the back of this heap and ruining my day."

"Paul!"

The deputy was about to slide into the driver's seat when he heard B.P. call out his name.

"Yeah?"

"Thanks! Not only am I going to get you subscriptions to Ladies Home Journal and Vogue; I'll have 'em sent to the substation to your attention." The pipes of the Cruiser rumbled to life and its rear tires sprayed gravel as it pulled out onto the road.

Paul dropped into the seat and closed the vehicle's door. "Now, that's more like it."

29

W. Bunting Esq. vs. the FBI

"I assure you Evan, I am about to lock in a bid on the property." As Bunting listened to one of his potential investors, he doodled little airplanes on his yellow legal pad. Each one had the numbers 228X on the rear of the fuselage; each was drawn either on fire or trailing smoke. "Other interested parties? No, we appear to be the only interested party. In addition, I've requested a thirty-day escrow."

When the conversation was over, Evan Wilkenson had finally expressed a verbal interest in buying into the Picket Ranch. Bunting happily checked his name off the list. He was about to punch in another number from his private address book, when his intercom beeped.

"Mister Bunting. There are two gentlemen at the desk who would like to speak with you."

"Sienna, I have a full schedule today. Have them make an appointment."

"Mister Bunting, they..."

He punched the talk button and rudely cut her off. "An *appointment,* Sienna. Have I made myself clear?" Normally, he would have been nice to the attractive young woman, but his attitude changed toward her a few weeks back. When T.J. made plans for a weekend at a spa, he asked Sienna to join him for dinner at a well-known restaurant in Sonoma.

She turned him down flat.

"Yes, of course, Mister Bunting." The voice over the speaker was oddly pleasant. "I'll ask these two gentlemen from the FBI to come another day."

As her words sank in, Bunting carefully placed his phone back in the receiver and fought down the beginnings of panic. "They can't know," he breathed to himself. After several deep breaths, he politely asked her to send them in.

Sienna opened his office door. "Agents Soble and Washington to see you, Mister Bunting." After letting the men into the office, she left the door ajar; she sensed this meeting was going to be interesting. She then headed to the office of Bunting's partner, Gary McNeil, thinking he might want to know about the visitors.

"Gentlemen." He shook their hands and offered them chairs. They declined coffee, and once they were seated, he leaned back in his comfortable leather chair. Bunting recalled a line from a recent movie. "Now, how may I help the FBI?" As he spoke the words, he suddenly realized the phrase came from yet another movie bad guy who died a horrible death near the show's conclusion. Bunting began to sweat.

"This shouldn't take very long, Mister Bunting." From inside his suitcoat, Agent Sobel withdrew a small black notebook.

"I appreciate that. I have a rather full schedule today." The agent's reliance on a simple notebook, rather something modern and electronic, gave him the fleeting impression of a thorough, yet not up-to-the-task investigator. While that slim hope was running through Bunting's mind, he noticed Agent Washington was studying his desk.

"Ah, yes."

Bunting's attention went back to Sobel, who looked up from the notebook.

"Perhaps you could tell us about your recent trip to Reno."

The attorney leaned forward in his chair. "Reno?"

When the agent simply waited politely, Bunting took the opportunity to stare at his ceiling, as if gathering his thoughts. "Reno. Certainly. I have a client in Reno."

"I see. That client would be Reno Mercedes and Audi?"

"What?"

"The service manager told us you brought in your SUV for replacing the front passenger side window."

"Oh, yes." Though Bunting frowned, he was inwardly pleased he gave the manager a made-up story about the window being smashed during a break in. He repeated it to Sobel, who seemed satisfied.

Gary McNeil stood in the doorway, holding a legal pad in his hand. "Warren, may I join you?" Bunting gave him a grateful look and waved him in. He stepped into the office, giving Bunting a questioning look as he closed the door quietly behind him.

"Gary." Bunting stood, then quickly introduced the agents.

"We were just going over Mister Bunting's recent trip to Reno." Soble explained. "Apparently, someone broke into his vehicle."

"A break in? I'm surprised something like that would require the attention of the FBI."

With McNeil's appearance giving him some measure sense of normalcy, Bunting began to relax.

"Actually, we're investigating a possible kidnapping. Involving an eight-year-old boy."

The sweat crept back. Bunting could feel the short hairs bristle at the nape of his neck. "A kidnapping?" His mind working furiously, Bunting folded his arms across his chest, tilting his head slightly in what he considered to be a look of concern. When no other words came to mind, he ended up simply repeating himself. "A kidnapping?"

Soble studied his notes for several moments. "You stopped at the Golden Doubloon Hotel. There was a dog show?"

Again the shift in topics caught Bunting by surprise, but he rallied. "Ah, yes, the dog show. Golden retrievers, in fact. It's a little-known fact I'm dog lover." He wondered how they knew about his visit to the dog show.

"You have one of your own?"

Bunting looked Soble in the eyes. "No. Sad to say, I'm between dogs."

"A Mrs. Tina Bloom informed the police during their interview that you attempted to take a dog she was protecting."

"What?" Now, Bunting was totally confused. "This, ah, Mrs. Bloom? I'm sure she has me confused with someone else." He gave his law partner a weak smile and shrugged.

"She stated you attempted to take a retriever from her.

When she refused to give you the dog, you verbally assaulted her, while grabbing her arm. Apparently she was able to fend you off with a raccoon." Noting McNeil's bewildered look, the agent added, "a stuffed toy raccoon."

After writing a note on his legal pad, underlining retriever, McNeil broke in: "Surely she was mistaken. Warren may not always exercise the best judgment in the world, but he would not steal a dog, or assault someone."

"We determined it was Mr. Bunting because witnesses saw the man flee to a black Mercedes SUV parked at the curb." After rattling off the license number he looked up expectantly.

Bunting's stomach was beginning to twist into a tight little knot. "The dog broke loose from his actual owner. I was only trying to, ah, restrain him."

"Is this by any chance the same dog for which you filled out the forms at the animal shelter?" Soble flipped the page and continued. "Mister Bunting filled out the forms to pick up a dog he claimed to be his at the Reno Animal Shelter. He left without the dog as it had already departed with his true owner."

McNeil wrote down a bit more before breaking the short silence that followed. "I'm afraid I'm not following this line of questioning. What on earth does a dog have to do with a child's kidnapping?"

Soble rose from the chair and closed the notebook. "Interesting question Mister McNeil." He folded his arms across his chest, his attention on Bunting. "Following the visit to the shelter, and the confrontation with Mrs. Bloom, the *child in* question called from a payphone near a hanger in the General Aviation section at the Reno Airport. We have videotape of Mister Bunting's vehicle breaking through the electronic access gate to the hangers about that time. The license number on the SUV matches the one given by Mrs. Bloom. Then, there is the matter of the cage in the back of his SUV."

"A cage?" McNeil looked at his partner with a look of absolute disbelief. "Warren?"

"Cage?" Bunting chirped. The knot began to expand into a cold queasy feeling.

Agent Soble continued. "When Mister Bunting's car window was repaired, the afternoon following the phone call, the technician noted a large cage in the rear of the vehicle."

Agent Washington added to the conversation, "At first, we thought the fingerprints on the payphone were left by the kidnapper after he took the phone from the child."

Pale and shaken, Bunting tried to figure out how to explain his Mercedes at the airport. He attempted to buy some time. "My fingerprints could not possibly be those on the payphone."

"Hmm, yes. The handset and numbers were wiped clean."

"Ah." Bunting began to relax a bit. His mind began to explore the idea that he could explain away his presence at the hangers by saying he'd been meeting with the client he mentioned a few moments before. Or even better, a potential client who failed to show.

"A print of yours, however, was found on one of the five quarters in the coin box." Soble smiled a crooked smile and shook his head. "Then there is another odd thing. The, ah, child, gave the 911 operator the number off the fuselage of the aircraft being used to abduct him. But the aircraft departed almost fifteen minutes earlier, piloted by Ms. Aemea Rand, a former Air Force pilot. We verified the times with the Reno tower. A golden retriever was the only other occupant of the aircraft. The tower operator also reported a large Black SUV on the taxiway, apparently attempting to keep Ms. Rand from leaving."

"As we were initially under the impression Ms. Rand was a suspect in a kidnapping, we were able to ascertain she was planning to land at the Sonoma County Airport. When she declined to land two of our agents borrowed a plane to pursue her. Unfortunately, she fled, but was able to land at a small private airstrip. Our agents, for reasons as yet undetermined, were not able to land at that location." He looked up with a frown. "During a subsequent pursuit by land, a civilian truck was badly damaged, along with an agency car."

McNeil cleared his throat. "The agents, are they all right?" When Soble answered that they hadn't been injured, McNeil asked another question. "If she were innocent, why did she run?"

Agent Washington stepped in. "It appears the dog accompanying Ms. Rand didn't belong to her, however, for reasons we haven't determined, she feared for his safety. We believe due to her earlier encounter, or encounters, with Mister Bunting, she took us as his accomplices when she saw vehicles from our agency along with the Sheriff's department at the airport."

The agents stared at McNeil, who looked up from the legal pad to stare at Bunting, whose eyes had gone to his doodles. "It was a simple misunderstanding. A mistake."

"Warren. I believe you should wait to explain this simple misunderstanding to an attorney."

"It was the damn dog! He took my keys, locked me out of my car," Bunting wailed. "He left me in the desert to die. I would have perished if I hadn't been able to finally find a signal on my cell phone."

"We believe the dog in question, the golden retriever I mentioned earlier, belonged to one Gabriel Picket, recently deceased." Sobel shut his notebook.

"You!" Gary McNeil backed away as he pointed a finger at his partner. "You kidnapped Trumpet! You left him alone in the desert!"

30

A RACCOON, ACTUALLY

"Hi. I'm here to drop off a Will with Mr. McNeil." B.P. held up the envelope for the receptionist to see.

"It looks like a dog tried to bury it." Sienna smiled at the young man holding the dirty envelope.

"A raccoon, actually. His name is Reggie."

"A raccoon?" Sienna held out her hand. As she read the return address she looked up at him. "I'm sorry. You would be?"

B.P. indicated the name above the address on the envelope and introduced himself simply as, "B.P."

"I'm Sienna," she nodded to him and slipped the Will from the envelope. "Just let me run a copy of this." She quickly scanned the document before running a copy and returning the original. "If you'll just wait here, I'll be right back."

"Sure, I'll..." But he was talking to an empty desk.

Less than a minute passed before she returned, trailing an earnest looking man in an expensive looking dark suit. He held out his hand. "Mr. Pfeifer, I'm Gary McNeil."

A few minutes later, B.P. was with Gary McNeil in a comfortable corner office, a cup of coffee on the small table next to him.

"A raccoon," McNeil chuckled. "My kids are going to love that one."

"If Aemea hadn't come along, none of this would have happened. I wouldn't have known there was a Will and Trumpet would still be wondering out in the desert." B.P. took a drink of his coffee and stared out the window.

"For a man who has come into an inheritance like this, you don't act overly, well, happy."

"I guess not." He gave the attorney a careful look. "I suppose nothing much will happen to Bunting?"

McNeil leaned back in his chair and made a steeple of his fingers. "Well, I can pretty much guess what you're thinking. However, Warren Bunting is currently, shall we say, up to his ass in alligators with his pants pockets stuffed full of hot dogs." He shook his head before turning the subject back to B.P. "You were saying that you're not thrilled with the outcome after finding the Will."

"It's sort of a long story."

"I'd love to hear it." He buzzed Sienna, asking her to tell anyone calling that he was in an important meeting.

B.P. slowly laid out the events of the past three days, including Paul's recent advice while at the side of the road. When he mentioned the FBI and their response to his phone call, McNeil smiled pleasantly, commenting they always seemed to get their man.

"It looks to me like you've got the ranch, but didn't get the girl. You, being the honorable type, will allow the girl to take Trumpet with her."

"Yeah." B.P. sighed and looked into his coffee. "That's about it."

"From your story, B.P. I'd say you're a romantic." The attorney leaned forward in his chair. Knowingly dipping his head, he smiled. "You need to do something romantic. Something, which will spell it all out if words fail."

B.P. mulled it over while he looked out the window. "I'm not sure I can find the right words to even get a chance to fail."

"What's the worst thing that could happen?" The attorney raised his eyebrows.

"Yeah, I see your point."

❦

"B.P., wait a moment." As he passed through the reception area, Sienna rose from behind her desk and waved him over.

"Hey, thanks for everything." He offered a smile as he held out his hand.

"Just doing my job." She glanced toward her boss's office before fixing her gaze on the deputy. "You definitely hurt her, so it has to be spectacular."

"Yeah, I've sure figured that out." He gave her a puzzled look. "What does?"

"Your romantic something. It can't be simply a gesture."

"You were listening?"

She pointed to the heater duct near her desk. "The acoustics in these offices are funny. If the register is open, like it has been this afternoon, I can hear quite a lot." She smiled at his look of surprise. "Nothing I hear goes past me. If there is something legally important between a client and his attorney going on, the register stays closed."

"You listened just now."

"I've been here long enough to know when someone could benefit from my advice."

"Why would..."

She cut him off with a chuckle and a wave of her hand. "You seem like a nice guy. Sometimes nice guys need an edge. Your friend and Mr. McNeil have given you advice. Do you want to hear from an actual woman's perspective?"

He slowly nodded. "Go on."

"Aemea was counting on you to understand how much she loves Trumpet. You, you made it trivial."

"I was just..."

With a nicely manicured finger, she poked him in the chest. Just as Aemea had done at the cabin he thought to himself. B.P. looked from the finger to the earnest expression on Sienna's face. He dipped his chin for her to go on.

"I told my last boyfriend to take a hike when he slapped my Sadie." She gave a meaningful glance over to her desk. In a framed photo she was sitting on the ground next to a picnic table hugging a large black Lab. The Lab was smiling hugely into the camera, the picture of a happy and content dog.

"She's a BBD, a big black dog I rescued from a shelter last year. Sadie is loyal, loving, she doesn't judge me when I pick a total jerk for a boyfriend. Right now she is the only person in the world I can totally count on." The young woman's voice rose slightly as she spoke allowing B.P a glimpse of the same intensity of emotion he's seen so plainly in Aemea.

After a quick glance in the direction of McNeil's office, Sienna cleared her throat slightly. "You need to do something devastatingly romantic. It has to absolutely melt her heart." She poked him with her finger a second time for emphasis. "You have to let her know you're laying it all out."

He nodded in agreement. "Do you have a suggestion, I hope?"

"It has to be simple. It has to come from the heart, your heart, not your friend's, Mr. McNeil's, or mine." She smiled. "If you give it some thought, you already know what to do."

He liked her attitude. Her faith in him boosted his confidence. "You sound like one of those shrinks on the radio."

"One more thing. No flowers." Sienna shook her head to emphasize her words.

"No flowers?"

"In a situation like this, flowers will come off as completely, totally lame, and you could get hurt if the vase is as heavy as the one my ex-boyfriend....." The young woman stopped herself, a dark cloud passed across her face. Closing her eyes, she took a slow calming breath before opening them and continuing. "Anyway, they're way too low on the romantic scale for something like this." Then her eyes focused on something far off for a few moments.

B.P. considered Sienna's advice as he rolled onto the freeway. During his discussion with McNeil he'd thought about showing up with a beautifully arraigned bouquet. Well, Sienna certainly shot that idea down. "And don't forget, the "devastatingly" part." As he drove he noted the wildflowers growing along the side of the highway. By the time he was back on River Road, 'The Plan' was forming in his mind.

31

TWO SEATS IN PARADISE

As Gabe rested in the blackness behind Trumpet's closed eyes, he wondered what meaning he could attach to the whole adventure. Though he thought he came to Trumpet's aid, and Trumpet at times listened to him, he was truly his own dog and came through mostly on his own. In the end, I guess that's what I wanted. I witnessed an adventure of a lifetime, and though I did help, I now know my friend can take care of himself and will be with people he loves. The floating sensation was getting more pronounced.

Gabe called up a vivid image of himself and Sarah sitting together on their two tractor seats, sharing their morning coffee as they looked out over the valley. She set aside her cup. Sliding an arm around his shoulder, she drew him to her. Around them, the yellow daffodils poked their heads up. A few yards away, Trumpet cavorted in the deep grass. He was playing a game with Yogi, jumping up, then tossing it into the air, catching it again and whirling around. They both laughed, shouting out his name at the same time. "Trumpet!"

Trumpet's eyes came open as if someone nearby had called his name. Instantly awake from his spot at the foot of the bed, he could hear soft breathing telling him Aemea was sleeping. Satisfied she was safe, he slid off the bed landing on his feet, stretched, and peered about. He paused to rest his chin on the bed, his eyes alert, but she slept peacefully on.

In the early morning light he trotted into the kitchen, then over to the front door. Cocking his head, he listened. With a soft whine, he whirled, hurrying back into the bedroom. At the mirrored door, he sat and stared hard at his image, his eyes locking on the eyes in the mirror.

"Wuff." He rested a paw against the cool surface of the mirror, leaning forward until his nose touched his image. "Wuff!"

Gabe stared back into Trumpet's eyes. "I'm leaving you now buddy. Sarah is waiting for me, and it is time for me to go. I can now rest in peace knowing you will be safe and loved. I will always be with you, just as Sarah is also there for you when you think of her. We are a part of this land; you can hear our voices in the wind and feel us stroking your fur."

❧

"Trumpet?" Startled from her sleep, Aemea sat up in bed. She heard his soft bark, and watched him pawing at the mirror. As he bolted for the living room, she tossed aside the bedcovers and swung out of bed, her bare feet feeling for her shoes on the wooden floor. "What's wrong?"

Again at the front door, he reared up, slapped at the door's handle, pulled it open, and darted out into the yard. The sun was just rising over the mountain, bathing the yard in a warm golden light.

From the front door, Aemea watched Trumpet run through the gate toward where she knew the lone tractor seat overlooked the valley. She couldn't see him but heard his frantic bark several times before he raced back to the cabin. Still holding the door open, Aemea stepped aside as Trumpet ran back onto the porch, edged past her, then rushed back into the house. She found him shivering and whining at the mirrored door, his nose pressed tightly against the glass.

"Oh, god." She squatted down next to the distraught dog. "Gabe?"

"Arrourr."

"I don't understand." She reached out and stroked his head. "Gabe isn't here?"

Trumpet suddenly ducked his head from under her hand. He ran from the room after letting out several sharp "Arrks!" Moments later she heard the front door opening and closing again. She quickly dressed and went out onto the porch. At the bottom of the porch steps, Trumpet sat facing toward the pond.

"Hey, boy." She settled next to him, and began a thorough inspection of his shoulder. "You could have pulled your stitches out, you know that?"

After a moment, Trumpet sighed heavily and leaned against her.

"Gabe?" She spoke quietly as she put an arm around the dog.

"Arrourr."

"Maybe he's just away for a little while?"

The retriever's long look into her eyes ended with

another heavy sigh, as he turned away.

"Trumpet. Are you alone?"

Trumpet whined softly.

"No Gabe? Is Gabe gone?"

Accompanied by a gentle, 'woof,' he slowly turned his face back to her.

She stared into the deep brown eyes. "Trumpet, do you still understand me?"

Listening to her words, his ears came forward, his head tilting first to one side then the other.

"Do you know what I'm asking?"

Again, he tilted his head, his eyes hard on hers.

She moved her arm until her hand rested on his neck. "No Gabe?"

Lowering his head, Trumpet, again, leaned against her.

Aemea didn't know how to comfort Trumpet, or fill the hole left by Gabe no longer existing in him. She wanted, needed, B.P. to be there to comfort them, to comfort her. He saved them from the boar's attack, had been there to get Trumpet to the vet, and took her side against Bunting.

"Things would have been so simple if we hadn't found the Will. It was like a switch was suddenly thrown. I am so afraid of losing you, I just couldn't think." She hugged him, wishing fervently she had controlled her anger the previous day, that she hadn't chased B.P. away.

They sat quietly together until Aemea spoke. "I've only known you for a week, yet you've changed the entire predictable, gloomy direction my life had taken." She held up her closed right hand. "Somehow, you released me from the nightmare I was having almost every night. Now I don't dread going to sleep." Counting, she extended her index finger. "The people I've worked with, and pretty much ignored, are now my friends." A second finger was extended. "My flying has gone from just going up and grinding around for an hour or so a week, to evading government agents and looping bridges." This statement brought out a smile, and a third finger was raised as she waved her hand, then pulled Trumpet close for another hug.

"You know, I've always thought of myself as a rational, logical person. I only met B.P. three days ago. My logical mind tells me I don't know him very well, and I need more time. But I gave *you* my heart." Letting out a quiet sigh, Aemea rested her chin on Trumpet's head. "Why can't I give it to B.P.?"

Trumpet had no answer.

～

After a while they returned to the cabin's porch, sitting together on the couch, Trumpet with his head resting on the padded arm. Aemea blocked the door open to allow Trumpet to easily enter the house because every few minutes he would get up and hurry back to stare at the mirrored door. Finally, Trumpet climbed back onto the couch, rested his head on her lap and closed his eyes. "I guess it's just us now, isn't it?"

She continued to speak quiet soothing words to the retriever, when B.P.'s Land Cruiser idled into view, making its way through the gate. Aemea sat up straighter and ran her fingers through her hair. She also unbuttoned the top button of her shirt.

"Hurr?" Trumpet lifted his head.

"Yeah, hurr. I've decided I'm giving *logic* the day off."

❧

"Morning, Aemea." B.P. smiled cautiously as he eased out of the front seat. "Hi, Trumpet."

Trumpet turned his head slightly in the Deputy's direction, then dropped his head back down and closed his eyes.

"Morning." Pleased he arrived so early in the morning, she nodded her head, with the knowledge that this time if he didn't make a move, she would.

"I thought you might like some doughnuts." He held up a small white bag. "They were just out of the fryer twenty minutes ago." In his other hand he carried a small thermos of hot coffee.

Now, Aemea thought as she ran her hand over Trumpet's well brushed coat, there is a hopeful man. "Sounds good. Chocolate?" She felt a certain hope in herself too.

"Oh." His smile faded slightly as his eyes looked into the bag of doughnuts. "Maple old fashioned."

Seeing the look, she quickly replied. "I love maple. Maple would be perfect." With his smile back in full force, Aemea decided he was a pretty good-looking guy in kind of a rough around the edges way. "There's room here on the couch." She slid over a bit, pulling Trumpet back against her. Pointing to the thermos, she asked, "I don't suppose you would mind sharing?"

"My pleasure." B.P. went to the kitchen and returned with two mugs. He poured some coffee for both of them before settling in next to Trumpet on the couch. Sipping his coffee, he rested his free hand on the dog's hip. He reflected on all the words he'd been rehearsing for most of the previous evening, now evaporating like the dew in the sun.

They were both quiet for a time when B.P. cleared his throat. "I'm thinking of taking a leave of absence. Maybe, spend some time here on the ranch."

Her smile rallied his optimism. He was thinking about a way to lay it all out when Trumpet suddenly raised his head, glaring first at B.P., then at Aemea. With a snort, he got to his feet and eased himself off the couch.

"What is it Trumpet?" Setting her coffee cup down, she reached out to touch him.

The retriever turned to them. Slipping his nose under Aemea's outstretched hand, he nudged it hard. When she simply left it there, he continued to bump her hand until it was over B.P.'s free hand. That done, Trumpet sat off to one side, his eyes expectantly on them. "Uuur, woof!"

"Damn." B.P also set down his cup, and got up. Taking both of Aemea's hands, he pulled her to her feet.

"Deputy Pfeifer, is there something you want to say?" There was a light in her warm brown eyes.

"Come on." He pulled her toward the yard. "You've probably figured out there are times when I'm not the smoothest guy in the world with words, so there's something I want you to see."

"What is it?" She kept her hand in his as he walked purposefully toward the gate.

"A surprise. Just be patient." He glanced down at Trumpet who was happily trotting along next to them. "And you keep quiet."

B.P. was suddenly uncertain she would understand. As they passed through the gate toward his 'surprise,' he tried to read her through her grip of his hand, hoping it was tightening up for a good reason.

They stood at the edge of the little valley. All around them and across the hill the morning breeze rippled a sea of grass in ever-changing patterns.

But Aemea wasn't watching. Her eyes were on the pair of tractor seats attached to the old railroad tie. Her free hand went to her mouth as she stared.

"Gabe hung Sarah's seat in the barn. I spotted it while I was looking for the keys. This morning I came up before sunrise to bring it here, to fasten it back where it belongs." Her silence was killing him. "Would you say something, please?"

"Deputy Pfeifer, this is the most romantic, the most devastatingly beautiful thing I have ever seen in my entire life."

B.P. let out a sigh of relief. Pulling her to him he grinned. "Those are the words I wanted to hear." When he kissed her, Aemea offered no resistance and wrapped her arms around his neck.

With a contented woof, Trumpet leaned against his new two people.

About the Author

This book reflects Kim Crumb's numerous interests and vast experience. Growing up in northern California, at the age of twenty he joined the Army and is proud to be a decorated Viet Nam combat Veteran. After returning home, he obtained his pilot's license while working at a small airport in Sonoma County. He enjoys all things mechanical, including his 1958 VW transporter, and riding his motorcycles (one with a sidecar).

Kim has worked in many professions: as a graphic designer, artist and cartoonist, and as an engineer designing fire trucks. He uses his craftsmanship skills for his own home projects and as a handyman building for others. With his wife of forty-three years, Sherrie Owens, he owned a doggie day care. Much of his insight into canine behaviors comes from hours observing their body language and play dynamics. He is fortunate to have known the best dog ever, his red golden retriever, Triumph.

www.ingramcontent.com/pod-product-compliance
Lightning Source LLC
Chambersburg PA
CBHW051215130726
47988CB00001B/108